Books by Eric Smith
available from Inkyard Press

Don't Read the Comments
You Can Go Your Own Way

ERIC SMITH

YOU CAN GO YOUR OWN WAY

inkyard PRESS

Recycling programs
for this product may
not exist in your area.

For my creative writing professors,
Susanna Rich and Robin Black.
Games of pinball start with a pull and a push.
Thanks for getting me onto the playfield.

For Nena and Langston.
For keeping me level,
and never letting me tilt.

"What will you carry with you, when the lights are out, all is quiet, and the game is over?"

–THE ART AND ZEN OF PINBALL REPAIR
BY JAMES WATTS

CHAPTER 1
Adam

The playfield is truly the heart of every pinball
machine. All of the player's goals are right there,
splayed out in front of them. And like life, it's up to
you to find a way to reach them, with the tools you're
presented. In this case, it's a ball.

—*THE ART AND ZEN OF PINBALL REPAIR*
BY JAMES WATTS

The sound of collective screaming and a massive crash shake
my entire workshop, and I almost stab myself with a piping-
hot soldering iron.

"Adam!" my mom yells from inside the arcade. If another
pack of junior high kids from the nearby Hillman Academy
"accidentally" flip over a machine trying to get it to tilt, I
am going to lose it. I grip the iron, the cracked brown leather
wrapped around the metal handle squeaking a little against
my skin, and shake my head, trying to refocus. Maybe I can
finish this before it's time to pick up that custom piece—

And another crash rattles the walls. A few parts tumble off my shelves, tiny intricate pieces of metal and glass, bits of copper wire, all clinking against my table.

I attempt to catch a few of the electronic pieces, trying not to burn myself with the iron in my other hand, and then a hammer falls off the perforated wall of tools in front of me. It collides with a small cardboard box full of pinball playfield lightbulbs, and I wince at the small crack and pop sounds.

"Goddammit," I grumble out. I toss the soldering iron aside and try to clean up the mess. At least those lightbulbs are like, ten bucks a dozen on arcade wholesale websites. But pinball machines have a *lot* of lights.

"Adam!" This time it's Chris. "Dude, where *are* you?"

I'm about to bolt from the workshop when I remember Mom is out there. I reach for the latest read I promised her I'd finish—*We Built This Gritty* by Kevin Michaels, a book on launching small businesses by an entrepreneur here in Philly that one of her colleagues is teaching at the county college— and immediately yank my hand back. The soldering iron had gone right in between the pages when I tossed it, and the book is already smoking. I pull the iron out and set it aside and flap the book around wildly, little wisps pooling up from inside the bright orange book. I flip it open.

It's burnt right down the middle. Great. Something tells me she won't be able to trade this back in at the campus store.

I glance over at The Beast and give the forever-in-progress Philadelphia-themed home-brewed pinball machine a pat, the glass still off the surface, wires and various parts splayed out over the playfield. My well-worn copy of *The Art and Zen of Pinball Repair* by James Watts sits smack in the middle of everything. I've still got a way to go before I can try playing Dad's unfinished machine again, but if anyone is gonna get me there, it's Watts. If I could just get a free chunk of time in between the studying and the arcade and the—

An array of swears echoes from inside the arcade, snapping me back.

Right. Chris. Mom. Chaos. Potentially broken and nearly irreplaceable machines worth thousands of dollars.

I unplug the soldering iron and place it in its little stand, like a quill pen in an inkwell. I wedge the now-toasty book under my arm and take a few steps to pick up some speed, to get a little force, and I push my shoulder against the dark red wooden workshop door. I push, gritting my teeth. The splintering surface presses into my arm, stinging with the pressure, until finally, the wood squeals against the frame, shrunken in and wedged together due to the sharp Philadelphia winter.

The whole workshop is like that, really, casting a major contrast to the polished, well-kept-despite-its-years pinball arcade. The cracked workshop table that is *way* more rickety than it has any right to be, tools showing their age with hinges that refuse to move and metal pieces falling off shrinking wood and weak plastic handles, vintage pinball parts that *maybe* still work, a concrete floor with a surface that's chipping away, revealing dirt and dust, lightbulbs I don't even remotely trust. My sad excuse for a drafting table sits off to the end of the workshop, and I've never really used it, preferring to fuss with plans right on the messy workshop table, next to all of Dad's scribbles.

We could clean it up, have this room match the rest of the arcade. But I love it. It reminds me of him.

The door swings open suddenly and hits the wall inside the arcade with a loud bang.

And it *is* absolute chaos here.

A bunch of little kids are rushing outside, and I see a couple of adults gathering coats and their small children, who are likely about to join the exodus. The afternoon light that's pouring in from the wide-open front door and the large plate-glass windows lining the wall make me wince. The glare hurts only slightly less than the idea of customers hustling out of here on a Saturday, easily our best, and *only*, solid day during the wintertime off-season. Especially now, at the end of the year, with so few days left before we close for the New Year holiday.

People don't come to pinball arcades in the winter. Well. Maybe they do, but not when your arcade is located near all the tourist stuff in Old City, all the college students are away on break, and you don't serve any alcohol. No tourists, no college kids, no booze, no pinball. It's a neighborhood for expensive restaurants and niche boutiques, old-timey candy shops and artisan pour-over coffee. Not an arcade with a poor excuse for a snack bar inside that mostly serves soda, chips, and reheated chicken tenders and fries.

If it wasn't for the upcoming Old City Winter Festival, I'm not sure we'd be able to keep the lights on come January. And there's a businessman out in West Philadelphia who would very much like to see that happen, and there's no way I'm going to let him do that. I've eaten way too many burnt chicken tenders that were "well, these are still kinda good, Adam" according to my mom, but not good enough for the customers. I've paid my dues.

"Mom!" I shout, looking to the back of the arcade. "Chris, what is—"

But then I see it.

On the other side of the arcade, my mom has her hands on her hips and is glaring intently at a handful of college guys who are sheepishly milling about near one of the windows. And Chris is trying to lift up a machine that's currently knocked over, the glass that would normally be covering the playfield shattered across the floor. Another machine is tilted, leaning against a support beam, and looks okay from here. But judging by the angle and the amount of force it would have taken to get it off the legs in the first place, I'm betting we're going to have some dents on the light box (the back of the machine that juts up over the area where you actually play, and displays the score and art).

"What the hell?" I snap, kicking the workshop door closed and storming across the arcade. My thick black boots squeak loud against the worn, polished hardwood floor, all the imperfections of the ancient Philadelphia wooden boards permanently glossed in place. A few more guys, these ones my age, weave around me, fiddling on their phones and oblivious. Bits of glass crunch under my feet, and I glance down at a bumper, red and black and looking like one of those crushed lantern fly bugs that litter the city sidewalks.

"What happened?" I ask, tossing my burnt book onto the floor. I nudge the tilted machine upright and then bend down to help Chris, who is straining to move the machine on the floor. I manage to wedge my fingers under the side, carefully tapping the metal, trying to avoid any extra glass, and lift. Chris lets out a groan and I grit my teeth as we push the machine upright, and it nearly topples back over the other way, but Mom reaches out and stops it.

"*They* happened." Mom nods back at the guys who are standing about awkwardly. "Any updates there?" She points at one of them, and that's when I realize they're all sort of keeping an eye on one vaguely familiar-looking dude in the middle, who is fussing with his phone.

"Just a second," he grumbles out, and he flicks his head to the side, his emo black bangs moving out of his eyes. I can't help but squint at him, trying to place his face. Half his head is shaved, and he has this sort of Fall Out Boy look that would be cool, if he and his pals hadn't clearly destroyed a pinball machine in my family's arcade. A splash of anxiety hits me in the chest as I realize I don't know what game has been to-taled, and I turn to look at the machine.

Flash Gordon.

I exhale, relieved that it's not one of the more popular or rare games in the arcade. But still, it's a machine from the '80s. One of the first games in the industry to use the popular Squawk & Talk soundboard, a piece of technology that is wildly expensive to replace, since it isn't made anymore. That's the sort of pinball trivia both Chris and my mom tend to shush when I start rambling too much, telling me "that should be a tweet," which translates to "shut up" in the nic-est way possible. I'm almost positive that's the reason they pushed me to get the arcade on social media—to have a place to share those musings.

The machine didn't deserve this, even if that awful movie maybe did.

I run my hand along the side of the other machine that

was just bumped into, leaning on one of the wooden beams that are scattered throughout the arcade, you know, holding the building up. It's the *Terminator 2: Judgment Day* machine, and thankfully, it looks undamaged. A little dented along the light box, as I suspected, but the glass and everything else seems fine. It's a popular one with the Millennial crowd, and I'm relieved.

"How much is it going to cost to fix?" the familiar guy with the hair asks. He must catch me staring at him, 'cause his eyes flit over to mine, irritated, and I look away, focusing back on the machine.

I pluck at some of the glass on the surface, nudging around some of the broken obstacles on the playfield, and feel a sharp sting in my hand. I quickly pull away and spot a thin line of red trailing along my palm.

"Adam?"

I glance up, and my mom, Chris, and Emo Hair are all staring at me expectantly.

"What?" I ask, focusing back down at the machine and then back at all of them.

"The cost," my mom presses. "That machine. How much do you think it'll cost to fix all of this?" She gestures at the floor and shakes her head, her mouth a thin line. All that brewing frustration that she's trying to bury down. Kids mess with the machines often, and we've certainly had a few hiccups like this before, but I've never seen her looking this wildly angry. I didn't even think she *liked* that machine.

"Oh." I swallow and clear my throat. "I don't know. It depends on how bad the damage is?" I scan the playfield and then the side of the machine, which has a sizable dent in the

steel that I can probably hammer out. But the shattered glass,
the pieces, and who knows what's going on inside it. I think
back to Watts's *The Art and Zen of Pinball Repair*, my holy
tome, written by my hero.

"If you think it's broken, it is. And if you think it's going
to be cheap to replace, it's not."

I stare at the broken glass.

"You know what, how's a thousand dollars?" the familiar guy holding the phone asks. He looks around at his dude
friends, their faces awash in expressions that are essentially
shrugs, each nodding at him. "Everyone Venmo me two hundred after this or I'll kick your asses."

Some of the guys laugh while the rest break out their phones.

"Why?" scoffs one of them. "You're the one with the money."

Emo Hair snorts out a laugh and shakes his head, and
glances back up from his screen. The fact that all of them
are so relaxed about that much money irks me. The arcade is
barely scraping by these days, and it's no wonder other businesses have been sniffing around the building this year, leaving painfully awkward notes and emails for Mom. I've seen
a few of them, here and there. The worst ones come under
the guise of pretending to be supportive. Do you need anything? We're here for you. Just checking in. And then in the
same breath, bringing up property values and plummeting
interest in arcades.

And despite frequent requests to stop mailing us, a local
real estate developer loves sending us physical mail about the
benefits of selling real estate in Old City now, and they're always addressed to Dad. Assholes.

"What's your Venmo?" he asks, looking at my mom and then at me. My mom and I exchange a look. He huffs. "How about PayPal? Apple Pay?"

"I mean…we could take a check?" My mom shrugs, wincing. One of the bros groans like this has somehow physically *wounded* him, and before I can say anything, my mom snaps a finger at the guy. "Hey, you five are the ones who broke this machine. If I want you to go get that thousand dollars in a burlap sack full of coins at the bank down the road, you'll get it."

"Sorry, ma'am," one of them mutters.

"Just Venmo it to me," Chris says, pulling out his phone. "I'll hit the bank when I run out to pick up sidewalk salt for the snow, and get it taken care of, Mrs. Stillwater." He glances at my mom and shakes his head at me. I know that look. He's about to force another freaking app on me, and I don't think I'll be able to talk about pinball on Venmo. It was bad enough when he tricked me into joining Pinterest, convincing me it was a pinball thing.

He steps over to the pack of guys, and they're all looking at one another and their phones and his, and I really shouldn't be surprised that he knows how to handle this. Him and his apps. I wish he'd just run the social media for the arcade, but he says it wouldn't sound "genuine" or something. If typos make someone sound genuine, I am *very* genuine.

A year behind me at Central, a junior, Chris has this whole Adam Driver look about him. Same sharp cheekbones and bits of facial hair, only a little shorter and with thin square glasses, and as geeky as you can get without actually being in a *Star Wars* movie. My best friend since I was eight, and

our only employee in the off-season, as everyone is either a
college student heading home for the break or a fellow local
high schooler who has no interest in working over the winter.

He nods at the guys, looking at his phone.

"All right, I got it," he says and then turns to us. The bros
stand there for a beat.

"You can leave," my mom snaps and points toward the door.

"Right, right," the familiar guy says and gestures for the
rest of his pack to follow. They amble out of the shop, their
feet crunching the glass on the floor in a way that makes
me feel like it's on purpose. I take a step forward, but Chris
reaches his arm out, his hand pressing against my chest.

I glance up at him, and he just shakes his head.

I huff and bend down to sift through the glass and pieces
of machine, while my mom disappears into the back office.
There are some bumpers on the ground, and a few small white
flags, little targets meant to be knocked down for bonus plays,
are scattered about like baby teeth. The glass, though, that
really bothers me. A good sheet of playfield glass can go for
a little over a hundred dollars, and while I know that's not
technically a lot of money in the grand scheme of things…we
don't have that much to spare these days.

Jorge over at NextFab, the makerspace that Chris practically lives in when he isn't here, has been great at helping me
replace some parts, as well as teaching me how to build some
of my own, which is way more helpful than YouTube tutori-
als. But a whole sheet of glass? Bumpers with *intricate* circuitry
and copper coils? That's not something easily 3D printed, especially when he keeps doing it for free. And I don't know

how much of that I can manage in my workshop. Or afford, for that matter.

I look around the dirty playfield for the remaining flags but…dammit, they are nowhere to be found. At least the back glass, the lit-up artwork on the back of the machine, isn't damaged. Flash is still there, looking dead ahead at me, alongside Dale and the…ugh, wildly racist Ming the Merciless.

Hmm.

Maybe the machine *did* deserve this.

Chris squats down next to me.

"Want me to grab the broom?" he asks, picking at a broken bumper.

I look back to my hand. The line in my palm is ugly but clean. I flex my hand a little, and the cut widens, and I see just how far up and down my hand it goes. I wonder if I'll need stitches or if it'll scar.

"Sure." I clear my throat and both of us stand up. I glance toward the arcade's exit, the place now empty, as Chris walks over to the snack bar. "Must be nice," I say, "being able to drop that much money without thinking about it."

"Yeah, well, not like his dad isn't good for it."

"His dad?" I ask, peering over. Chris is behind the bar, some paper towels already scattered out in front of him, a broom in one hand. Heat lamps keeping fries and onion rings warm tint his face a reddish orange for a moment before he ducks back out.

"Well, yeah?" He shrugs, walking over. He places the paper towels in my hands and nods at the cut. "Apply pressure." He starts sweeping, moving bits of glass and broken parts into a small pile. "I swear, one more incident like this, and that is what's gonna make me finally try to get a job at the maker-space. Or a coffee shop…" He looks up at me as I stare at him. "What? You know I can't work in here forever, bro."

"What do you mean *what*? I know *that* part." I laugh. "Who is his dad? You're just gonna leave the story hanging there?"

He nearly drops the broom but reaches out to grab the handle.

"Are you serious?" he scoffs. I shrug and he shakes his head. "Adam, that was *Nick*. That's why I thought you were so mad, looking like you were about to charge after him and his goons." I shrug again. "Jesus, Adam. Nick *Mitchell*."

The stress on that last name.

Mitchell.

It sends a shock through my entire system, and I turn to look at the exit, as though he and his friends might still be there. I tighten my hand into a fist, and the pain from the cut sears through my palm, lighting me up through my forearm. And I swear, for a moment I can feel it in my head, bouncing around like a pinball against bumpers.

Nick Mitchell.

Whitney Mitchell's *brother*.

And also the oldest son of the man trying to buy my father's arcade from my mother, with plans to make it into another one of his eSports cafés. He's been poking around all year, like a vulture circling over something that might just die any minute. But this place still has a little life in it. A little *fight* in it.

And dammit, so do I.

Did he even recognize me? Did he know this was our arcade? Back when me and Whitney were supposedly friends, before high school changed everything, I don't think I ever saw him come around. But I saw him all the time at school and before her dad's career took off, when we'd play at Whitney's old house in South Philly. And when we were kids, everyone had their birthday parties here at the pinball arcade. With so many mutual friends and the like, he had to have been in here at some point. Until they forgot about us, like the entire building was just one giant toy that fell behind a dresser.

"All right, well, I can tell you know who he is now," Chris says, walking back toward the snack bar. He grabs some more paper towels and thrusts them at me, nodding at my hand. I look down, and the paper wad is an awful dark red, soaked through from my rage. "Go take a seat. I'm gonna get the first-aid kit out of your workshop."

"What about *Flash Gordon*?" I ask, glancing back at the messed-up machine.

"It's a problematic racist relic. Who cares? Come on." He laughs, reaching out and grabbing my shoulder. "Besides, if you want some replacement bits, I'm heading to the makerspace tomorrow—we can rummage for parts. Go grab a seat." He nods at the snack bar and walks off. I turn around and pull my phone out, snapping photos of the broken pinball machine. The scratched-up metal exterior, the dented places around the playfield. I bend down and snap pictures of some of the crunched glass still on the floor, the broken parts scattered in a neat pile thanks to Chris. I even take a few photos of the dented *Terminator 2: Judgment Day* machine.

I stroll over to the arcade's snack spot, Dad's last great idea for the place, and sit down. The chairs aren't exactly the pinnacle of comfort, and the hard wood digs into my back, but it's what my family could afford when we first put this spot in here. It's still passably cozy enough that local writers will drop in to play a few games, drink our bad coffee or nurse a soda, and spend the day staring at a blank screen while scrolling through Twitter instead of writing.

I sigh and glance up at the wooden shelving that looms over the café corner, a shabby-chic display that Chris's parents helped build. Tons of Mason jars, full of coffee beans and loose-leaf tea, illuminated by strings of white Christmas twinkle lights, sit on nearly every shelf. Decor meant for hip college students and artsy creatives in West Philly, pulled from a Pinterest board someplace and made real. I think it looks pretty, but if Gordon Ramsay made an episode about our arcade's little food corner, it would just be a twenty-eight-minute scream.

Chris walks around the side, a little first-aid kit in hand, and gestures for me to give him my hand. I hold it out and he glances back at the *Flash Gordon* machine.

"Real shame," he says, wistfully looking at the shattered game.

"Yeah." I nod. "I took a bunch of photos to post—"

Psssssssst!

There's the sound of spraying, and I scream, yanking my hand away. I glare at him, and he's sporting the widest grin I've ever seen, a bottle of spray-on rubbing alcohol in his hand.

"Argh!" I groan. "Why!"

"Kidding, fuck that game." He laughs.

"You could have *told me* you were going to do that!" I shout. He tilts his head a little at me. "Fine, you're right—I would have made a scene over it."

"Everything okay?" Mom's in the doorway to the office, peeking out.

"Yeah, Mrs. Stillwater," Chris says.

My mom scowls at the two of us before breaking into a little smile, but that expression disappears as her line of sight moves toward the broken pinball machine. She closes the door, and I look back at the exit to the arcade again. I feel like with every setback this place has had this year, it gets us one step closer to my mom putting the pinball machines in storage for good and selling the place to Mr. Mitchell. And two damaged machines, one of which is basically destroyed, isn't going to help.

"And I'm gonna need you to stop it," Chris says, reaching out and grabbing my hand, slapping a large Band-Aid on my palm. I wince and suck air through my teeth, and he just gives me a look. He pulls out some of that gauze-wrap stuff and starts to bandage up the big Band-Aid, keeping it pressed to my palm. "That guy isn't worth it, that machine isn't worth it, and that family definitely isn't worth getting all riled up over."

"He *had* to have known this was my place," I grumble. "Whitney probably *sent* him here. If not her, then definitely her father."

"Oh, come on," Chris scoffs. "I'm not her biggest fan either, and I know you two don't get along, but she isn't some nefarious supervillain. And her dad isn't going to send henchmen here. When was the last time you and her even talked, outside of snarky social media posts? You like pinball, she likes playing *Fortnite* and *Overwatch*. Not exactly a blood feud."

"I'm not even sure she's into the video games at her dad's

places or whatever," I grumble. At least, she wasn't into video games when we were kids, always so irritated when we'd retreat inside to get in games of *Halo*. "Besides, you don't understand." I shake my head, trying to chase away the memories of that summer before high school and those first days wandering the halls at Central. Her and her new friends, leaning against their lockers, matching jean jackets and bright lip gloss. She was like an entirely new person, and the way she laughed with them when I walked over to say hi...

"Anyway." I clear my throat. "I wouldn't put it past her."

"You need to spend more time worrying about the people who are there for you and less about those who aren't," he says, fastening the gauze together with two little metal clips. "Maybe go on a date with someone or something."

"How do you even know how to do this?" I lift my hand up, flexing my fingers, ignoring the dating question. "There's no time for that, between the arcade and school. If I kiss a girl by the end of my senior year, it'll be a miracle."

"Please, my dads are carpenters and you know how I spend my free time," he says. "It's best to be prepared in case someone loses a finger at home or in the shop or at the makerspace."

I laugh and again find myself looking toward the door. I let out a long exhale through my nose.

"You think we're going to get anyone else in here today?" Chris asks. "It's just, you know, maybe I could duck out early to go work on stuff?" There's this beat of silence that doesn't need to be filled, and I sigh.

"I think we both know the answer there, right?" With the snowstorm we all know is coming, the brutally cold gusts of wind, and the fact that business slows to a crawl right before the Old City Winter Festival, there's not much to even say.

I lean back in my chair a little, the sharp pain of the wood digging into my back weirdly comforting, distracting me from my hand and thoughts of Nick and Whitney and that whole terrible family.

"Do you need to talk?" Chris asks, and I glance back at him. "I mean, I can hang a bit longer if you need me." He digs around in his pocket and pulls out a little candy bag and waves it at me, the plastic crinkling. Swedish Fish. Not the regular kind either; the tropical sort, with orange, pink, purple, and off-white fish in the mix. He shakes it until one drops out onto his hand, and he holds it up between his fingers. "I grabbed a bag at the CVS before I came over here, for my dads. Didn't realize *we'd* have to use it, though."

"Oh, God, no," I whine. "If you're gonna do that to me, just leave."

Whenever Chris's parents want to talk about "big feelings," they break out these Swedish Fish candies. Have something important to say? Out comes the candy. It's usually something critical that might make someone feel upset, but it's the way you're feeling, so it's good to get it all out. Then pair it with something that makes you feel good while you're hearing something that might make you feel bad.

It was a tradition Chris first told me about when we were really little, and one that's been ongoing. I'm not quite sure why Swedish Fish are the candy of choice, but I'm guessing it's because you can buy them in bulk at the South Philadelphia IKEA. He's since introduced it to me and all our friends. Tell someone how you feel, let them eat the candy, and take

in all those thoughts and emotions. Or, give someone the opportunity to say how they're feeling, and take it all in. Simple
enough. And while we don't practice it at home, my mom
often likes to say, "Do you need a fish?" when she thinks I
have something I need to talk about.

I hate it so much.

"I hate this so much," I grumble and pluck the fish from
between his fingers.

"Listen," he says, reaching out and closing my good hand
around the candy. "You're upset. You're thinking about Whitney and the Mitchells. Nick and the boys. Both of those sound
like terrible West Philadelphia indie rock bands. And you're
thinking about maybe going on Twitter and saying something snippy on social media. That what those pictures are
for? Yeah?"

"N–no." I barely stammer the word out. "It's for…insur-
ance."

He gives me a look.

"You're the worst." I glower at him.

"Nothing good ever comes out of these little fights you
have with Whitney online." He presses, pointing at me. "All
you do is get all the stores in the neighborhood riled up,
dunking on one another. As if you get points for dunking on
people online."

"You're the one who *taught me* how to use social media."

"Don't give me the whole 'I learned it from watching you'
thing. Resist the urge to go online. It's a waste of your energy," he says, nodding at me. "Save your online presence for
posting your pinball puns and facts. Now, eat your candy."

"No." I glare at him.

"Fine, fine." He smiles, shaking his head, and pulls out his phone. "I'm gonna head off to NextFab. You behave."

"Ugh, can't you just work on your weird woodworking coffee things in the workshop?" I groan and gesture toward the red door on the other side of the arcade. "Then you could just be here all the time."

He laughs and then sighs. "What are you going to do here without me?" he asks.

"Hmph," I huff. "Probably have a meltdown on the regular."

He reaches over and taps the screen of my phone, and my eyes flit up to him. "Don't do it, and you'll be fine," he says and then bends over to grab his backpack. It's this beaten-up leather thing that looks straight out of an old movie. I half expect to see it filled with vintage books tied together in beige string, but I know it's just full of woodworking tools, and depending on the day, some glassblowing stuff. It's not lost on me that my best friend spends all his time creating beautiful new things out of nothing, while I stress over repairing machines older than I am every single day.

He walks out of the snack bar and toward the door but stops and turns around.

"And hey, if you need to talk—" he throws something, and I reach out to catch whatever it is that is flapping its way toward me; the plastic bag of Swedish Fish makes a loud crinkling sound as I grab it out of the air "—text me. But I'm gonna want pictures of you eating your candy. It's important that you trust the process."

He's out the front door, and I'm alone in the arcade with his candy and my phone.

I glance back toward the office, and slide myself out of the wood café chair, the legs squeaking loudly in the empty space. We'll probably have to call someone in to do something about the *Flash Gordon* machine. From what I recall, there's not a lot of room left in the office to store any other broken or not-in-use machines, and it's definitely not going to fit in the workshop, with Dad's unfinished game in there. If no one will take it for free or for scrap after I pluck out the worthwhile parts, who knows how much that's going to cost, lugging away three hundred pounds of steel and glass and—

I stop walking when I reach the office door.

I hear…crying? I think?

"Mom?" I venture, opening the door. Generally, I know better than to pester Mom when she's holed up back there, going over our books and trying to figure out new ways to keep us afloat. She's usually either doing that or, during the school year, grading or fussing over lesson plans. How she balances working as an adjunct at the community college while running the arcade with me, I have no idea. All I know is she drinks a lot of coffee, forgets to water all the plants in the house, and never seems to sleep.

She's awesome.

"H-hey," she stammers out and looks up at me from my dad's old desk, wiping at her face. We have a lot of the same features, me and my mom, even though I'm a little tanner from Dad's Sicilian side. Our thick black hair and sharp Palestinian cheekbones betray how soft I know we both are, even if we try not to show it. The apple doesn't fall far and all that.

"You okay?" I ask, even though I can tell she isn't, walking into the office. Some mascara is running down her cheeks.

I lean against the wall, the cold exposed brick nipping at my neck, and I can't help but think of the Swedish Fish in my pocket from Chris. The old rickety windows, with faded glass that looks as old as the building itself, tremble a little from the wind outside, a soft dusting of snow already sticking to the gritty outside panels. "What's going on?"

"It's nothing." She sniffles; my fingers twitch for the candy. "Just, you know. *Another* mess we have to clean up, *another* rough day." She practically shouts the *anothers* and runs her hand through her hair and sighs, looking back down at the desk. "You shouldn't have to worry about any of this, Adam." There are a bunch of papers and notebooks splayed out over the surface, marks in black and red pen, and way too many neglected succulents, drying up to the point that they look like those bundles of tea that unfurl when you plop them in hot water. Dad's old aging PC hums louder than it should next to her, like it's trying its best to do an impression of an air conditioner.

"It'll be all right," I say, trying to swallow back the anxiety brewing in my chest. "I mean hey, we got a thousand dollars for that old machine, right? Maybe I can fix it. It'll be like we *made* money off it breaking." I look around the space, which is mostly taken up by some of Dad's old metal filing cabinets, packed with ancient pinball manuals and circuit blueprints, and shelves with boxes full of miscellaneous parts that never seem to be the pieces I need. Three out-of-commission machines stand pressed together along the wall, *Monopoly*, *Batman Forever*, and *Star Wars: The Phantom Menace*, overdue for a wildly expensive repair that's a bit beyond my skills or the arcade's finances.

"Maybe we just put it behind the café?" I look back out the office door. "Rope it off?"

She smiles up at me, but that smile barely reaches her eyes, and quickly turns back down, like she's trying to hold back a sob.

"That thousand dollars is nice, Adam, but—"

"Or we could unload the broken machine on someone who might want to fix it?" I shrug and rub my chin, a little bit of stubble scratching against my fingers. "I know that coworking space up the block has an old arcade cabinet that they refurbished. Chris goes there sometimes for makerspace meetups. Maybe they'd want—"

"Adam… Adam, just stop." She exhales, looking down at the notebooks and up to the old monitor. She reaches out and picks at a dead plant. "It's fine, we *can* get rid of it and just hold on to that extra money. I just…your dad liked that machine, is all. And I got a little too in my head about it, what with…" She sniffles and gestures her hand around in the air. "You know. This week."

"I know, I know."

I walk over and sit on the edge of the desk. Dad's carvings are all over the surface. Numbers. Random words. Bad attempts at drawings of characters found on various pinball games. I grab a crispy air plant out of a little brass planter dangling from a small basket on a hook.

"Aren't these supposed to be impossible to kill?" I ask, shaking it around.

"Yeah." She coughs out a laugh, shrugging. "I'll probably go bother Jill over at Krumm's this week. Restock on some plants to torture." The name of that place sends a little chill through me. It's Whitney's mom's plant boutique, and I try to avoid walking by that storefront whenever possible. It's practically right across the street, just down the block and around the corner near all the other Old City boutiques that dot Market Street. I've definitely spotted Whitney in there from time to time, while grabbing a slice of pizza or some tacos across the street. Places the two of us used to go to together, now just places I go to alone where our friendship haunts.

"I'm… I'm gonna go work on The Beast and think of what to do," I venture, wondering if Mom knew that the guy who knocked over the machine is her pal's son. I didn't recognize him, and I saw him in the school hallways for a full year, so maybe not. "And I'll leave the workshop door open. In case anyone comes in."

My mom looks up at me and nods, exhaling.

"You do know if things keep going the way they are, we're going to have to take one of…his meetings." She slides a pamphlet across the desk, and my eyes widen at the sight of the eSports café out in West Philly. It's bad enough I see them all around town, in coffee shops and restaurants, tacked up on bulletin boards. I never thought one would work its way into my home.

"Mom, no, come on—"

"We're not there yet," she presses. "I don't think. But I need you to be open to it."

"I can't make any promises," I grumble and lean in to give her a hug. I move to leave when she clears her throat.

I turn around, and she's got my lightly toasted copy of *We Built This Gritty* in her hands, a little smirk on her face. She throws it at me, and I just barely catch it.

"Saw it on the floor. Go talk to Dev at The Book Trader down the block. Maybe she's got a copy." She spins back to the computer. "I know you feel like you need to keep these… these unsaid promises to your dad, with the arcade and his unfinished game, but…" She glances up at me. "You need to keep the promises you make to yourself, too. How's the drafting going?"

I feel like it's my turn to start crying, and I really don't want to prove Chris right with his Swedish Fish right now.

"Good, good." I nod, thinking about the mostly unused drafting table in the workshop. Designing circuit schematics by drawing them out really isn't my thing, or anyone's thing in the year 2021, but Dad thought it would be a good idea to get me a whole drafting table when I started showing the slightest bit of interest. "I'm mostly just guessing at it on the computer, but I'm learning. I've got another workshop at NextFab next month on using that TinyCAD software."

"Great." She smiles. "Your dad would be so proud of you." She waves me away, dabbing at her eyes. She looks back down at the flyer and over at her dead plants, flicking a dried air plant off the table with her fingers. It skitters across the hard floor like an insect and she sighs. "We'll talk more later."

I wave the book at her and leave, shutting the office door behind me. I hurry by the snack bar, pass the broken game, and duck into the workshop after struggling with the old door.

I keep it open, the front door to the arcade in plain view, but my mom knows as well as I do, with that look she gave me, that no one else is coming today. Might as well lock the place up, or grab another copy of this book, and get some reading done in the dog park around the corner. It's a good place to watch for corgis, the pinballs of dogs, always bounding around all over the place.

I stare at my dad's old machine for a beat, before I grab a pair of pliers to fuss with one of the ball catches toward the top. Jorge emailed me this morning, to say the bumper I'd designed should be done in the next day or so, and I'm so eager to get back up to NextFab to see what he's done. I pull my phone out and look at the photos of the broken machine just outside.

There's this swell of... I don't even know. It's not quite anger. But there's this twinge of...jealousy, I think. The Mitchells, Whitney and her whole family, they've always just thrown money around to make their problems go away. Anytime her dad failed at some startup idea, he just threw himself into a new one, and there he would be. In the news, all over the place. When someone crashed into Whitney's parked Acura outside school, her dad got her a new one the very next day. Not that she told me about it. Everyone at school was talking about it.

Her dad is like the Philadelphia startup tech bro version of Batman, and Batman is the worst. You're not a superhero if you can buy away your problems, while we're here stressing over a hundred dollars here and there.

I tap over to the arcade's Twitter and check out the general news feed. It's mostly local shops here in Old City hyping up their plans for the Old City Winter Festival in a few days. Vagabond posting about their discounts, AKA Music with a series of pictures of discounted $1 vinyl that Dad would have just gone wild over, and Brian and Rob over at Brave New

Worlds, my favorite comic book shop, shooting videos of the graphic novels they're planning to put on sale for half off.

And of course, there's Whitney and that damn eSports café of her dad's, getting tons of attention and interaction. Things are fine; no one is running in there and breaking their computers or monitors or whatever. It's so easy for them. For Whitney, for Nick, for her family. People just show up at their cafés for something they could do at home; meanwhile we're here and no one comes. And you can't play pinball at home. Well. You can, but who owns several dozen pinball machines in their house?

Whitney's asshole dad probably could. Whitney could probably ask for a few for Christmas, just to spite me.

I peek out of the workshop, at the destroyed pinball machine. A couple stops in front of the entrance to the arcade, peer inside, and walk away.

I dart back into the workshop and pick my phone up.

Fuck it.

Sorry, Chris.

I go through and find the best photos from the smashed machine and get ready to unleash a little slice of Hell.

CHAPTER 2
Whitney

West Philly eSports:

Rumor has it there's going to be a big announcement this week from Blizzard? What does everyone think it's going to be? And would you want to have an announcement viewing party at the café? Vote below!

Yes	3,457

No 0

The music thrums from someplace deep within the historic brick row home, and as I place my hand on the railing leading up the white marble steps, I feel the vibrations in my hand. When I let go, my hand is still shaking.

I'm so mad.

It's bad enough that Dad jetsetted across the country for a conference I know he doesn't really need to be at, leaving me to take care of the café and my siblings all weekend, when

I should be relaxing. Nope, he had to go and neglect to tell me he wanted to have a big viewing party at the café for the surprise Blizzard announcement.

It's only a surprise to me and gamers everywhere. Him? He knew. He always knows that sort of stuff, and all I get for all the work I've been doing this weekend is a hastily written, typo-filled email, to "pleaz" make sure the café is ready for tomorrow.

Pleaz.

I heft my backpack up over my shoulder, the speakers inside jostling about a little against my back, and press my hand against the ajar front door.

"Watch out!" some boy shouts, stumbling out of Patrick's house, a girl's arm around his waist. My bag swings and clangs angrily against the cast-iron railing, and I wince and grit my teeth. Dad doesn't exactly keep track of all the slightly dated gadgets and tech he leaves stashed in the closet at the West Philly café, but I'm not in the mood to explain that I broke a handful of year-old Bluetooth Bose speakers on my way to a house party at my boyfriend's.

Especially when his parents are out of town, and I'm supposedly over at Helen's house. Not that I'd necessarily want to be at her house in the first place, but she's one of "my" girls, my little crew that I spend most of my time with. Me, Helen, Sophie, and Andrea, the four of us, connected at the hip since freshman year. Though I feel like I've been trying to get away from them the past two years.

It's hard when you start to realize the toxic friendships you're warned about in every movie and book are the kind you've surrounded yourself with. And no one seems to see it but you and the people on the outside, who aren't particularly interested in being friends with you, toxic by association.

And they're all in there. But so is Patrick. So away we go.

I recognize the dude from Patrick's hockey team, all checkered flannel and bedraggled chestnut hair and unearned confidence.

"Hey, watch where you're—"

Him and the girl start making out, leaning against the decorative iron fence that lines Patrick's parents' small patio garden, filled with barren azalea bushes and holly shrubs. Before I can say anything else, both of them give me the finger without looking, a feat both impressive and insulting. Their arms wrap around one another again as I suck at my teeth and turn to walk inside.

I hate Patrick's hockey bros, but I love him. I try to push back thoughts of my girl gang, Patrick's sports dudes, and everything going on with my dad and the café, for him.

I swing the door back open, this time without anyone making out tumbling out from inside, and the interior of Patrick's home is absolute chaos. There are piles of jackets and backpacks and boots in the narrow hallway that leads to his living room, the small area rug covering the hardwood floor is absolutely drenched from the little bit of rain and snow flurrying outside. I suppose the shoes of several dozen people will do that.

Whatever drum and bass *boots-and-cats-and-boots-and-cats* song is playing switches, and Taylor Swift's "Shake It Off" blasts, promoting cheers from somewhere inside. Despite how furious I am with my father and how this whole weekend has spiraled away from me, I smile, and nudge my way around a few people I vaguely recognize from our class.

Well, our old class. *My* old class, what with me wrapping up the school year somewhere new in the spring. Thanks to the move, I can walk to Patrick's house now, but not all my friends are so close. Whoever determines district lines in this city is the worst; how my house in South Philadelphia was somehow in the same space over two miles away, but now that I'm just a couple blocks away and on the wrong side of a certain street, I'm off to a whole new high school. I wonder if the break away from the girls will be the thing I need, to start over. To hit reset on my social life.

In the narrow living room, there's a whole DJ booth setup, and I wave at Carlos, a senior at Central and one of Patrick's good not-sports-bro friends, who is operating the tables. I'm not sure if he actually DJs live in front of everyone, or just plays music on his iPhone, but whatever the case, his music picks at his parties are always fantastic. And it doesn't hurt that he can snag his cousin's equipment whenever he wants.

Some of the multicolored lights held up precariously by thin metal stands flash, splashes of red, orange, and blue lighting up the exposed brick walls and plush West Elm furniture. It annoys me that I know that, recognizing the furniture. But Dad wanted a whole new look in the new house, and I spent way too much time poring over catalogs and fabric color swatches with him in our old South Philly kitchen. And as irritating as it was developing an encyclopedic knowledge of fancy furniture and the differences between bumblebee and pineapple yellow, it was nice to actually have him spend time with me outside work.

Which is, honestly, the only way we ever seem able to connect. Not like when I was a kid, and we'd spend hours fussing over wildly complicated LEGO sets that he'd buy secondhand. Substituting missing pieces with others. A roof of a small castle could be a shark. A wheel, a tree. It didn't matter that the homes we build were empty, as long as ours wasn't.

But things change.

There's a flurry of motion, and someone stumbles, spilling some kind of reddish drink on the burnt orange living room couch. Everyone around us moans an "ooooh" in the guy's direction, and he fumbles to cover the stain up with pillows.

Pretty sure that's the Leon, which is like a $1,500 couch.

Smooth move.

I inch my way around the crowd, a few classmates muttering solutions to get the stain out that sound bound to fail, one of which involves root beer and apple cider vinegar, and hop up to Carlos's mini booth. It's not so much a booth as it is a small, emptied-out bookcase with his equipment on top of it, and I glance around the room really quick for the books, which are nowhere to be found.

Jesus, Patrick.

His parties do always get a bit out of hand, but from the soaked hallway to the stained couch to the missing books, this is definitely out of control. Even for him.

"Hey." I tap the mixer, or whatever it is, and Carlos's eyes flit up to me. He grins and nods, pointing in the air as the song switches to something by The Chainsmokers, and he smiles as though this was an excellent decision. I wince and he shrugs, looking back down at his console. I tap the board again and he glances up, finally taking off his headphones.

"What's up, Whit?" he asks, running his tongue over his teeth. "I'm not taking requests, but for you I'll—"

I unzip my backpack and pull out one of the Bluetooth speakers, holding it up to him like I'm a witch offering up a poisoned apple.

"No way—" He lunges, and I pull the speaker back. "Hey!"

"Two conditions," I state, leaning on my hip a little, the speaker in my palm. "One, change the song. Two, where's Patrick?"

"Ugh, fine, fine," he grumbles, fiddling with something on the console. I'm tempted to peek over and see if it *is* his iPhone, but I don't want to hurt his feelings and break the illusion. An electronica remix of a Haim song comes on, and there are a few groans of protest, but I absolutely do not care. Perfect rocker girl group is perfect.

He holds out his hand and I give him a look.

"In the kitchen!" Carlos whines, pleading, his hands out. I drop the speaker in his hand and dig into my bag to find the other two. I scowl as my fingers brush something sharp, and when I pluck it out, one of the speakers has a crack in the plastic on its side. He winces at the thing and I shrug.

"Let me know if it works."

"Here, take this one with you." He hands me the not cracked one, which lights up with a soft blue light, music humming through it as it connects. It vibrates in my hand, and I wave at him with my free fingers and make my way toward the kitchen, weaving around some more classmates. People who know me and I vaguely know, but no one who is really a friend. There are a lot of quick nods and smiles as I squirm through another skinny hallway that opens up into

Patrick's kitchen. It's a bright space, with huge bay windows that overlook their surprising backyard, with the sort of massive trees you can spot from the street and wonder where they're planted, tucked behind row homes and brick.

He's standing in the middle of the kitchen, against the little kitchen island his parents have made me endless breakfasts and snacks on. Sophie, Helen, and Andrea are there, as well as a couple guys from school, all looking at him. I'm not sure what he's saying over the music, but he commands the space in the kitchen like he's holding court. I spot my brother Nick, right outside the back door to the kitchen. He's fiddling with something on his phone, and talking to one of the guys he's always out and about with. Steven, I think. Former high school baseball star turned disappointing college undergrad.

I look back to the kitchen island, to Patrick, and his eyes flit up to me, a smile breaking over his face.

The girls look up at me, and let out a shrill squeal and bound over, enveloping me in hugs that smell like vanilla-orange shampoo. It's warm and wonderful, and a welcome escape from the frigid atmosphere both outside and around the house. I can feel it, even though no one is saying anything, and maybe that's part of that. The silence, the nods, the eyes that look away and the conversations that quiet themselves when I get nearby. And it's so easy, so easy, to forget how I want to step away from these girls, when they're the only ones who seem comfortable with me stepping toward them.

"Hnnghhh!" I groan, feeling a little crushed. Patrick peeks into the group snuggle, and the girls inch away. He gives me a soft kiss and hugs me tight, before holding his hand out to the side, a bottle immediately landing in it. He hands it to me, a grin on his face, and leans back to grab his own drink off the kitchen island that's normally home to wholesome family meals, as opposed to high school debauchery.

"To winter break!" he crows, and everyone around him cheers. Bottles clink together, and he wraps his arm around my waist, pulling me tight against his side. He warms me up from the cold winter chill outside even more than the house does, and smells like a mix of sandalwood and wood shavings, like someone threw a bar of Old Spice soap at him and it just exploded against his chest. I glance at the bottle he handed me and around at everyone sipping. It's some kind of hard cider, and I take a swig, tasting the overly tart apples.

The song changes, some dance song I don't recognize, and Patrick groans, leaving my side and bounding toward the living room.

"Carlos, I told you to play some Mumford and Sons!" I hear him yelling as he stomps down the hall. "It's *my house!*"

I love Patrick, but his music tastes mostly consist of groups where dudes play banjos and acoustic guitars, with beards that are impossibly large, likely grown to hold guitar picks, harmonicas, or bird nests. I laugh and turn to the girls, and all three of them are mid eyeroll, smiles on their faces, though Sophie seems particularly annoyed. I catch another glimpse of Nick outside, who is looking in at all of us, but once he catches me staring at him, he turns away really quick, focusing back on his phone in the cold.

Weird. Whatever.

"What's up?" I ask, stepping over to the island and leaning on it. Something sticky is on the surface, and I nudge back, my skin squeaking against it. Great.

"Nothing." She sucks at her perfectly white teeth. Sophie

has the look of an Instagram model, with her dark red hair and bright green eyes, like a forgotten member of the Blossom family just stepped out of *Riverdale*. "He's just been pestering Carlos all night for music no one else wants to hear."

"Seriously," Helen scoffs. "We all love Patrick but could live without his beard rock."

"Is it him just projecting wish fulfillment?" Andrea asks, tapping her chin with a perfectly manicured nail. "That facial hair of his is…not great."

"Wish fulfillment?" Sophie laughs. "You get one B+ on a short story in creative writing, and now you talk like this. Besides, I like his scruff."

"You would," grumbles Andrea, and Sophie swats at her.

"What's going on with you?" Sophie asks, looking me up and down. "You look a mess."

"Ugh," I groan. "Stuff with my dad's café." Andrea and Helen turn toward me, suddenly a bit more interested, and inch closer. I glance up at them, and they nod, like they're eager to hear more. "I'm just tired, you know. Have to prep the place for a launch party."

"You and those video games." Helen shakes her head. "And them, am I right?"

She nods over at a crew in the corner of the kitchen. I recognize some of them vaguely from their appearances in the café…four boys who always have their Nintendo Switches out and about. The one time I managed to get a look at what they were doing, it seemed like they were playing that *Animal Crossing* game and working on each other's gardens.

"Fucking nerds." Helen rolls her eyes, looking back at me. "Why even come to a party?"

"I don't know." I shrug. "It's kinda nice. Those games are pretty relaxing and social—"

All the girls just stare at me.

"What?" I scoff. "They are."

"You're starting to sound like we're in freshman year again," Andrea says, and smirks at Helen. Sophie just shakes her head. "What was that game you were obsessed with? With the aliens?"

"Mass Effect," I grumble. "It has a good story."

"Right," Andrea mutters, looking off into the milling crowd of classmates for whoever her next target is going to be.

I fucking hate this. Why am I sitting here—?

My phone buzzes, and I pull it out of my pocket, feeling grateful for the interruption. At least I can focus on work instead of—

Wait.

What is this?

Old City Pinball:

This afternoon we lost one of our vintage pinball machines due to some pretty serious vandalism. Shout out to Nick and his friends, who took the time to tip over a Flash Gordon machine, shattering it on our floor. And hello to his family at West Philly eSports!

Also, if anyone is in the market for a broken Flash Gordon pinball machine, we'd like to rehome it. We won't be able to fix it, but we really don't want to just throw it away.

1,257 Likes, 97 Replies

No.

No, no, no.

Nick, what the hell did you do? Of all people to mess with, Adam and his damn pinball arcade? The biggest headache of my life? It can't be that bad. It can't be—

Click to Load Media

GODDAMMIT. How do you even do that to a pinball machine? Those things weigh like a million pounds from what I remember. I look up and outside, and Nick has disappeared from where he was leaning against the back door. When I get a hold of him, I am going to let him have it.

Technically Philly News:
Are you saying that Nick Mitchell vandalized the arcade? Can you email or message us? Can we have permission to share these photos?

32 Likes

Old City Pinball:
Absolutely.

3 Likes

Philadelphia Weekly:
Can we have permission to share these images?

25 Likes

Old City Pinball:
Why not. Sure.

4 Likes

Oh, my God. I press a hand against the counter of the kitchen island, steadying myself.

My breathing gets quick and I grit my teeth.

"What is it?" Helen asks.

"Probably Patrick sexting her from the living room." Andrea laughs.

"Oh, my God, shut the fuck up," I snap, my hands up. The kitchen gets quiet and I look back down at the screen, ignoring everyone's whispers.

Chris Makes Stuff: WHAT ARE YOU DOING I SAID NOT TO GO ONLINE.

2 Likes

> **Old City Pinball:** _(ツ)_/
>
> 6 Likes

Brave New Worlds:
Yo dibs on the machine! Me and Rob will swing by tomorrow, I'll message you. We'll trade you something.

37 Likes

> **Old City Pinball:**
> Done
>
> 4 Likes

Well, all right. Here we go. I can't just let this spiral out of control.

West Philly eSports:
Excuse me? You've got a lot of nerve publicly disparaging my business and our family like this. Where is your proof? Who do you think you are?

237 Likes

Old City Pinball
Oh, hi Whitney. Been a while. Tell Nick we at Old City Pinball
say hello. He doesn't have to come back to help or anything.
We clean up our messes.

198 Likes

West Philly eSports
Oh, hi ADAM. See my previous post.

128 Likes

Son of a Mitch:
What the hell man, I paid for the machine. It was an accident.
You didn't have to put me on blast like this.

1,928 Likes

I almost slam my phone down against the kitchen island.
I look back up, and there's Nick, walking inside from the
backyard. He flicks a cigarette into the wind, turns, and his
eyes meet mine.

"You," I growl.

"Oh fuck," Nick says, staggering back as I stomp over toward him. He moves to try to make it back outside, but he
struggles with the door and isn't nearly fast enough to escape.

"What were you thinking?" I snap, resisting the urge to
straight up lunge at him. He scowls at me and scoffs, but
squirms a little, his eyes darting around.

"Oh come on, Whit, chill out," he grumbles, still looking about.

"None of them are going to save you." I dart in front of
his line of vision, and I hear a couple of giggles around me,
and look over quickly to see the girls and everyone else in the
kitchen zeroed in on us. "You and your friends are assholes."

"Oh whatever." He crosses his arms and leans against the door, glowering at me. "Like you're one to talk." He points at, the girls.

"Hey!" Sophie snaps.

"I paid for the machine," he continues. "It's over."

"What?" I scoff. "It's absolutely not over!" I shout back, and he starts to walk out of the kitchen. I follow, weaving in between some classmates walking toward me, and pull my phone out of my pocket. "Get back here!"

"Why, so you can yell at me? We're at a *party*!" he shouts back, heading toward the living room and Carlos. The booming music is some kind of folky indie band, and I spot Patrick near the DJ booth nodding his head, while everyone else in the room looks wildly annoyed. I even spot some people getting their coats. It's not that bad, but I suppose if you showed up at a party to drink and dance, a bunch of people airily singing with a cello playing in the background isn't going to do that.

"Yes!" I shout back. "You're fueling the fire!" Some guy brushes by me, glaring. "You need to fix this."

"I. Paid. For. It." Nick is at the front door, wrangling his jacket from the piles of them on the ground. He flings a few this way and that, not caring.

"Money doesn't fix everything!" I exclaim.

"People who say that don't have it," he says back, in a tone so flat that I want to reach out and slap him across the face. He acts as though we weren't just living in a crumbling row home a few years ago, barely scraping by before Dad finally had a big break with something. He hefts his jacket up and pulls his hood down, his face curled up in a snarl. "I'll see you at home."

"Nick!" I shout as he bolts out the door, slamming it shut behind him. I'm too late as I dart toward it and just slam my fist against the wood. I'm not about to chase him. Not when my boyfriend and seemingly half my class are here. I want to try to enjoy some semblance of normalcy before I start at the new school in January.

I lean against the wall in the narrow hallway by the front door, typing madly on my phone.

West Philly eSports:
Nick get off of here, you're only making this worse.

342 Likes

> **Old City Pinball:**
> No, stay! This is just getting fun.
>
> 834 Likes

> **Son of a Mitch:**
> Fuck you man, that thousand dollars is more than your place makes in a month.
>
> 32 Likes

> **West Philly eSports:**
> Old City Pinball, I'm going to private message you. Okay Adam?
>
> 17 Likes

> **Old City Pinball:**
> Feels a little late for that.
>
> 593 Likes

Nick. I just can't believe him. I'm clenching my jaw so tight that I feel like I'm going to chip a tooth.

Before the money, before Dad's success, he wasn't like this.

We went thrifting; he rummaged at the Center City flea markets with me. When Dad's ventures failed, as they often did, we skimped and saved our money from our shitty part-time jobs, so Mom wouldn't have to carry us all on her own before he managed to wrangle more funding for whatever new idea he was kicking around.

My brother, who once couldn't wait to go to the county college and mostly ate out of food trucks, now brags about his Ivy League school that my dad paid to get him into and turns his nose up at any restaurant that isn't Steven Starr or Jose Garces. But I remember the two of us, how different things were.

I turn around, and everyone is looking at me.

"It's fine!" I exclaim, holding my hands up in the air. "Everything's fine. My brother's still a dick."

I walk back up the hallway, staring down at my phone as people part ways like the Red Sea for me. My inbox is quickly filling with direct messages from angry people I don't recognize and local media outlets that I absolutely do.

Adam. Fucking. Stillwater.

It's bad enough it's already spiraled into real life, here and now, with a fight with my brother. Embarrassing me in front of all these classmates and the girls. This online disaster that Adam's causing me isn't going to disappear if I just sit here and ignore it, and let myself, I don't know, actually have a good time at this party—if I let myself stay late, stay over, stay on the couch making out while watching terrible Netflix movies. No. He's assured that the night, the entire holiday, the whole winter break, is going to go up in flames.

All because of my idiot brother.

I fire off a quick text to Patrick to let him know I'm heading up to his room to take care of some work stuff. I watch the little bubbles pop up where he should respond, but they fade. It's fine, though. I know he'll rush up the stairs and scoop me up when the party is over, or things quiet down.

I make my way up the stairs, passing photos of his family lining the narrow staircase. The second floor opens up to a slim corridor that breaks off to the right and straight ahead, one to his parents' master bedroom, the other toward his room and the bathroom. Classic Philadelphia row house, huge downstairs, small rooms on the tiny second floor. I head toward his room when I hear some giggling and peek back, just in time to see two girls walking out of his parents' room.

Dammit. I should be the one kissing up here, but instead I'm dealing with this.

I walk into Patrick's room, which is also a disaster, clothing all over the floor, sheets on his bed totally rumpled. It looks like people downstairs came up here to change or—

My foot gets caught in a bra and I stumble. I don't want to know whose that is, or what couple was just in here.

I kick it, and some other clothes, into the center of the room and walk over toward the window, flopping down in the massive papasan chair right near it, sinking into the outrageously comfortable cushion. I feel like the chair could straight up swallow me, leaving me to swim inside the stuffing, and right now I fully welcome that. Just envelop me, please. But alas, my arms and hands remain undevoured, and my phone beckons.

People are still coming after me. It's so unfair. I wasn't even there; it was Nick. But the internet doesn't care. And I know,

I know in my heart, that they aren't raging against me, the person. It's the café they're furious with, and by proxy, my father. They don't see the person behind the online brand, the online personality. They see a target.

I always feel bad for the people behind accounts that get like, roasted online. Restaurants. Airlines. Phone companies. Not the actual corporations, but the social media manager who has to deal with all the vitriol. That's me.

And I'd quit. I really would. God knows Patrick wants me to. Mom absolutely wants me to. But with Dad as busy as he is, it's the one way I can still feel connected to him. The eSports cafés are the center of his focus; not me, not Nick, definitely not our little sister who looks up to him like he's a rock star. If I let go, if I let him hire on an actual social media manager who would get paid a salary and all of that, would he even see me anymore?

I need this. And I need it to go well.

The music hums from downstairs as I flip through Twitter, hopping back and forth from there to Instagram and Facebook, where folks are leaving us negative reviews and tagging us in the worst rants. I've got to figure out a way to smooth all this over—

"Hey."

I almost fall backward out of the cushiony chair, which is built in a way to purposely avoid such an accident, when Patrick grabs the back of the chair's wooden frame. His hands are on both sides of me, and he slides down onto the top of the chair, his chest pressed against it, his head nestled on top of mine. He drops down to my shoulder, nuzzles my neck, and stands up, walking around to face me.

"Come on." He holds a hand out and nods at my phone. "How about we put that away and go downstairs and dance."

"Patrick, no, the café—"

"We could dance a little in here, if you want. Just you and me?" He winks and I roll my eyes, nodding at the bra in the center of the room.

"Someone else was already doing that," I huff. "Who are you letting fool around up here?"

"What?" he asks and looks over at the pile of clothes. He must spot the bra because he winces. "Oh." He steps aside and nudges it farther into the mess of outfits with his foot, like he's just gonna make it disappear. "I think that was Kashif and that new girl he's dating." One of his hockey bros, then. He slides down to the floor, looking up at me. "Forget all that. What's the deal there? Someone downstairs said you and Nick were fighting?"

"It's Nick," I groan, looking back at my phone. "He's messing up everything. Messed up." I get up and pace the length of his small bedroom. "I mean, here, look at this." I hand him my phone, and I take a few deep breaths, trying to calm myself down again before sitting down on his bed.

"What is he trying to do to me?" I ask. "Why would he do this?"

"Do what?" Patrick asks, staring at the screen. He looks up at me, his hazel eyes full of confusion, his kissable lips turned down in a frown. "Babe, I don't know what you're talking about or what this is. Is this the account for your dad's place?"

"Yes!" I grab the phone and look back, my heartbeat quickening. I shouldn't have looked back at this. I should have just sat here and hung out with my boyfriend, stayed downstairs, danced, had some drinks, and—

"Oh, my God, every local news outlet is sharing this. I need to think." I look around the little room, and feel my breathing getting a little too heavy. "I need... I need to get some air. Can we go outside?" I wave my hands in front of my face. "It's just a little too constrained in here."

"Yeah, sure," Patrick says, getting up from the floor. He kicks at the clothes, nudging them even farther into a corner. We walk out into the hallway and just manage to catch another couple sneaking into his parents' room.

"Hey!" Patrick snaps, shooing them away from the door. "Come on, don't be gross. That's my parents' room. Go do it in the bathroom or something."

I turn and scowl at him and he shrugs.

Such a romantic.

I grab my white jean jacket off the floor, a boot print right in the back of it, the footprint almost cartoony in how perfectly placed it looks, and swing it over my shoulders, annoyed. That's gonna be a pain to get out, but I'll do it. It's my favorite coat; me and the girls all have matching ones. I wonder how it'll feel on my back, when they're not around to *have* my back anymore, at a new school in the spring. Am I still going to want to wear this, a relic of that old life?

The couple who was previously making out against the patio fence is sitting on the curb now, holding hands and chatting. I sit down on Patrick's white marble steps. I take a breath, the cool autumn air a nice replacement for the atmosphere inside the house, full of perfume, cologne, alcohol, and hastily snuck cigarettes, but it doesn't do me much good as I stare down at my phone.

I swear with every exhale, there's a new major local media outlet popping up, sharing Adam's photos. Inhale. There's a post. Exhale. Another retweet. And of course, they're all the ones in the demographic our place caters to. The geeky outlets. *Technically Philly*, with all their local tech and startup coverage, being the one that concerns me the most. We are an eSports café. Video games. Those are our people, and I need them wanting to cover our events and post about them online. I don't want them hating us more than some people already seem to, the big, bad startup that revitalized two failing storefronts in West Philadelphia and Camden. Such absolute villains.

And if Dad gives the social media accounts over to someone else, God, if he fires me, how am I supposed to get him to see me? Between the possibility of that and leaving my old school behind halfway through my senior year, I'm looking at having no one but Patrick, and Mom on the weekends.

I could get Nick to post something…some kind of public apology. Maybe Dad could donate a pinball machine to a school. The Hillman Academy down the block, perhaps. I can still fix this. Or maybe—

The front door to the house opens, and Patrick peeks out.

"You closed the door behind you," he says, drily. "Am I invited?"

"Sorry." I snort out a laugh and scoot over.

I motion for him to sit with me. I reach out to grab his hand, but he shirks it away, rubbing them together.

"It's cold out here. Can't we just go back upstairs?" he

grumbles. "My living room? Anywhere inside the house, you know, where an entire party is happening?"

I start swiping through all the notifications on my phone. He mutters something and inches away from me on the stoop, pulling out his own phone, texting away. I do a double take as he stares at his screen, away from me.

"Hey," I start, reaching out. "Hey, I'm sorry."

"You know, it would be great if when you came over, you just existed here with me," he says, sharply. "You're always just staring at your phone. What is so impossibly important right now?"

"My brother! My dad's café! Ugh. He broke a pinball machine at that arcade in Old City, and they put it out on social media, and everyone is—"

"Did he die?" Patrick snaps, looking back at me.

"What?" I laugh.

"I'm just saying, is it that critically important and world ending? I know your dad's business is important to you, and it keeps you all close. I mean, sometimes I feel like I only really stick with hockey because it makes my parents so happy, but at least I like it."

"Hey, I like doing this stuff," I grumble, wiggling my phone. At least, most of the time I do. Not right now.

He sighs, and then a little flash of realization washes across his face, and he looks back at me, his eyebrows quirking down. "Wait. Pinball arcade? Adam Stillwater's place?"

"Yeah," I mutter.

"Jesus, Whit." He rubs his forehead. "How many times am I going to have to keep hearing about this guy?"

"He trolls my dad's cafés!" I exclaim. "It's not my fault he's out there blowing up my mentions on Twitter, making my family look like we're monsters."

"Is it, though?" Patrick asks.

"Excuse me?"

"Nothing," he huffs, getting up off the stoop. He leans against the iron railing leading up the steps. "So what, people are giving the café crap because your brother did something wrong? I really don't know what the big deal is. It's the internet. People will forget about it *tomorrow.*"

"It's the *optics,*" I stress. "And while the internet might forget, people don't. Dad is going to lose it when he gets home. People are already leaving the West Philly location bad reviews on Facebook and Yelp and seemingly everywhere else, because of what he did at the arcade! It's not even connected to the cafés! God, and who knows what they're saying about the Camden spot. I still need to check that. Reviews—that stuff lasts longer than random social media posts."

I open up Growth, my favorite social media tool, and swipe around. It feeds in just about every single network into one convenient "hellscape" as my brother likes to call it, so I can keep an eye on everything.

Most of the time, I love it. I really do. Even now, when putting out fires.

I just…hate how this one was set.

This is worse than someone who hated their latte or had a bunch of lag while playing *League of Legends*, or maybe missed out on a livestream they wanted to catch after we ran out of space. No one dives in to support some random user who is grumpy there was too much sugar in their coffee.

This is different.

People are coming after us in multiple places, even on the photo-sharing apps, just tagging us in rage-filled posts. And we're getting mentioned in a bundle of quickly written news blips, covering what Nick did, sharing the photos from Adam. There are a few more in some of these, other than the ones he'd posted originally, and they are better quality than the ones he put online, so I'm guessing he took quite a few and sent them over.

Dammit.

The story is just spiraling out of control, making it look like it was some kind of coordinated attack on the place. The big, bad new tech business across town tucked in the big sprawling campus that is West Philadelphia and University City, sabotaging the small mom-and-pop arcade in the historic district of Old City. It just writes itself, and I'm honestly surprised Dad hasn't texted or called me about it yet.

"All this—" I wiggle the phone around before looking back at the screen "—helps keep my family in business."

"People would find out about your dad's video game cafés without your posts," Patrick grumbles, taking a step away from the stairs, standing in the sidewalk. "You could easily let someone else run that show, and you know it."

I let out a huff and keep going through. If I reply to too many of these, it's just going to spiral out. We're going to need to address it once and move on, and hope the damage is contained there.

"Are you even listening to me?" Patrick asks.

"What?" I ask. "Yeah, of course, babe." I get up and walk toward him. He's wearing his corduroy jacket, a dark sandy color that brings out his hazel eyes, a bright yellow enamel pin on the collar. It's some local band called The A-Sides, who broke up over a decade ago. Pretty sure neither of us really knew what music was back then, but he listens to them all the time, on vinyl records left behind by his sister before she went off to college.

"I don't...think I'm happy," he says.

"What?" I scoff. "What are you—" My phone buzzes and I pull it out, and Patrick huffs. "It's my mom, hold on. Mom!"

"What did your brother do?" my mom asks, laughter in her voice. I'm jealous of the lightness there, and the sounds of her shop and people chatting and humming in the background. "I have people from boutiques all around the neighborhood coming by and asking what's up."

"I'm sorry," I groan. "He broke a machine at Old City Pinball with his idiot friends. And then Adam—"

"Adam," Patrick scoffs. I glance over at him, and he's facing the street, texting on his phone.

"Oh, Adam." My mom sighs. "That poor kid. Maybe I should go talk to his mother. Maybe she's at the arcade. Did you two talk about it?"

"Yeah, sure, I guess we did," I grumble. "*He's* the one who posted all the photos, you know." A few snow flurries flutter by and I glance up at the sky, a foreboding light gray. The gust chills me through my jean jacket. The news keeps talking about an upcoming storm, but right now I have to quiet *this* one.

"Well, he's upset!" my mom exclaims. "And you know, the girls at the Smak Parlour boutique offered to launch a Go-FundMe for him, to pay for that machine?"

"Cool, great," I huff. "So everything is fine for him after

like, what, half an hour? I get dragged on the internet, and he gets showered with money and affection."

"Whit, come on now. People aren't attacking *you*. They're taking their anger out on your dad's video game coffee shops," my mom says, and I can just hear that smile in her voice. She knows they are eSports cafés, but okay, Mom.

"It's the same thing!" I shout.

"It's not." She sighs. "And the sooner you realize that, the happier you're going to be. Are you swinging by this week at all? You could maybe drop by his arcade, apologize for your idiot brother?"

"Apologize?" I snort. "In person, to him?" I scoff. "Not a chance, not after what he did online. He knows what he's doing."

"Well, then at least come help us prepare for the winter festival." She sighs. "There's a lot to do, and you need a break from all your dad's drama. Besides, it'll be fun. We have a lot of terrariums to make."

The Old City Winter Festival, when all the boutiques and restaurants set up their wares and dish out food on the street, in the chilly and blustery Philadelphia winter. It always happens right before the New Year, and sometimes when we're lucky, with a dusting of snow…though this year seems to be hinting at more. After her and my dad split, Mom threw herself into creating the yearly event, meeting with the Old City District and neighborhood associations to make the thing happen, finding "a bit more warmth in the winter as opposed to with your father," which is a great thing to tell your kid in a house still reeling from being fractured.

"Yeah, yeah," I tell her. "I'll probably swing by on Monday. Dad's still away until tomorrow."

"Great! Bring Patrick," she says, and I hear her co-owner, Alison, squeal an *ooooh!* somewhere in the shop. "We have a few terrariums to finish up, and he's got those musician hands." I can hear the grin in her voice at the end of that sentence and roll my eyes.

"Pat, my mom wants help setting up for the festival next week. You want to come?" I ask, talking off to the side. He's silent, and I peek over.

He's texting still, looking away from me.

We go every year. Last December they had a temporary ice-skating rink set up right in the middle of the dog park on Second and Market, where we held hands and drank hot chocolate. I feel like I took a million photos that night.

"Pat?" I walk over and nudge him, and he shirks away. "Mom, I gotta go. I'll see you Monday." I hang up and slide my phone in my pocket.

"I'm not even here," he says, turning to look at me, his face turned into a scowl. "I don't even exist when you're on your phone, taking care of your dad's stuff."

"Come on, of course you are." I reach out and he steps away again. "Who were you texting?"

"Oh, like you care," he snaps.

"Pat." I reach out. "I just had to talk to my mom about—"

"I'm not happy anymore, and honestly, neither are you," he says, crossing his arms, his eyes flitting about, not meeting mine. "I haven't been happy for a while, and I deserve to be with someone who wants me to be."

"What?" I snort a laugh. "Yes, I am. How can you say I'm

not happy?" I stop for a beat, because there is a part of him that's a little right, but he doesn't understand. His family is there for him, constantly surrounding him with affection and attention. I need him. "And what do you mean *someone who wants you to be*?" My eyes flit to his phone. "Are you texting with some other girl?"

"You're not happy and you just don't realize it." He shakes his head, completely bypassing my question. "You're so wrapped up trying to hear people who don't care that you're listening, that you're missing out on everyone who actually cares for you."

"My dad cares," I push back. "Who were you texting?"

"Yeah, right. And all those followers?" He scowls, shoving his phone in his pocket, like I somehow don't notice. "Your little…internet wars with Adam Stillwater? They don't matter. None of it matters."

"You don't know what you're talking about." I step forward and grab his hands, and he tries to pull away, but I hold on tight. "I'm here. I'm listening."

He pauses for a beat.

"Who were you texting?" I ask.

He tosses my hands away from him, and stomps toward his house.

"I'll…see you around school in January, I guess," he grumbles, reaching for his door.

"January? *January*?" I snap, following him toward the stairs. "I'm not going to be at our school in January." He tenses up at his front door but doesn't turn around. "So you do remember."

"Whitney," he says, exhaling. "Come on. I'm sorry, but—"

"Patrick…" I take another step toward him and his home, toward the steps we'd spent endless hours sitting on. Snuggling, drinking pumpkin spice lattes and eating breakfast sandwiches piping hot from food trucks, talking about our plans. Him at Penn, me at Drexel, going to different colleges in the same city and not making the mistake some of our friends did, burning out as couples at the same school. Follow one of those awful bands he loves around on tour, the summer before college starts. I could learn to love those stupid beards. I could. I *would*.

He glances back at me from the doorway and shakes his head.

"Look, I'm sorry, but this—" he gestures at himself and then to me "—this is done."

And he shuts the door.

I sit down on the stoop, my heart racing, blood pounding in my head. He's being ridiculous. I don't only think about my dad's eSports joints and all the social media. And even if I did, it's important. It's the family business, and my dad needs me. And Adam? Barely a passing thought; he's an irritation, like a mosquito or a pimple. And I definitely don't sit on my phone all the time. He's over here talking like some kind of out-of-touch boomer, like I'm addicted to being online, when I'm *working*.

And who was he texting that he just tried to brush away from—

Wait.

My phone.

"Hey!" I shout, standing up and facing the door. I bang on it with my fist. "Patrick! My charger is in there! Come on."

After a beat I hear a window open, the noise of old wood clacking angrily against a hard surface and look up.

My iPhone cord goes sailing out Patrick's window, and onto the sidewalk. The window closes with a bang.

Asshole.

West Philly eSports: Well, my boyfriend just broke up with me BECAUSE OF YOU.

Old City Pinball: What? I don't see how that is even possible.

Old City Pinball: Do I know him?

Old City Pinball: Oh no. Is your boyfriend a pinball machine?

Old City Pinball: Did he see what your brother did? Was he upset?

West Philly eSports: I hate you so much.

Old City Pinball: Block me then.

West Philly eSports: Why don't YOU block ME?!

Old City Pinball: Ah yes, this dance.

Old City Pinball: ♫ ♪ And I've...

Old City Pinball: Had

Old City Pinball: The time of my liiiife. ♫ ♪

West Philly eSports: You and your old movies. And music. And everything.

Old City Pinball: Old things have character.

Old City Pinball: Soul.

West Philly eSports: Do old things have friends?

Old City Pinball: Wow.

Old City Pinball: Nice. Real nice.

West Philly eSports: Whatever. You know you could actually just text me. Not like my number changed.

Old City Pinball: Like I even have it anymore.

Brave New Worlds: Hey we'll swing by tomorrow morning.

Old City Pinball: See you guys then. Gotta warn you, it's super broken, it'll cost money to fix. Do you have the new Wendy Xu graphic novel? I'd love that and anything like it as a trade.

Brave New Worlds: Deal, brother. We'll hook you up with a whole stack of books.

CHAPTER 3
Adam

"A good game of pinball and a good friendship have one key thing in common. They should be built to last. The trick is to keep your eye on what matters, splitting time between what brings you joy and what obstacles you'll have to face. The lights, the buzzers, the bumpers, the pitfalls…you and the player are in it all together. Keep the player in the same place you keep your loved ones…in your mind and in your heart."

–THE ART AND ZEN OF PINBALL REPAIR
BY JAMES WATTS

A winter-worn Philadelphia passes by me in the large, cloudy passenger window. I barely feel my phone buzz against my leg, as the SEPTA bus rumbles up Girard, jostling me about in the faded white plastic seat. If it's another direct message from Whitney, trying to make me feel like a monster, it's not going to work.

Because I…kind of already do.

I don't like her. I don't like her father, definitely don't

like her brother, and those eSports cafés that are basically a modern take on arcades. Why try to fix or upgrade something that isn't broken? But...I have some regrets about that post. All those attacks. Whitney is a lot of things, but she's not what all those people are saying. And I know, *I know* the posts aren't about her, but when you try to pretend living, breathing people aren't there behind social media accounts, you start to dehumanize everyone.

I should delete that post, but it's not like she's ever apologized to me. There's no deleting her comments, her treatment of me online and in the corridors of Central. The way her and her friends laughed, in their white jean jackets, in the school hallway.

I pull my phone out, and there are a bundle of notifications, on Twitter and Instagram, and a few emails have piled up. My phone buzzes again, and that's when I realize it's text messages lighting me up, not more DMs.

And mercifully, it's Chris.

CHRIS

Hey. You almost here?
Jorge has your bumpers printed.

CHRIS

And I know what today is.

CHRIS

Let me know if you need to talk.

CHRIS

🐟

Ugh, is that one of his fish candies? In a text?

I shove my phone back in my pocket and keep watching the cityscape rolling by. Every now and again, some wildly out of place new building is being built, smack in between old row houses and shops. There's the occasional swath of construction, large chunks of the city block gone missing, big lot-for-sale signs replacing whatever was there before.

Some things should stay the way they are.

Arcade games. Vinyl records. Old row houses.

Families.

Friendships.

But that's not how life works.

Maybe that's why I like pinball machines so much. Real ones, old ones. You can restore them and fix them up as much as you want, but you can't get rid of the grit. The scuffs and scratches in the plastic, the dings and dents along the steel edges. You could buy new plastic buttons or metal doors, but then it isn't the same anymore. You've changed it.

Then again, I suppose that's what this project with Jorge is kind of all about. Breathing life into something old. Second chances. The latest plans in my messenger bag are proof of all that.

I stretch, the leather of my jacket squeaking against the plastic seat, and lean my head against the cold, rattling window. Dad's old R.E.M. jacket doesn't exactly provide a lot of warmth in the traditional sense of the word, but it'll do. Especially today.

The year is almost over. We've barely broken even, and there are things we need to fix, like the rumbling bad water heater that sounds like one of the monsters from those *Quiet*

Place movies my mom hates but for some reason always watches. But the one thing I don't know how to fix is how to get people to come back.

People don't come back, after they've left.

I see where this road is going. For me, for the arcade.

And I'm not ready to say goodbye just yet.

The smell of sawdust and ozone fill the air as I sign in at NextFab and walk through the large wide doors into the workshop space. People are hustling about. An older guy wearing a thick leather apron, the surface blackened and scratched to all hell, brushes by me to work on who knows what. A few nerdy younger women stroll past, talking excitably to one another, long trails of lights in their hands. I walk along a line in the middle of the floor, colored yellow and black like warning tape, meant to keep anyone passing through the busy makerspace from crashing into any of these busy people with their metalwork or wearable tech or lasers.

Some guy has a huge-looking drafting table, with electric schematics spread out like he's planning to build a house, but it's probably just some kind of circuit board. I think about the poorly sketched-out ones in my bag, and immediately feel some kind of impostor syndrome settle in. What am I *doing* here?

I spot Chris over in the woodworking side of the space, a few people scattered about the area, busy with their respective projects. He's sanding down some long-curved piece of wood, and I shout for him from the line. The last thing I want is to sneak up and tap him on the shoulder and get a face full of sandpaper.

He turns around and waves excitably, motioning for me to come over.

"Hey, man!" he exclaims as I get closer, my eyes flitting around cautiously to the people nearby with their tools that look like they'd fit neatly in my chest. He lifts his goggles up and sticks them on his forehead, gesturing at his workspace. It's this large table with tools and wood and glass just scattered about, in seemingly no order. "What do you think?"

The piece of wood he was sanding sits neatly in the middle of all the mess. There's another just like it nearby, both of them shaped like question marks without the dot.

"I'm not sure what I'm looking at?" I shrug.

"You have no appreciation for my art." He groans and grabs the other piece. He leans them together and reaches underneath his bench, plucking out a third one, and all three pieces come together in an odd tripod with a curled base and a center holding space. He turns and looks at me, smiling, his hands out.

"I still don't—" I start.

"Ugh!" He sighs. "Why are you like this? I'll tell you why. It's that Keurig you keep underneath the snack bar at the arcade. It's ruined your vision!"

"What does that have to do with anything?" I laugh.

"Watch," he says and grabs a curved glass vessel from his pile of stuff, placing it gently in between the wooden slats. It sits there comfortably, the glassware tapering off in the middle kind of like an hourglass. "It's a new one of my pour overs!"

"Ah, okay." I nod. "I see it now."

"Listen, this thing is going to make amazing coffee," he says, taking a step back, admiring his own work. "It took me forever to get that shape right on the vessel. Maybe this is the month I convince one of the local cafés to use it, or your mom to let me give these a test run in the arcade."

"Good luck." I laugh. "All we need is someone to bump into the bar and send all that coffee soaring onto somebody's head." I shake *my* head and keep checking out the work on the table. There are shavings from his wooden pieces, I'm guessing, and a cast-iron glassblower and some tongs. Between the woodworking and the glassblowing, Chris has got to be the single most handy person I know, and maybe the only person in our school with hobbies straight out of ancient times. I feel like the rest of our class just got really into photography using their phones.

After a beat, he grabs my shoulder. "Hey, you okay?"

I look over at him and shrug.

"Is it dad stuff? Or Whitney stuff?" he asks.

"A bit of both, really?" I shrug. "I'm feeling...not great about the other day. The post and all, I don't know."

"Well, I mean, I told you...but come on, I know just the thing to cheer you up. It's what you're here for anyway, right? Got those schematics?"

"Right here." I pat my bag. "Calling them actual schematics is...generous, though. They're more like drawings on a paper towel."

"You're too hard on yourself. Come on, I'll walk you up and then wrap up what I'm doing." He throws his arm around my shoulder and gives me a side hug and starts walking along the caution tape leading out of the space. I follow along, making a sharp right up a set of metal stairs toward the second

floor, skirting carefully around a guy carrying a pile of circuitry down the steps in a hurry.

The upstairs opens up into an entirely different setting,
leaving behind the woodworking and construction scene
for gadgets, computers, enormous laser printers, and etching
tools. I follow Chris along the line, spotting a familiar face
across the room in front of a thick plastic-looking cube with
rounded edges. It's an odd choice for a desk, looking more
like an oversize storage bin or an aquarium, but through the
transparent plastic I can see all the gadgets he's been putting
together, on display for anyone who walks by. Jorge looks
up, and grins, motioning the two of us over, and then ducks
behind his table.

"Just a sec, friends," he says, digging around for something
inside.

"Hey, I'm gonna go back down. There's a glass mold I ordered from Farah that I gotta scoop up," Chris says, already
walking away. "I'll meet you back at my table." He rounds a
corner and disappears down the steps. Farah. She's a program-
mer who spends her free time here smelting out of a mini
forge in the very back of the makerspace, and her Instagram
is wildly popular. A few years ago she made a set of chainmail
armor using soda cans thrown out at Wawas around town.

So cool.

"Here it is!" I turn back just as Jorge pops up from behind
his cube. He hands me a Liberty Bell, about the size of a computer mouse, that fits perfectly in the palm of my hand. It's
got a little weight to it, and I lift it up and down, feeling the
heft. I turn it on its side, and I just can't contain my smile.

"Well?" he asks, crossing his arms. "Not bad, right?"

I run my fingers over the rubber along the edges and tap it, feeling the light bounce. Underneath there's the solenoid, a coil of copper wire that activates a bumper when a pinball hits it, and the Liberty Bell bounces up and down a little bit on the plunger.

It's the perfect piece for Dad's machine.

And on today of all days.

"I don't even know what to say, Jorge," I practically whisper. "It's exactly what I pictured." I look up at him, blinking away what feels like tears. "I mean, it matches the bell on the mural outside the arcade exactly."

"I tried my best." He shrugs, a little smirk on his face. He knows it's good.

"How much do I—" I start fussing with my wallet when Jorge reaches out and stops me.

"Come on, man." He shakes his head. We go through this every single time he's helped me with a part or given me a lesson in electronics. "No way. It's a joy to work on this stuff during my downtime."

"Sure, but—"

"None of that," he says, walking back around to his workstation, patting his large 3D printer. "When me and my friends were getting priced out of our little coworking space in Old City, your dad was the guy who rallied to try to keep us there. I'm only sorry I can't make more of these things faster."

"I don't deserve you." I smile, looking at the Liberty Bell bumper again.

"Sure you do," he says, reaching out and patting my shoulder. He steps back, arms crossed, looking at me expectantly. "Well?" He holds out a hand. "Let me see it."

"Ugh," I groan, lifting my bag up onto his table. I push aside a few weathered paperbacks, including a backup copy of Watts's *The Art and Zen of Pinball Repair* and a novel called *Ziggy, Stardust and Me*, the last book Dad gave me with one of the most beautiful David Bowie—inspired pieces of art I've ever seen on the cover, until I find the folded-up paper buried at the bottom and wriggle it out.

"Hey," Jorge says as I hand him the note, not taking it. "What is it?"

"What do you mean?" I ask, nudging the paper toward him. He gives the folded-up plans in my hand a look and crosses his arms, nodding at it.

"Are you not into this anymore?" he asks. "What's going on?"

I turn around, looking about the space. Chris is off downstairs, and there are a few people milling about, working on their various projects. No one I recognize.

"I don't know," I huff. "With everything that's been going on, that mess with the machine and today's…anniversary, I'm just not feeling it lately. Besides, I don't know if this is even any good."

I hand him the note and he takes it, looking at me intently. He briskly unfolds it, spreading the paper over his desk next to his printer.

"Hmm," he mutters, his head tilting back and forth as he reads. "This design is good, Adam." He glances up. "I don't know why you don't feel a little more confident in this stuff. Come here."

I walk over and stand in front of his drafting table, staring at my own electronic blueprints. What it lacks in straight lines and proper symbols, I hope it makes up for in how much I care. It's a design for another bumper, that I hope Jorge will be able to work out and print here in the shop.

"Here's what I want you to do with the next thing you bring, okay?" he says, opening a drawer. He pulls out a steel protractor. Not the sort they'd give us in high school geometry, plastic pieces of junk that frequently snapped in half in backpacks, but one made of actual metal. He holds it up to me. "Take it."

"Oh, come on, Jorge, I can't—"

"Taaaaake it," he emphasizes, smiling. "Don't forget what I actually do for a living, kid. I can afford to give away a thirty-dollar protractor."

"Fine." I take it, and it has some heft to it.

"Use that with a ruler, to make your next set." He digs around in the drawer again, pulling out some papers. "And draw it on some actual schematic paper this time? This feels like you sketched it on the back of packing paper."

I smile.

"Okay." I nod. "Okay, I'll try."

"Don't try." He gives me a look and pulls some graph paper from his table, rolling it up briskly into a tube. "Just do it."

"Thanks." I take the paper and snatch a rubber band off his desk to secure it all in place.

"I gotta get back to it. I've got some orders to fulfill and some designs to send out before I head to the office tomorrow, but you let me know when you have another piece in mind from your dad's notes. Or you know—" he taps on the desk, on my sheet of paper "—something you've whipped up."

"Absolutely." I nod, and then salute him with the roll of paper. "Thanks!"

I start to walk back down the caution line when Jorge shouts out again.

"And let me know when you're ready to talk business!" he exclaims. I turn and look at him, and he shrugs. "I'm just saying, it's a good idea. And it won't be too hard to register." He smirks and points at himself. When he isn't busy playing with circuit boards and his 3D printer at the makerspace, Jorge is a lawyer downtown, so I'm guessing we won't have to use one of those register-your-business-in-ten-minutes-or-less websites that I keep getting ads for.

Search "how to start a small business" just once in Google, and this is my online life forever now.

With my mom teaching and managing the arcade, Chris working with me while crafting his pour overs, and Jorge creating while lawyering, I surround myself with people who have a hustle while chasing their dreams. Dad was so laser focused. And sometimes I wonder what it is I'm missing out on, keeping my focus so narrow like him. And if this idea, figuring out electronics and engineering, might be the right way to go.

I turn around and there's Chris, with what looks like a chunk of iron in his hands. He's looking toward Jorge and back at me, a quizzical look on his face.

"Business?" he asks, a little frown on his face. "What's this all about?"

I shrug, feeling a bit embarrassed.

"I just… We'd emailed a bit about the part, and I had this idea…" I walk toward the stairs, but Chris stops and flops down in a comfy-looking, egg-shaped chair, setting the iron piece on a side table with a heavy thunk. He stares at me expectantly.

"We're gonna miss the bus," I whine.

"This is Philly," he scoffs. "There's always another bus." He reaches out and pats the chair across from him, and I grab it, sitting down.

"It's stupid, but I thought maybe we could do something with pinball parts?"

"Parts?" he asks, crossing his legs and tilting his head.

"Yeah, like…" I exhale. "My dad had all these ideas for his custom machine, right? The Liberty Bell bumper that rings, a light-up arch of Penn's Landing, like in the opening of *It's Always Sunny*, that awful—"

"The pretzel on the end of the plunger?" Chris laughs.

"Yeah." I chuckle, thinking about how ugly that thing is. "You can't exactly get those made by a pinball manufacturer, right? There aren't even that many left. So while Jorge was making this, I brought up the idea of a custom shop. He did this one, that fun water ice bumper, and those printed flippers we needed for those older machines. I just don't really know how to do something like that yet. Maybe make an Etsy store? There's got to be more to it than that, though."

I think about the half-burned book sitting in the workshop now, and how badly I need a new copy. I've got to hit The Book Trader later to scour their used stacks, maybe say hi to the cute bookstore dog, Coco, or head over to Fishtown and order one from Harriett's, one of my favorite indie bookshops.

"Interesting." Chris nods, getting up. He grabs the mold,

which slides loudly across the table. "Why didn't you tell me about it? Does your mom know?"

"Oh, I don't know," I huff, and we start walking down the stairs. "It's another pinball thing, and I know you two want me doing something else."

"*Anything* else."

"Shut up." I nudge Chris as we get to the bottom of the steps. "We'll see. I feel like maybe I'm more into designing the stuff, figuring out the circuits, than I am trying to make it my life."

"Hey, I'm just glad you've got something outside of the arcade. And you know, you *could* go to Drexel for electrical engineering, and I could go there for industrial design…just think about it." He grins. "Our dorm room would be so cool. 3D printers and woodworking and glassblowing—"

"We'll be so popular." I laugh.

"Might actually kiss a girl." He shrugs.

"Ugh, stop it." I swat at him. "You know I just don't have the time. Dating? Hmph."

Chris shrugs and I nod, a little silence hovering between us. "You really want to go back there and put that bumper in the machine, don't you?"

"I do. I really do." I grin and have to force myself not to squeal with excitement.

"*That* you have time for." He raises an eyebrow.

"Yes," I say, short. "I'm sure you're excited to make—" I glance down at the mold "—whatever that is."

"All right." He sighs with a quick roll of his eyes. "Let me pack up my stuff, and we'll head over. I need to head home soon, anyway." Chris lives over in Queen Village, just

a fifteen-minute straight-shot walk from the arcade in Old
City, which made for the most convenient sleepovers of all
time when we were kids and…well, now. "Go hit the rummage bin. See if there's anything good."

I rub my hands together and make my way to the entrance
of NextFab, weaving between some folks here and there, until
I come to two large Rubbermaid plastic bins overflowing
with gadgets. I don't know what half the stuff is, but I flip
through, nudging wires and little plastic boxes that clearly
do *something*, but I have no idea what, searching for anything
that might be useful.

There are a few little resistors that look like they're maybe
burnt out, but I'm not sure, and some loose LEDs. One looks
like it has a magnet attached to the bottom, and when I press
the battery that connects the two wires, it lights up. I toss
it at a nearby desk, and it sticks there with a bang, glowing.

"Cool," I whisper to myself.

"It's called an LED throwie," a voice says, and a chair rolls
out from behind that desk. I glance up at a woman with
dark, slightly spiked hair and a nose ring. She nods at the bin.
"There are a few more in there if you want them."

"Yeah?" I turn back around and rummage about, finding
a bundle more. "How do you make these?"

"Come here," she says, motioning me over with her hand.
I walk over to her desk, which is full of wires and circuits, as
well as bits of clothing and fabric. She must catch me staring
at it all because she leans back in her chair and gestures at all
of it, her hands wide. "Behold my little kingdom." She sticks
out a hand. "Olivia… You're one of Jorge's projects, right?"

"Adam." I shake. "And I'm not sure I'm a project."

"No one ever is." She smirks.

"So what's this?" I nod at all the stuff on her desk.

"Wearable tech," she says, plucking a piece of fabric. "Lights up when you're say, riding your bike. Or on your wrist when you're on a nighttime walk along the Riverwalk, and you maybe don't want to lose your group."

"Wow." I brush my fingers against the fabric, and it's wildly soft, like something you'd wear to the gym. A trail of light pulses down a strip of it, and I jump back, laughing. "That's really cool."

"All you need," she says, plucking the throwie off the side of her desk, "is an LED, a rare-earth magnet, and a lithium battery." She scours around on her desk for a few and sets them out. "Put the LED wires on both sides of the battery, tape together with a magnet, and voila!"

The little bulb lights up, and she throws it in the air, sticking to the ceiling above her.

"It'll last for a good three weeks. Sometimes a month—"

"Dammit, Olivia!" I turn around, and Chris is walking toward us, staring up at the ceiling. "It took me forever to get those down!"

Olivia leans back in her chair, smiling.

"Sorry, champ." She shrugs.

"You had to get them down?" I ask, looking up at the ceiling. "How? That's like…two stories." The interior of Next-Fab is like a warehouse, and I think once was.

"Ugh. Paper airplanes the first time. A series of cheap dollar store bow and arrow toys the last." He groans, looking up at the LED again, and then at me. "Did she teach you how to make them?"

"Yeah. They're pretty cute, I think." I pull the few I found in the rummage bin out of my pocket. "Could be something fun at the arcade, maybe. Light up the ceiling, maybe the awning out front."

"Great," he moans, and then glares at Olivia. "When I'm working here and not an intern, I'll have my revenge."

"Sure you will, champ." Olivia grins, reaching out and patting the side of his face. "Now, can you get that down for me?"

Chris glares at her and then looks at me, before grabbing a piece of paper. He starts folding the angriest paper airplane, grunting with each crease.

"I'll just be a minute, and then we'll get going." He grabs a paper clip and sticks it on the front and aims at the ceiling.

"Oh." Chris exhales as we stand in front of the arcade.

"I swear to God, if you take those Swedish Fish out, I will throw them into the Schuylkill River," I growl.

There are flowers and little trinkets lining the mural outside the arcade, the one that's covered this side of the building since I was a kid and has been restored a handful of times over the years. Most notably, a year after Dad died. And on the anniversary, it's become something of a tradition for the community in Old City, all the boutique owners and restaurant workers, to leave a little something here.

And that's today.

It's a lot. But I know Dad helped a lot of people here, like Jorge. He's not just mine alone to grieve, which is a sort of comfort, I guess. It's nice to know people haven't forgotten about him.

I pull the Liberty Bell bumper out of my pocket and hold it up, comparing it to the bell painted on the expansive mural.

"Hey," Chris says, patting my back. "He'd have loved it."

I nod, walking along the mural, Old City Pinball in big wild lettering, bold red and orange, with a Philadelphia-inspired playfield all over the surface. The Liberty Bell in the center. Ramps that look like the I-95. A back glass full of water and walking paths and trees, like Fairmount Park. It mirrors Dad's homemade machine, or at least his vision of it, and I run my hand over the surface of the wall.

Feeling for home.

"Should we pick some of these up?" Chris asks, standing above some of what's been left.

"Nah." I shake my head. "They're not really for us, you know?"

"Yeah." He pauses. "But maybe tomorrow morning? I'm just saying, the nightlife scene isn't going to be kind to all this. Or, you know, the snow that's coming."

"Good point."

I fuss with the keys in my pocket and unlock the door to the arcade, the inside dark and feeling extra empty considering the day. Chris flips the lights on as he walks in ahead of me, basking us in their warm glow. He stands by the entrance while I stroll over to the workshop, pulling the door open, the wood squealing loudly against the frame.

"I'm gonna head out, unless you want someone here?" he half asks. "I just don't know if you want to be left alone, you know, today."

I reach inside the workshop and flip on the lights, which slowly flicker on, the aging halogen washing out just about everything.

"It's all right." I shrug, turning around to look at him. "I'm just gonna mess with this a bit and then hop the El home."

"Is your mom okay?" He leans against the wall.

"Yeah, she's out with some of her girlfriends." I shrug, wondering if one of them is Whitney's mom. Her and Ms. Mitchell still have a pretty good relationship, despite their kids despising one another. "We had a little breakfast this morning and talked about Dad a bit. She's good. Might pick her up a plant or something."

Chris tilts his head to the side.

"From—"

"Come on, the chances of her being there are astronomically small," I scoff. "Besides, I'll make sure I peek in the window."

"All right, well...tread carefully."

"Definitely." I smile.

"Love you, brother." He ducks out toward the door and stops. "Hey, what was the design you brought with you to Jorge this time around?"

I smile and shrug.

"It's for a food truck." I look at the machine next to me. "Bumper for up in the corner, with a light-up series of signs on the top of it."

Chris shakes his head and points at me.

"I'm telling you. That. That's your thing. Design. Electronics. Doesn't have to be pinball, though." He pats the front door and waves and heads out into the Philadelphia afternoon.

Doesn't have to be pinball.

I don't know.

I pluck the Liberty Bell bumper out of my pocket as the

front door snaps shut and look over The Beast. It's in the same messy condition that I left it in the other day, with wires and bits all over the play area. I also drop all the LED throwies on the workshop table, and the maybe-burnt-out resistors. I activate a few of the throwies and toss them against the back of the table, little glowing balls of orange, red, and yellow illuminating the steel backing. I'm definitely going to have to make more of those.

I scoop up my copy of *The Art and Zen of Pinball Repair* and flip through it to a random page, the paperback cover so worn and old that the book flaps around listlessly in my hand.

"In life, as in pinball, there's no removing the ramp. It is going to be there whether you want it there or not, preparing to drop you off someplace. It is up to you. Are you going to enjoy the ride, or fight against it and come out unprepared for what's to come?"

Jesus, James. I shake my head and put the book down on the workshop table, grabbing some of my tools. It takes me a minute to clear off the surface of the machine before I can try putting in the bumper. There are still a lot of little projects left across it, but all of them pale in comparison to actually getting the thing working. Connecting the displays, getting everything powered. Part of me just desperately wants to finish building this machine, but there's this other piece that just wants to…I don't know, put a sheet over it. It's hard to look at, sometimes. Dad put so much time into it, all the tiny, intricate little details he did manage to finish. Fairmount Park up on the back glass, the playfield full of side streets and the Benjamin Franklin Parkway, various museums dotting the ramps. He left one of those Moleskine notebooks, drawn inside like a bullet journal, full of his ideas for the game...including a poorly drawn food truck.

I run my hand along some of the bumpers, shaped like water ice pints, and reach down for the plunger. Who, who would possibly want to start a game of pinball with an ill-shaped Philadelphia pretzel on the knob? I scoff and roll my eyes, remembering the argument about it. I thought it looked silly, made the machine look gimmicky. Dad said it added personality. Flair. The plunger is where the game begins, with a pull and release that sends the ball up into the machine.

I squint, looking under one of the ramps at one of the ball catch drop-offs, and debate turning the machine on to test it out before putting in the Liberty Bell bumper. It's the latest piece I was working on, and I can't quite get the timing right, and sometimes when the ball gets caught, it just sits in there until the thing overheats. Last time a bit of smoke pooled up, which is a special effect that simply doesn't work when it comes to underneath the I-95 interstate.

Hmm.

Okay, well, maybe it does. I grab one of Dad's old multitools, a bundle of gadgets ready to come unfolding out of the heavy metal handle, and get to work.

When I look up from the machine it's nighttime. The Liberty Bell bumper is tucked away inside, right in the middle where it's supposed to be, and the entire arcade is dark. Lights on a timer and all. I run my hand over the machine, walk over to the back, and plug it in.

With a few electronic chimes, it hums to life.

The display flickers out a few bits of orange lettering and images, whatever Dad was trying to program in there when he last worked on this. A couple lights and bumpers illuminate on the playfield, including the Liberty Bell bumper, much to my surprise. It beams a golden yellow.

I pluck a pinball from off my workbench and slide it down on top of the plunger, and pull what is an arguably ugly pretzel.

And I let go.

It soars up over the ramp and down onto the playfield, and almost immediately hits the Liberty Bell bumper. The steel ball collides with the rubber with a resounding loud *ka-chunk* noise…and promptly soars out of the pinball machine and across the workshop, embedding itself in the particleboard holding up all my tools with a bang.

Well. That could have killed me.

I quickly unplug the machine.

I pry the pinball out of the wood with a multitool. For some weird reason it's hot.

There's…a lot of work to be done. And I know it can't be Jorge's design. Everything he's made has worked so perfect. It must be something inside the machine, meaning there's even more to do when it comes to making this thing actually work.

My phone buzzes, and I pull it out. It's Mom.

"Hey," I say, clearing my throat.

"Adam, what's all this on social media?" she asks, and I can just hear the annoyance in her voice. "I know you and Whitney still aren't getting along, but this is a bit ridiculous."

"She started it," I grumble. "Nick broke the machine and—"

"I'm aware," she huffs.

"You knew who he was?" I ask. "While he was in the shop?"

"Of course," she says in a way that I can almost hear her crossing her arms. "I've known that little shit since he was ten and you were six, running around first grade with Whitney."

"Mom!" I laugh.

"What?" she scoffs. "He used to steal cupcakes at the bake sale. He was a shitty kid then, and he's not so great now as a kind-of-adult." She sighs. "Okay, but listen. I know today is a hard day. But your dad, he wouldn't want all this... I don't know, drama, for you. *Either* of you. And I think you know that. He loved Whitney, and Whitney really adored your dad, especially when you were all little."

I don't say anything.

"Adam?" she asks.

"Yeah, I'm still here." There's a bit of brewing anger in my chest there. She didn't care about Dad. If she'd cared, she would have been there.

"All right, well..." She inhales and sighs. "Kinda wish I had some of Chris's Swedish Fish right now. Do you have any on you? You should eat one. We just dug into feelings."

I feel the bag in my pocket.

"N-no," I mutter.

"Right." I can hear my mom's smile on the other end of the phone. "How's The Beast looking?"

I glance over at the machine, no more smoke pooling out of the ball catch.

"Fine, I suppose," I say. "I got that Liberty Bell bumper installed, thanks to Jorge. It looks really great. I'll send you a picture. And I'll post one. I dropped off my latest design to him, too, while visiting Chris."

"Nice, I'm glad," she says. "I want to make sure you look at

Drexel over break. We talked about this. Maybe go up there with Chris. Oh, and be sure to lock up when you're done tooling around with that thing." She yawns. "And remember. You two used to be friends."

"Me and Chris are still friends!" I say, sarcastic.

"You know who I'm talking about," she snips back.

"I know, Mom," I sigh. "I'll see you soon."

I hang up and I toss the multitool down on the workbench with a little pang, and run my hands through my hair, trying to think of what might be wrong with the machine...and thinking of Whitney. And Dad. And the future, school choices looming in the distance. I pace the length of the small workshop, small posters and flyers decorating the walls, tools dangling from hooks, Dad's old books everywhere. "Total Dad books" as Chris likes to call them, novels by Nick Hornby and essays by Rob Sheffield.

My eyes flit to the photographs tacked on a corkboard near the door.

The three of us. Mom, Dad, me. Looking happy. I've got on a band T-shirt from the last concert me and Dad went to, one of those Summerland tours full of '90s alternative rock bands. *Feeling Strangely Fine* written across the front, the name of a Semisonic album. Even though Dad was mostly trapped in the late '70s and early '80s with his rock-and-roll tastes, he had a soft spot for '90s alternative, and whenever one of those nostalgia tours hit, there we'd be. Watching bands like Everclear, Soul Asylum, Gin Blossoms, Marcy Playground, and Fastball at venues like the Electric Factory, surrounded by a bunch of other people who honestly also looked like dads.

I reach out and lift a corner of the photo up.

Me. Dad. Mom.

Whitney.

There she is, wearing an American Hi-Fi T-shirt, the band's name written in typewriter font over a cassette that has the tape sprawling out. She's got pink hair and braces with little green rubber bands on them, multicolored leather bracelets on her wrists. I remember her mostly being excited to see that band because they were Miley Cyrus's backup band when they weren't playing pop punk. She changed so much when high school started, and her dad's business took off. New looks, new friends, new outlook. I barely recognize the girl in that photo.

There's a small tear in the bottom of the photo, from where I started to rip it years ago, but had stopped.

I sigh, and let the other picture cover it back up. She disappears.

So much about pinball is about letting go. Pulling the plunger and taking the journey.

And there's a lot I need to let go of.

But it's so much easier playing a game than living a life.

Old City Pinball: Hey.

West Philly eSports: What.

Old City Pinball: Just seeing if you're okay.

West Philly eSports: Is this some kind of joke?

West Philly eSports: Of course I'm not okay.

West Philly eSports: Look at all your mentions, they're still talking about me.

Old City Pinball: Ah. Yeah.

Old City Pinball: I'm sorry, I don't know what I'm doing.

Old City Pinball: Have a good night.

CHAPTER 4
Whitney

My senses are awash in the smell of leather, sandalwood, and soil. I inhale and exhale, resisting the urge to close my eyes to just take it all in, as the door to Krumm's closes behind me. I'm so eager to erase this afternoon, hell, this entire weekend, with something else. Something fresh.

Like some more plant babies for my tables and planters at Dad's café. Or my room.

"Whitney!"

I look over at the register and smile. There's Mom, her eyes bold and bright in her oversize glasses, dwarfed only by her grin. Ali, her coworker and co-owner, peeks out from the back room of the shop and waves. We follow each other in a few places online, and of course I follow the shop, and just adore all the artsy plant pictures she takes. Her arrangements are gorgeous, from the stunning bouquets she sells on Etsy to the little pots she puts together here. Sometimes I try to work on my own floral arrangements, even plotting and planning how the succulents will look in Dad's café, but they are nowhere near as good. I still take photos, though, posting them on my personal Instagram. Ali and Mom never fail to leave encouraging comments, while I'm not even sure Dad knows I do it.

"Hey, Ali." I wave and walk toward the register and Mom with a smile, passing by a massive wooden table made from what looks like a single piece of polished oak—thick, smooth branches as legs. The cracks are filled with some kind of silver metal, and a number of little clay pots dot the surface, different plants inside. "I was going to ask if there was anything new and exciting today, but that certainly is."

"Lovely, right?" Mom grins, walking around the register. She runs her hand over the surface of the table. "It's a reclaimed piece of wood from an old shipwreck out by Petty Island, in the Schuylkill?"

"Whoa." I exhale. "And Petty Island, huh? Sounds like a place I could settle down."

"Oh, stop it." My mom snorts. "Me and Ali sanded it down, varnished it, used a little old silver in the splits, and here we are." She puts her hands on her hips and looks over at Ali, who is still lingering in the back doorway. "We'll do a whole video share of the process soon."

"It's awesome."

"I know, I know." She grins. "Give your mom a hug. Come here."

And of course, I do. She squeezes me tight, and lets me go, looking around the store for a second. "Where's your sister?" she asks. "Or your idiot brother?"

"Ah, Lily's home with the sitter, Leandra." I shrug. "Not sure what Nick is doing. Not sure I really care."

My mom shakes her head.

"Are you doing okay?" she asks.

"Sure?" I shrug. "I feel like all the comments have died down a bit."

"Good, good." My mom nods. "Is your dad still...you know, poking around at trying to buy the place? I can't imagine that makes things easier between you and Adam."

"There is no me and Adam," I grumble, crossing my arms. "Or me and anyone else, really."

"Oh?" My mom raises an eyebrow and glances over at Ali, who strolls over. The two of them stare at me expectantly, their eyes wide and searching, like two overly concerned owls, and I try to wave them off.

"We just—" I grumble and stammer before exhaling "—want different things."

My mom gives Ali a look.

"What?" I snap.

"Have you talked to your dad about it yet?" Mom asks, crossing her arms. "Or, you know, anyone?"

"Not really." I shrug, pressing my foot against the floor. "I keep thinking...maybe he'll change his mind? It feels like it's really *over* over this time, though. But it's fine. I'm fine. He seemed upset but I'm sure he'll be fine, too."

"Usually, when people say the word *fine* three times in a sentence, they aren't," Ali says, walking back to the other side of the shop. My mom smirks and Ali shrugs. "I'm not wrong."

"If you want to talk about it, I'm here. I know your father isn't exactly the best with those kind of chats, and maybe I'm not either, but I'm around for it, as best I can be," my mom says, squeezing my shoulder. "Come on, I've got something to show you."

"So that table? That's not all we've got that you'll be hyped to see." My mom smirks and wiggles her eyebrows around, and looks off to the side, toward the workshop area of the plant shop. They host classes here, for arranging terrariums and the like, and I glance over at the tables. There's some little setup on the one closest to the register, some rocks and bags of sand scattered about. I stroll over there with her, past the empty tables and shelves full of plants, to whatever it is she's working on with Ali.

I feel my eyes go wide.

"Is that a sand dollar cactus?" I hustle over to the edge of the table, pressing my hands to the surface and staring down at the chunky little green plant. It looks like a little green pincushion with white spots, speckled with a few fuzzy dots. Perfectly round with little lines up and down the sides, it's easy to see where it gets the whole sand dollar name.

They're my favorite.

"Where did you get it?" I ask, unable to hide my smile. I take my phone out, snapping a ton of photos.

"Oh, I know a guy who knows a guy." My mom crosses her arms and smiles…and then shrugs and drops the act. "There's someone in Roxborough with a nursery growing them, if you can believe that. John—" She stops herself and winces.

"It's okay." I shrug. She always gets weird, bringing up her new partner, but he's been around for over a year. It's not exactly a new development anymore, since she left Dad for him. I used to be… I'm not sure if it's mad or not. Upset?

Disappointed? I don't know. I felt a little something about the whole thing, but she deserved better, and it was hard to get worked up knowing that.

But with her gone, and Dad's attention thrown into his work, I definitely got a little left behind by both sides. I've got my ways to hold on, though. Visits here whenever I can, handling Dad's social feeds. Though I can't help but feel if I stopped showing up here, my mom would come for me. Dad, I don't know if he'd notice.

"John met him at the last farmer's market of the fall on Main Street. Apparently, he has a whole heated greenhouse in his yard."

"I'm still waiting for you to get me his number," Ali grumbles.

My mom laughs and swats her hand at her.

"No one picked this baby out of Texas, promise you that," my mom presses.

"I know you'd never." I look up at her and smile, then back down at her setup. The terrarium she's got out is this big geometric hexagon, black metal bars outlining the hex glass shapes. There's a bit of sand sprinkled inside, little stones, a dollop of moss. A cozy little home for the sweet little thing.

It's beautiful.

Ali walks out from the back room and sets some pieces of wood down on the workshop table, all cobbled together in a Mason jar.

"What do you think?" she asks.

I'm looking through some of the pebbles Ali's got out, the mosses, the bits of driftwood in the jar, different colored sands, when I feel a hand on my shoulder. I glance over and see Mom there, little wrinkles stretching out from her bright eyes. She nods at all the materials.

"Go ahead," she says.

"No, I don't have time—"

"I see the way you're looking at it," she interrupts, and takes a step back, arms crossed. "Something is missing. I trust you. I know you can see it." I move to lean over the table when the chair next to me slides out with a squeak, Mom standing behind it, grinning. I can't help but laugh, and then sit down.

They know me. And it's what I do. Find what's missing; fill in the pieces. Try to keep the picture together, or at least, figure out how to take a picture in the first place. That's what you do, crafting terrariums like this. Make a setting out of nothing. A story.

I do it here, with my plants. At the cafés, running all the social media.

"You need to take time for yourself," she presses. "Between school and your job with your dad, you have to remember you also matter."

"I know I matter, Mom," I grumble.

"I just worry," she sighs. "I know you throw yourself into that work, same way your father does. And it's not going to make him…" She grits her teeth and shakes her head, exhaling.

"What?" I ask.

"I don't want to be that parent bad-mouthing the other parent," she says, and I give her a look. "Fine, fine. It's just not gonna make him give you the attention I know you're looking for. That you deserve."

"It's…what I've got, Mom." I shrug, barely getting the words out.

"You've got so much more to you than that." She puts her hands on my shoulders, and I wince, trying not to cry. "Just watch. Close your eyes. Breathe."

I do. I inhale and exhale, trying to push back what I think might be a sob. Just…push away everything with Patrick, all my insecurity around Dad, and focus. On the moment, on me. And when I open my eyes, I flip through some of the bits of driftwood on the table, their shapes and textures varying piece to piece. Thin, brittle beige pieces the color of sand, a few white sticks, looking like sun-bleached bones. And then there are some pieces of what look like newer driftwood, not left in the sun, not beaten by the dawn or the tide. I pluck one out of the pile. It almost looks like a tiny log an animal could hide in, albeit one that would have to be like, smaller than my pinky.

I slide it into the terrarium, nestled against the ball of moss.

"There we go," I breathe out, pushing the seat away from the table.

"There we go," Ali repeats, and bends down to look at the terrarium. "Now we just need to make like three dozen more for the festival. When are you just going to come work for us?" She looks at my mom. "Seriously, Jill, it's time, isn't it?"

I laugh and make my way over to another one of the displays, dozens of lovely terrariums on little elevated stands. I run my fingers over a large spherical one with a slice cut out of the top, perfect for carefully placing things inside. I do love it here.

But Dad needs me.

"You laugh every time one of us asks that, but I'm serious," Mom says, strolling in my direction. I look at her and she shrugs. "My holiday workers are all gone, and even though we don't get a lot of traffic in the shop at the end of the year, I mail out a lot of these, pre-filled and all. And we've been doing a lot of business with that."

"What?" I scoff. "How?"

"Very carefully." She laughs and huffs. "It's tedious, lots of packing paper and writing out careful instructions, and like… one out of ten usually ends up coming back because some overeager DIY-er is displeased with a piece of moss that got jostled about too much—"

I scoff.

"But I mean, Whitney, if you have time you know I'd love to have you here. You could work on your photo skills with Ali a bit, help with shots of the plants. I miss you being around more."

"Yeah." I nod, resisting a sniffle. "Yeah, me, too."

I glance toward the big window in the front of the shop, looking out to Market Street. I can see The Franklin Fountain from here, the cobblestone sidewalks outside. It's a Sunday, in the winter, and it's getting late. It's freezing outside, and the flurries, hinting at slightly more serious snow, are fluttering all over the place, sticking to buildings and a little on the sidewalk. Yet, in here, it's a blast of warmth.

"How's…" my mom starts, then swallows. "How *is* Dad?"

As distant as the two of them are these days, and as uncomfortable as I can see it visibly makes her, I like when Mom directly asks about him, instead of poking around awkwardly. Something about it makes me feel like there's still a connection there, to what our old family was. Even if I know that part of my life isn't coming back.

"And I'm out," Ali says, giving me a sideways glance and a smile, her eyes as bright green as the plants dotting the shelf behind her. I snort out a laugh and turn to Mom just as she vanishes behind the curtain in the back room.

"Fine," I huff. "He's away at some conference, should be back on Tuesday, I think. The plants in the café are doing well, you'll be happy to know."

"I've got no doubt." She beams. "I'm not worried about the plants, though."

"He does ask about you." I shrug. I'm not sure why I'm saying that, when he actually doesn't, and I want to stop the words as they're coming out of my mouth. "You two should, maybe, talk." I look around the shop, not really wanting to make eye contact right now. I hate tiptoeing around all this, like walking on eggshells.

"Yeah, well, speaking of people who should talk." My mom crosses her arms, smirking at me. I give her a look and she nods at the phone in my hand. She straight-up stomped on those eggshells.

"Oh no." I shake my head. "No way."

"Fine, fine." My mom shrugs. "But it's going to be another weird Winterfest with you and Adam dodging each other."

"If Dad comes, it'll be another weird Winterfest with *you two* dodging each other."

"Well, traditions are important." She shrugs with a little smile.

Someone walks by the shop, all bundled up, and stops, walking backward, their eyes fixated down. I stand on my tiptoes and look down and spot what he's looking at. The big plastic bin Mom and Ali keep outside the shop, full of giveaway items. Nearly dead plants, broken pieces of wood, warped stands, stuff that she can't sell, but can't quite bring herself to throw away.

"Here," Ali says, and motions for me to come over, walking out from behind the curtain, a little paper bag in her hands. "Couple of plants with imperfections that could use a little love, that I probably won't be able to sell or ship. You can give them a home in that café of yours, or at home, wherever."

"I mean, I practically live in the café, anyway, so home is—"

I peek inside, and it's practically overflowing with weirdly shaped air plants and succulents that are missing chunks of leaves. They're all way too good for the giveaway bin outside, but taking them for free?

"Ali, no way." I look up at her, and weirdly, something starts tingling in the bridge of my nose. "This is probably like, a hundred dollars' worth of—"

"Eh, they're not worth anything if people aren't going to buy them, or want them, in their kits." She presses the bag toward me. "You're my favorite customer. Your mom's, too, I guess." She grins with her whole face.

"I was going to buy stuff today, you know." I sniffle and shake my head, as though either of them would actually let me spend money in here. I'm pretty sure I could walk out the door with that fancy new table over my head, no questions asked. "Whew. Sorry. It's been…it's been a day."

"Need to talk about it?" Ali asks, and the genuine concern in her voice almost breaks me. I look back at my mom, her face awash in worry. Between Patrick and the drama with Adam I'm not sure how much more I can—

There's the sound of a bell, and then the door to the shop slams into my shoulder.

I hit the ground, and the air gets knocked right out of me. My ears are ringing. The little paper bag flutters out of my hands, small plants scattering all over the place.

I try to say "no" as the little plants skitter over the floor.

"Hnnghhhhh—" is all I can get out.

I struggle to catch my breath, making some horribly ugly wheezing sounds as I pull for air, and in the midst of the stars floating in front of my eyes, I catch Ali's and Mom's sandaled feet—it's snowing outside, what the hell—and someone else's. My mom bends down as the other pair of feet paces about, thick black boots squeaking angrily against the floors.

"Are you okay?" I'm guessing the voice behind the boots asks, weirdly familiar. He takes a few more steps, his clumsy, thick-booted feet crunching some of the plants Ali just gave me.

"Hnhhhghh!" I reach for some of them, and the feet hop back.

"Oh! Oh no, I'm sorry." I see hands plucking at them, a leather bracelet on one of them, a black leather sleeve to some kind of jacket. I roll myself over onto my back, enough air in my lungs, taking big painful gulps. "I didn't mean to—"

Ali helps me sit up, my mom behind me, propping me up. "I'm okay… I'm okay…" I swallow again and sniffle, then wipe at my face, tears just everywhere. "Ugh. Who—"

"Hey, sorry about that."

The voice squats down next to Ali.

And it feels like my breath is about to be sucked away again. Adam. Fucking. Stillwater.

The combat-boot-and-old-leather-jacket-wearing voice, the one belonging to the person sporting that leather bracelet, is the same voice that's been in my messages. Making my life hell this weekend. His eyes go wide when they meet mine, and he staggers back, his hair bobbing a little, a necklace nestled in his chest hair revealed by his v-cut band T-shirt, two women with guitars and the name "Heart" across them.

He's dressed a little like he just stepped off the set of *Rock of Ages*, or maybe *Grease*.

And I feel like *Grease 2*.

I haven't seen him up close like this in nearly four years, since the summer before high school. In the hallways here and there, sure. Online, definitely. Sometimes while walking by the arcade, okay. Here, in person, a few years older, never. And when I look at him right in his light brown eyes, I swear I can almost see his pupils dilate as he stares at me. I will every cell in my body to fight against the warmth I feel pushing to my cheeks.

I'm on the floor. The wind was knocked out of me. He's been nothing but a total jerk online. A meet-cute situation, this isn't.

What does he think he's doing here?

"Are you…" he stammers out, looking down at me and back to my mom. "Are you okay?" He turns away and starts picking up my plants, and I can't help but scowl at the back of his jacket. He still has that stupid R.E.M. jacket. He's scooping more of them up, broken stems and pieces of leaves and all, and none of it really matters. "I'll pay for these. Just let me know how much."

I glance up at my mom, who is smirking. Her eyes flit down to me, and then she gives her head a tiny nod in his direction. She winks.

Oh great.

I get to my feet just as he turns around, the little white bag in hand, plants, and what I'm guessing are now just *pieces* of plants, inside. The bag is a crinkled mess, not the elegant thing Ali handed to me earlier.

"Why are you here?" I wheeze out, taking a few more deep breaths.

"Um… I wanted to…" He looks like he's reaching for something in his pocket and stops. "I was going to get a terrarium for my mom." He looks over at Ali and my mom. "Hi, Miss Krumm, Miss Mitchell."

"Adam," the two of them say at the same time, grinning.

"I just… Um…" Adam stammers out. "I'm gonna go."

"No!" my mom exclaims, taking a step forward. "We'll have none of that. Come on, we can find you something. After what happened with Nick, it's the least we can do here."

"I don't know…" He looks at me and my mom.

"It's fine," I grumble and walk over to the other side of the shop with Ali. It's not fine. I came to the shop to get away from everything, not have to literally face it.

"All right." Adam nods. "Could you uh…help me find some like, impossible-to-kill plants?" he asks my mom, stepping away from me, but still glancing back. "My mom, she loves these things but there are dead plants all over our house and the arcade. Like, everywhere."

I snort.

"You know, Whitney," Mom says, a grin on her face. "Why don't *you* help Adam out before you leave?" The grin on her face threatens to *break* her face, and I know she is just loving every minute of this.

"It's okay—"

"No, it's fine—"

The two of us protest at the same time, and as he turns to look at me, a little smirk darts across his face. Him and that jacket, and… Heart on his T-shirt. Don't they sing that song about dreams or something?

"I mean, if you've got them." He shrugs.

"There is an art store a few blocks down that sells fake plants, you know." I cross my arms, thinking of the Old City Art Supply shop nearby. "Made of plastic? Very unkillable."

"You don't know my mom," he grumbles and I snort out a laugh. I actually do know his mom; she still hangs out with mine plenty. His eyes soften a little. "That's um…some laugh."

"It hasn't changed," I snip, my mind involuntarily flashing back to running around his neighborhood all those years ago, games of manhunt spanning city blocks, laughing under South Philly streetlights. "Let's see what we can do." I push ahead, trying to press past the pain that's swirling in my chest, from a number of things. Patrick. Literally having the wind knocked out of me. Adam being here in my one safe retreat.

I glance at him, and his eyes flit up to mine.

I can still see him. The boy he was, when we were kids. Who was so broken after his dad died, and how I just wasn't able to get through to him. I tried so hard, that winter, and those last few months of junior high. And the further we drifted apart, the more I think the two of us just resented each other for it. Me, for my friend who disappeared behind a veil of grief I couldn't pull him from, and him, clouded in all of it.

By the time September came, we were different people. I hadn't seen him all summer, and I'd started hanging out with a new bunch of friends those few months before we started at Central. Grief is like that, sometimes. Two people, pushing and pulling, with no one moving anywhere except away from each other.

I shake my head and stop at one of the wooden shelves along the wall opposite the register and workshop, more of that reclaimed wood look held up by upcycled black metal pipes. There are a bundle of different air plants lining the surface, their thin tendril-esque leaves pushing up and curling into one another, like slips of wrapping paper ribbon. My mom and Ali have all different shapes and sizes here, from the sort of tiny ones that line desks in offices to enormous chunky ones the size of a fist. There are a few recommended accessories framing a lot of these, small brass misters, little homemade pots, terrarium ideas.

"So these are tillandsias, which everyone calls air plants." I pluck one of the thick, fist-size plants off the shelf, the curled-up leaves scratching against my palm and one another, making a soft crunching noise. It's a bold shade of purple blended with an almost blue-green. "These are your unkillable plants. If your mom can kill these, then I'm not sure this place has got much for her."

He laughs, shaking his head, and reaches out to grab it. As he gets closer to me, I get a whiff of cedar and vanilla. He looks up at me and smiles.

"How do you know so much about this?" he asks, his eyebrows quirked up. "I thought you were only into like, video games and YouTube and social media these days?"

"I'm not just *all* about digital marketing stuff, you know." I cross my arms. "And I'm barely into video games."

"Really?" He looks at me like he's remembering something, his head cocked to the side. "I thought you at least liked *Animal Crossing* when we were…you know…"

He wants to say friends. I can just feel it.

"Younger?"

"I liked *Mass Effect*," I say, not really wanting to say much more, not up for this walk down memory lane or whatever this is.

"Oh yeah, that's right," he starts, his eyes looking down at the floor. His hands go into his pockets, and he's fussing with something. "You know my mom got really into that and… Well, there's… I just… So about those posts and—"

"Where does she usually get her plants?" I ask, stopping him right there. I hear my mom suck in air through her teeth, and I look over at her, and she looks disappointed. Whatever. I didn't ask her to throw me into all this awkwardness.

"She um…" He winces, scratching at the light stubble on his face. "She orders a lot of them in subscription boxes? Or like, off big online stores, sometimes even auction sites? They get delivered to our house in boxes that might as well say 'please kill these for us.' And they are way smaller."

I sigh and shake my head.

"So these—" I take the big air plant and set it back on the shelf, the thin, long leaves making it bounce a little like a spring against the surface "—have been pretty lovingly cared for. The ones she's getting in the mail, sometimes they've had a bad start. Usually, air plants are tough. Independent. Just need a little bit of water, maybe once a week, and then can be left alone."

"So you're saying I shouldn't just water plants whenever I'm feeling thirsty?"

"I'm gonna have to ask you to leave." I roll my eyes, fighting the urge to chuckle at that while setting the plant back down. "They can take a lot of damage, but still need a reminder that they're cared about, you know?" I reach out and scratch one of the leaves, and turn back to Adam, who is looking at me curiously.

"Well," he says, swallowing. "I, um, I guess I'll take four of the little ones here?" He glances lower on the shelf and plucks a few of the smaller air plants up. They're tiny, maybe about the size of a half dollar. "She has this—" he squints, and looks off to the side, clearing trying to remember something "—I don't know, an iron thing with candle holders at the house, but she puts plants in it?"

"Oh." The memory of that decoration comes back to me for whatever reason, fastened to the brick wall near the stairs in Adam's home. It hits me with a surprising blast of sad nostalgia, and again, I'm shook by the fact that he's even in the shop. "She still…has…*that*?"

"It's a *choice* when it comes to decorating, I know," he scoffs. "Ah!" His eyes widen, spotting something else, and he reaches by me, and I get hit with a blast of cedar and vanilla again. I try to wave it away.

"Excuse me," he says, reaching, and his eyes flit to mine. His arm comes back with one of the misters, a little bronze thing. He shakes it a little. "This. This might be the key to it all."

"Key?" I ask.

"To her actually watering them once in a while, properly." He grins. "She usually just like, shakes them over the sink and douses them with water, and I don't think that's the way of things. You know how some sinks have those little spray nozzles? She uses that."

I shake my head. Those plants.

Godspeed, little ones.

And of course I remember her sink. That sink. We used to tape the little spray lever on the nozzle, so it would be pressed on, and sit in his kitchen, waiting, giggling. I think his dad knew what we were doing, every single time we did it, and still turned the sink on, acting wildly surprised when he was sprayed with a blast of water.

I hate this.

It feels like every reference he makes, every little word, catapults me back there, to a place that doesn't really exist anymore.

I walk with him over to the register, where my mom and Ali are both waiting, standing side by side, practically sharing the same smile. They are so embarrassing. It's bad enough Adam Stillwater went and got hot. I don't need them hamming it up and forcing me to navigate this situation. I hate all of this. Everything going on here.

"Did you find everything you were looking for?" my mom asks, beaming.

"I think so," Adam says, looking down at the plants in his hands, and then briefly, up at me. My heart catches in my chest, and I hear Ali let loose a little squeak. What the hell?

Why is Adam Stillwater, of all people, making me feel like a walking blush?

"Do you want these wrapped?" Mom thankfully interjects before any more noises make this awkward.

"Oh yeah…" He pulls out his phone and puts it away just as quick. "Yeah. I've got time. Sure."

"How's your family doing? You know, today? This week and all?" my mom asks, wrapping up the plants. This week? I look from Mom to Ali to Adam, and they're all looking a bit solemn.

"It's…you know. A day," he sighs out. "Thank you for the flowers. I have to bring a lot of that stuff inside tomorrow. I guess I'll see you all at the festival?" He glances at the gift bag and looks back up. Stuff…outside? "And thanks for this. My mom is gonna love it."

He walks toward the door, that ridiculous R.E.M. jacket and logo moving farther away, his thick black boots clomping against the floor. He's had that coat since… I'm not even sure. All I know is it was practically attached to him the summer before high school, and he never seemed to take it off in the halls. He opens the door to the shop, the bell above it singing, and looks back at me one more time.

He smiles.

The door shuts behind him, and instead of walking by the window and heading down Market Street, he stops and leans against the shop, pulling out his phone. Then he slides down to the sidewalk, a little square bit of light illuminating the dark outside.

"What's he doing?" Ali asks either of us.

"I'm not sure—"

My phone buzzes, and he looks back in the store with a little smirk.

Oh. Oh no. I feel my heart start racing; he probably posted something. Poured more gasoline on what's already a massive online fire for me. Acting bashful and awkward just to attack me at the right time. What fresh hell is—

Old City Pinball: Hey. I took down that post.

Old City Pinball: I'm sorry.

Old City Pinball: Thanks.

What?

I flip over to Growth and scour through my feeds, and while there are a few people still replying to the now-deleted thread, it's gone.

Old City Pinball:
Hey everyone. Me and West Philly eSports talked. We're cool. If you could all lay off, I'd appreciate it. I shouldn't have lashed out like that.

Old City Pinball:
And to everyone who left behind a memento for my father at the mural...thank you. It meant more to our family than I can really say in a post.

I glance up, just in time to catch Adam getting up from the sidewalk against the shop, and walking up Market. Today. Today was the anniversary of his dad's death. Fuck. I don't like him, not anymore; we left that connection in the past, but if I'd known...or at least, if I'd remembered, I don't know.

Maybe I would have tried to be a little nicer with him in here? Faked it? Maybe.

"Wait," I breathe out, and look around, and up at my mom and Ali. "I'll be… I'll be right back."

"Go get him!" Ali shouts melodramatically, and oh, my God, I want to scream.

I hustle out of the plant shop and glance up Market. Adam's a few shops down already, walking with his hands in his pockets. The snow flurries are starting to overtake the Philadelphia evening, dancing by the streetlamps and still-lit-up buildings, through the twinkling white Christmas lights and collecting in a fine dust along brick sidewalks.

"Hey!" I call after him, the cold gusts chilling my face, making my eyes water and burning my cheeks. "Adam, hey!"

He stops and turns around, his arms tightly on his sides, like he's trying to squeeze every possible bit of heat out of that leather jacket. He does that head tilt thing again as I get closer, like a golden retriever that wants to ask a question but can't, and looks back up Market and then at me.

"Don't you take the El up to West Philly?" he asks, nodding at the station stop on the other side of the street.

"Yeah but…" I sigh. "Why'd you take down the post?"

He laughs, shivering a little, and shakes his head.

"I mean, come on, Whit," he huffs, his breath pooling out in little clouds. "It's the holidays. The festival is coming up, it's the anniversary of…you know. What's it all matter? None of it matters."

He kicks at some of the snow on the brick ground, but there's a definite pang in my chest at that comment. It's the same thing Patrick said.

But it *does* matter.

"I shouldn't have posted that in the first place. Fed those flames. I knew what I was doing. What I was doing to you." His eyes look up at me and he shakes his head again, exhaling a cloud of chilly breath. "I hope um... I hope you have fun at Winterfest."

He turns to walk back up Market.

"I'll see you there?" I venture, and wince. He stops and looks back, and I try to recover quickly.

"Yeah. Yeah, you will." He turns and keeps walking, the snow flurries dancing around the Philadelphia streetlights. I can hear his boots clomping against the red brick sidewalks, and watch the R.E.M. logo vanish around other people wandering Old City at night.

I turn back toward the shop, all the other boutiques closed, a few restaurants still open, heat lamps out on the sidewalks. When I reach Mom's boutique, I see her and Ali fussing over some terrariums again, and they both glance up, catching me at the window. Mom tilts her head down and gives me a wide smile, and Ali squiggles around, grinning. I'm never coming back here again.

As I make my way toward the door, a spot of color on the brick sidewalk catches my eye. I glance down, a splash of yellow against the reddish brown.

I bend down and pick it up, the bag crinkling in my hand.

I glance back up the sidewalk, toward Adam, long gone, and snort out a laugh. Something I recognize from when we were kids, from Chris's "let's talk about our feelings" nonsense.

It's a bag of Swedish Fish.

West Philly eSports: I'm not sure why you did what you did, but thank you.

Old City Pinball: It's just not worth it, right?

Old City Pinball: And it's not a big deal, really.

West Philly eSports: It is though. Those kind of posts and that kind of online drama, it gets attention. It builds followers. You were getting so many.

Old City Pinball: Hahaha, what?

Old City Pinball: I don't care about that.

Old City Pinball: I'm only on here because Chris made me. I don't even have a personal account for myself on anything.

West Philly eSports: What? No way.

Old City Pinball: Shrug. It's just not for me.

Old City Pinball: Anyhow, hope it makes your life on here easier. Sorry again.

West Philly eSports: Thanks. You could have kept it up. Or should have. I mean, that's what builds up followers. Chris would tell you that.

Old City Pinball: Please, he was mad at me that I posted it. I don't really care about followers, and neither does he.

West Philly eSports: You should though.

Old City Pinball: I'm good.

West Philly eSports: No but hear me out. Followers are good for you. They boost your messages. They help make you popular. It gets you out there, in front of more people. I bet it would help the arcade.

Old City Pinball: Sigh. See this is where we're different, Whit. You care about that stuff. Popularity. People paying attention to you. I don't.

West Philly eSports: What is that supposed to mean?!

Old City Pinball: Nothing.

West Philly eSports: No, if you've got something to say, go ahead.

Old City Pinball: Ugh. I mean like, you and your little crew. Sophie and them.

Old City Pinball: All you care about is what people think about you. Whether or not they're focusing on you.

West Philly eSports: Right, right.

West Philly eSports: Like that jacket isn't your way of getting people to pay attention to you? All those old band T-shirts?

Old City Pinball: Jesus, you're still the same, aren't you?

West Philly eSports: Me?! What about YOU?!

Old City Pinball: Maybe I should have left that post up.

West Philly eSports: Yeah maybe you should have.

Old City Pinball: Thanks for the plants.

CHAPTER 5
Adam

"One of the core aspects of pinball, is the concept of letting go. The steel ball sits there, waiting for you to send it on its way. The possibilities that await it are endless. But it's up to you to pull and push. To begin the journey. To move forward and essentially, let go. Can you let go?"

–THE ART AND ZEN OF PINBALL REPAIR
BY JAMES WATTS

I close my book as the bus rumbles against the Philly streets, and shove my phone back in my pocket.

I tried.

West Philly eSports: Helen!

West Philly eSports: Where are you and the girls??

West Philly eSports: I've been trying to text you all weekend, after everything with Patrick.

West Philly eSports: Hello?

CHAPTER 6
Whitney

West Philly eSports:
We're open early! Swing on by to catch Blizzard's big announcement. Like the rest of you, we're all busy speculating over here and will be live streaming a set from I Fight Dragons on all our HD monitors around the café. Come rock out!

S Marshall:
Any updates about the weather? Are you staying open despite the snow?

West Philly eSports:
Yup, we're not going anywhere, Marshall! Sidewalks are shoveled, the heaters are on.

Helen Marie:
Is your dad going to be in?

West Philly eSports:
This feels like a text, Helen. No, he's at a conference. Are you and the girls coming? I can save a table!

Of course. Of course, Blizzard decides to drop a surprise an nouncement regarding an expansion pack for the latest *Starcraft* game today. A few days after a social media disaster that I'm barely done cleaning up, and now my feeds are full of people asking if we'll be open in time for the unveiling. Pictures of people waiting outside, wildly early. Videos. Folks who were just screaming at me less than forty-eight hours ago are now pleading for a seat online.

I think of Adam, his voice echoing in my head, under white twinkling lights, a face full of flurries.

What's it all matter? None of it matters.

I shake my head, his messages that followed later replaying, scrolling across my eyes like a marquee, and keep walking.

I appreciate the sentiment, but it does matter. It matters to me. I love this. I do.

I mean, I think I do. It keeps me close to Dad. Lily doesn't have to do anything except be sweet and doted upon, and Nick, he's at the school Dad wanted him to go to. Me? I need to make myself be seen.

"You don't have to hold my hand," Lily grumbles behind me, trailing just a little bit, her little hand vanishing into mine. "I can walk up the stairs by myself."

I look behind me at her and smile.

"I've got no doubt." I smirk but tighten my grip on her seven-year-old hand as a few people brush by us, bounding up the steps toward Market Street. The roar of the Market Frankford subway line, affectionally known as the "El," thunders in the tunnel below. I'm still not sure why people call it that, though my dad said it has to do with it being a subway that goes above and underground. An "elevated line."

Lily scowls at me and huffs, and keeps trudging up the

steps, her sneakers slapping against the surface. While I've got my mom's features, the jet-black hair and bright blue eyes, the freckles and the small pointed nose, Lily is all Dad. Dirty blond hair and eyes like emeralds, a look that seems eternally sand- and salt-kissed, even as a second grader who lives nowhere near the ocean. Her face tells the world she'd be at home on a beach with a surfboard.

Not that Dad has ever done a bit of surfing in his life, other than on the internet. Meanwhile I just *look at* a picture of the sun and my skin starts peeling.

"Why couldn't Nick watch me?" she grumbles. "It's way too early to be out."

"Because he's out with his friends, making life difficult for someone else today," I grumble back, thinking about the slowly-tapering-off-but-still-negative comments coming our way, due to his nonsense. I hold back, though. I'm not going to be the sibling who talks down about the other. Let her have her heroes.

University City blooms out in front of me, in front of us, a stark contrast to the gritty, white-and-blue tiled underground of the SEPTA station we're leaving behind. Large, gleaming buildings with shimmering reflective glass windows glitter in the sun, like hundreds of mirrors reaching up to the sky. Chain restaurants and small eateries line the street, the whole area catering to the bustling college community that calls this neighborhood home. Drexel and Penn, taking up almost all of this.

"I don't want to hang in the café," Lily whines as we make our way up Market.

"The sitter isn't around—" I start.

"I *hate* Leandra."

"Okay, well." I chuckle. "That very well may be, but she's not free, and I can't leave you at home by yourself now, can I?" I squat down, the two of us in the middle of the sidewalk. Some folks walk by us, and I feel like I hear an annoyed grumble or two, but I don't care. "I promise, I won't stay late. Just need to open, and then we can head home before lunch."

"Fine," she huffs and retakes my hand. "But I want to play *Magic*. With a headset!"

"Sure, whatever you want." I grin. The fact that my seven-year-old sister is destroying full-grown adults in online games of *Magic the Gathering* is an absolute delight. I'm pretty sure you're not supposed to play that game online unless you're like thirteen, but oh well. It makes her happy.

We make our way up Market and cross the usually busy street, heading toward Walnut, going deeper into the University of Pennsylvania campus. Despite the bluster of the chilly winter weather and looming threat of heavier snow, the campus still teems with signs of life, large evergreen trees and shrubs smattered between the towering bare oaks. I pull out my phone, and resist the urge to flip through all the social notifications while we're walking, when it buzzes. I stop and lean against a low brick wall, and see a few messages from Patrick coming through.

PAT

Hey, I'm out with the girls, grabbing breakfast.

PAT

Andrea wants to know if your dad is gonna be at the café?

PAT

They were thinking of stopping by.

PAT

Would it be weird if I came with them?
I don't want to make you uncomfortable.

My heart sinks. *He's* out with the girls? I've been trying
to wrangle them up all morning; most of the weekend, really, and even tried messaging Helen. I grit my teeth and try
to shake it off.

ME

No, he's at a conference.
Just me running the show with Dana.

PAT

Cool, okay. I'll let her know.

PAT

Hey. Hope you're doing okay.

I angrily slide my phone back in my pocket, and try not to
let it bother me that he's out with Helen, Sophie, and Andrea
without me. I grab Lily's hand and keep strolling.

It really is over.

Signs for the big Van Pelt Library and the Perelman Quad-
rangle point in the direction we're going; we pass by the
People's Books & Culture bookshop, a huge display for the
latest Celeste Ng book in the window, promising an upcoming signing on campus next month. I smile, my well-read
and worn copy of *Little Fires Everywhere* tucked away in my

bag somewhere. It's a favorite read, and the title is a good reminder. Running Dad's social media for the cafés, there are little fires everywhere online, all the time. This weekend was just another example.

And it's my job to put them out.

Patrick liked to say I was missing the point of the book and the television series, but whatever. This weekend just proved he doesn't understand anything about me.

Me and Lily zip around the corner, the bookstore behind us, and I nearly gasp. The pictures and videos on social media weren't lying. People are here.

We don't even open until 10:00 a.m., which is early for us, and yet, there they are, lining down the street to get in. I hope Dana, one of our baristas and also one of my favorite people, is here today, and maybe a bit early, considering the news. The line trails enough that some people are pretty close to the bookshop, and if the bookstore was open at this hour, I'd try to nudge them inside there. I love it there, my one place to hide away on my lunch breaks, tucked between paperbacks and the cookbooks shelved upstairs in the small loft.

"Why are so many people here already?" Lily asks, tugging my hand a little.

"There's a new game announcement," I groan. "People are excited."

"Why can't they watch it at home?"

"It's the *experience*." I look down and smile at her. "They want to be around their friends and community."

"Whitney!"

Through the corner of my eye I see a hand reach out, and I swat it away. I stop and turn around to spot Aaron, a local who goes to college here, wincing, and cowering away into the line.

"H-hey," he stammers, all awkward and cautious. A student at Drexel studying something in the video game design department, he's at the café just about every other day to talk and game with his girlfriend, who lives in Jersey someplace. I know way too much about their relationship due to the fact that he's almost never early enough to get one of the private, soundproof booths that line the back of the place.

He rubs the back of his head and smiles awkwardly at me, shrugging. With his sharp jaw, stubble, and random emo band T-shirts he always has on, he'd be cute if he wasn't almost *always* here, looking at me with the pleading wide eyes of a Pixar character. I look down at today's shirt, some local group called The Wonder Years that I recognize from stickers all over town. I glance back up at him, and he's grinning.

"One day you'll take me up on making you a mix," he says with a smirk.

"I'm good." I snort. There's a beat of silence, interrupted mostly by the people around him in line, chatting amongst themselves and fiddling with phones that aren't on silent, the clicking of virtual buttons like a symphony of typewriter keys.

"Is this your sister?" he asks, breaking the quiet.

"I'm Lily." She perks up, but leans in closer to me, pressing against my leg and waist.

"Nice to meet you, Lily." Aaron smiles. "I have a sister about your age."

"Is she here?" Lily asks, lighting up.

"Oh no." Aaron winces. "Sorry. Maybe next time?" he

ventures, looking at me with an apologetic glance. "Everything okay? I saw some stuff online about your brother?"

"Is Nick okay?" Lily gasps.

"He's fine." I try not to snap at her, and glare at Aaron, and I'm convinced his face is just going to freeze in that wince. "Come on, man," I whisper.

"Sorry." He shakes his head. There's a pause for a beat, and he fidgets around. "So—"

"Nope," I say, shaking my head. I know where this is going. "Come on, Lil'."

"Please, Whit?" he pleads. "You *know* me."

"If I let you in before everyone else—" I nod at the people in back of him, who suddenly look up from their phones, interested "—people will complain. It'll be all over the place online. Especially on an announcement day. Are you kidding me?"

"But…" He glances backward at the folks in line, and they stare back at him, a girl with short red buzzed hair and a number of piercings, standing with a guy with a jean jacket on decorated in just as many enamel pins, glaring back, their mouths a thin line. "It's just…" He turns back to me. "It's her *birthday*. And my headset at home just isn't good enough to keep up with—" But I've already tuned him out.

Oh, God.

I am *getting him* in one of those soundproof booths.

It's bad enough I have to hear him swooning in the middle of the café, giggling and saying all kinds of compliments that are entirely one-sided, because it's not like I can hear what she's saying in return…but a birthday makes it sound like that'll be turned up from ten to eleven.

I lean toward Red Head and Jean Jacket, who are clearly listening in on this exchange.

"I'll comp an hour of your time today, on the headsets," I whisper. Red Head's green eyes flit toward Jean Jacket. The two of them look older than me, but not by much.

"Two hours," she says back, quirking a smile. I bite my lip at the sight of her lip ring and shake it off, but she definitely notices and winks at me.

"F-fine," I stammer out before I turn as red as her hair. That wink was a brutal, unfair attack. I try not to glare too hard at Aaron as I nod at him. "Come on."

"You should talk to her," he whispers as we walk, and it takes everything in me not to elbow him in the side.

We stroll up the rest of the block, about half the thing, and there standing at the front doors to West Philly eSports are a few people staring down at their phones and—

"Dad!" Lily wriggles from my grip and bounds over, and sure enough, it's him. He's looking down at his phone to the pile of boxes surrounding him. A handful of college-age kids are standing around him, muttering things and peering through the glass doors. I see Nick, swaying on the balls of his feet, staring at his phone.

Dad's dressed in his black turtleneck and jeans, attempting a tech startup look even though we live in Philadelphia, not Silicon Valley. I can't help but roll my eyes at the whole getup, when just a few years ago we were still living in our old house in South Philly, where he wore ancient jeans and ripped flannel, like some kind of lumberjack software developer.

"Dad?" I pick up my pace, and he looks up, along with the faces of several other people, in my direction. A smile beams

across his face, and his eyes completely light up as Lily dives
into his leg, hugging him. He wraps an arm around her and
hugs her, and then holds up his phone toward me, looking
like a kid eager to show off a new toy.

"Hey, little pixel." He smiles down at Lily, messing with
her hair, and she just beams at the nickname. "Whit!" he exclaims. "Come take a look." He gestures at the boxes. "Oh,
and meet Sean."

"It's with an e-a," he says, nodding at me as though I was
interested enough to ask. He's older than me, maybe in his
twenties, with half his head buzzed on one side, a smattering
of you-should-really-give-up facial hair, and what looks like
a permanent smirk stapled to his face.

He looks like a walking vape pen.

"Cool?" I mutter at Sean, my attention on Dad. "What
are you doing here? I thought you got home tomorrow?" I
glance over at Nick, who peeks up at me, makes a face, and
looks back down at his phone. This whole weekend was his
freaking fault, and he can't even say hello.

"Oh that." He waves his hand about dismissively. "There
was no way I was going to miss this viewing party. Flew right
home and overnighted a few new high-definition monitors,
once the news hit. Sean here was dropping them off. Do you
think we'll need better HDMI cables?"

"I'm sure we're fine?" I venture. I'm irritated that he
couldn't be bothered to text or call me that he was coming
home earlier, but could absolutely take the time to tell me to
help wrangle this together and post about it online. It's not
entirely surprising. I guess I should have expected him to
drop everything to make it back here. Being ambushed like

this really sends my heart pounding, though, wondering if he's going to flip out over everything that went down online. "Did you get *my* texts and emails, though? About the pinball arcade situation?"

"Hm?" He looks at me, confused, and then he nods. "Oh yeah. We paid for the machine, right? Nick told me. Sounds like we're okay." He waves his hand around like he can physically brush the words away. I feel someone walking over to us and glance aside to see Nick, rolling up next to me.

"What's up, sis?" he asks.

"Shut up," I snap at him. "It might have been paid for," I say, turning back to my dad, "but everything online has been a disaster," I press, grabbing for my phone. "Apparently, it's an old game, vintage. Hard to find. People are not happy and are still demanding an apology."

"For what?" my dad scoffs. "Besides, once we buy that place and fix it up, none of those people will matter."

"Yeah, I'm pretty sure there's no way in hell Adam's family is going to let it go," I huff.

"We'll see." He shrugs. "Whitney, if running the social media is starting to wear on you and take over your weekends like this, we should really talk about bringing someone on here."

My heart slams against my rib cage.

"Give you more time to run around with your friends, maybe get another part-time job?"

"No way." I shake my head. "I can handle this and I'm good at it. Besides, it's only making my résumé and future college applications look better."

Dad gives me a skeptical look before nodding and looking back at his phone, and over at Sean.

"You know, Dad, I have this idea, with the Old City Winter Festival? The thing Mom runs, maybe we could donate something? To the arcade?" I venture. "Do a public thing about it online, get some good favor—"

"Hah!" He chuckles and looks over at me. "Please, whatever you're thinking regarding your mom's little party, it's a resounding no. And besides, I'm gonna buy the place. Why would I give them a pinball machine that I have to buy back?"

"Dad, if you'll just listen—"

That's when I spot Dana, our barista, strolling towards us, and a warm wash of relief just courses through me. Her outfit is a cobbled-together array of vintage bits, probably from the Buffalo Exchange shop in West Philly, ripped jeans and sweater with an open shoulder, revealing a bright blue-and-pink Circa Survive tattoo under her collarbone.

Ugh. She makes me want to sigh with my entire body. She's so cool.

One of the first employees my dad hired here, she's been at this particular café for well over two years now, while wrapping up a degree at Drexel. I have these vague memories of her at Central, when I was a freshman and she was a senior, but we didn't really hang in the same group. It always felt like her crew of popular girls left just as mine were coming in, and I wonder if she's still friends with any of them. I'm not entirely sure what I'd do without her.

"Hey, guys," she says, swinging her patch-covered bag over her shoulder. "What's going on?"

"Hey, Dana," Nick says, tilting his head and smiling.

"Nope," she says, lifting a hand up, and Nick's expression sours. Takes everything in me not to burst into tears with laughter. "So what's happening here?"

"New monitors, Dad's ignoring my ideas, the usual," I grumble.

"Are you okay?" she asks, nodding at my phone clutched in my hand. "This weekend looked…rough. You know, on the internet and all that. I'm here, if you need to text, talk, whatever."

"We bounced back." I shrug, but there's a twinge of guilt there. Dana's one of the few other people I'm really close to, other than the girls and Patrick. I should have called her. I glance back at my dad. There's a beat of silence, and he looks back at me.

"Oh. Whit, we'll talk more about…whatever the idea is later." He waves his hand around. "Come on, let's get all these monitors inside and set up before everyone rushes the doors."

Dana gives my shoulder a comforting squeeze, before she bends down and scoops up a monitor and looks at me expectantly, a little grin forming on her face.

"So uh…what are the plans for the old monitors?" Dana asks, still looking at me with a smile, as my dad unlocks the café, the smart lock opening with a satisfying *thunk*.

"If you're asking so you can sell one on eBay, under the guise that you need a new one for your dorm, the answer is you can have one." He looks back at her with a smirk, and Dana squeals, dancing around with the screen in her hands.

I'm leaning against the reclaimed-wood countertop of the barista station, water spray bottle in hand, as my dad makes the rounds inside the café. He's smiling and chatting with as many people who will pay attention to him as he can, though it seems like just about everybody is laser focused on their screens. I thought he was going out with his friends, but Nick is sitting at a table in the back, his feet kicked up on another chair, taking up the space three potential customers could have. The announcement should hit in the next hour or so, but Blizzard has all kinds of fun entertainment lined up, and the band I Fight Dragons is playing a live, streamed set.

I turn to spritz some of the plants that grow out of the grooved-out surface along the bar. It's a beautiful thing, the dark, blackened spaces in the tan natural wood perfect for putting little plants, and a piece of the café I know my dad absolutely picked out just for me. There's no way Mom didn't give him advice on it, but that's not something worth asking.

"Whit, come get some photos of me for the feeds," he says, waving me over. "Maybe a few of your brother, too. Nick! Get your feet off the tables!" I push myself off the coffee bar and turn to look at Dana, standing behind it, grinning as she polishes a mug.

"Don't," I grumble, pointing the spray bottle at her. She holds her hands up in a faux surrender, the coffee mug dangling from one finger inside the handle. I pull out my phone and take a few pictures of my dad wandering the café, chatting with people sitting down, all very posed. Nick doesn't move his feet, and when I kick them off the table, he scowls at me, just in time to get an awful photo of him. He rolls his eyes at me and I stroll back over to Dana.

"Wasn't going to say anything." She smiles, giving the mug a little twirl and setting it down with a satisfying plunk on the wood surface. She grabs for a pour over and gets herself situated, while looking back and forth at the tablet facing her, where all the orders from the folks using headsets come in. I post a few photos of Dad.

> **West Philly eSports:**
> Getting ready for the big announcement from Blizzard today! The café is full, the seats are filled, and Randall Mitchell is here, talking to guests, ready to celebrate!
>
> > **Glen Liggett:**
> > Tool. He doesn't even play the games.
> >
> > **Steve Arnold:**
> > Total fake gamer.
> >
> > **Elle Mathur:**
> > If he really cared about the community, he'd have fixed that pinball machine, right Old City Pinball?
> >
> > 1 like

I squint at the like that pops up on that comment and tap on it.

A like from Old City Pinball.

What the fuck, Adam? I thought we were moving past all this. I'm not surprised by the comments from all these people, but liking and encouraging any of it, come on—

Dana sucks at her teeth, and I spin around.

"Are you seeing this, too?" I snap, shaking my phone.

"What?" Dana asks, confusion on her face, her eyebrows quirked. "No?"

"Ugh, people are raging at my dad and the café again!" I

grumble, staring back at my phone. "Even though Adam got rid of that post."

"Ah, okay," she says, not really fazed. "I feel like I remember Adam...he always had those old band T-shirts and that vintage jacket, right?" I glance up and she's looking toward me, her eyes searching thoughtfully. "Rage Against the Machine or something?"

"R.E.M." I snort.

"I mean, both are political bands, right?" She nods, angrily squeezing a bottle of syrup into a mug. She quirks up an eyebrow and looks at me, placing the syrup on the counter. "You two should just make out already."

"Oh, my God!" I snap, and Dana responds by laughing loudly. "It's bad enough my mom and her best friend are busting my chops, but you, too? There is *nothing* there."

She shrugs, still grinning.

"It just feels like the two of you have more in common than you think."

"Please, like what?" I scoff.

"Okay." She straightens up. "One, you both help run businesses owned by your parents, and hopelessly throw yourselves into them. Two, you both just want to make out with each—"

I throw a bundle of napkins at her before she can finish, and she erupts in laughter. She's abruptly cut off by a chime from the tablet embedded in the table, and she looks at it with pure disdain on her face.

"What's up?" I ask, peering over.

"These kids," she grumbles. "Here I am, making these wildly perfect drinks, and they all want to drown it in sugar and—" she pulls her head back, an exaggerated look of disgust on her face *"—creamers."*

I snort a laugh and look out over the café. Several dozen plush chairs are scattered about in a way that seems disorganized, on purpose. Thick wooden tables with steel black supports are dotted around, long metal arms folding out from under them, some of them holding our large monitors. Others sit empty, with laptop stands. Ceramic square pots hold little plants, splashes of purple and green and deep red bright against the grain-and-steel surfaces, and a few crouched hangers sway gently near the windows. Even from here, I can see the small LED lights pulsing along the metallic stands, showing off charging keyboards and computer mice.

"You're bad at this game and you should feel bad about it!" shouts Lily, from where she's sitting just a few feet away. She's glaring intently at the monitor in front of her, a headset that's way too big for her head covering her ears. Her small hands are balled up around her controllers, little fists of rage. An older guy is sitting at the table with her, who has this professor sort of look about him, and looks away from his tablet to her and huffs out a laugh, shaking his head. You're supposed to go inside a soundproof room for gaming like that, but she *is* the owner's daughter.

Nick laughs from the back of the café, and I glare at him, though he doesn't see it.

It's a busy morning.

It's hard to say who everyone is, here in the café right now. I recognize a few college students from the area who are regulars, and a few young new faces, though I say that like they all aren't my age. Probably enjoying their winter break, not here, stressing about social media meltdowns in desperate pleas to be noticed by their family.

My phone buzzes.

PAT

Hey we're here.

I swallow, a well of anxiety brewing in my chest, and look up, just as Patrick walks in with Helen, Sophie, and Andrea. His eyes flit over to me and he nods, and I dash his way... and then push myself to walk. There's this strange urge to just run to him and hug him tight, despite everything that just happened. The way he just threw my iPhone charger out his freaking window, for one. The tether he knows I need.

"Hey," I manage to get out.

"Hey." He nods and clears his throat. He's got a wild curl twisting down his forehead, but it's not mine to brush away anymore. "We um...missed you at breakfast. You should come next time."

"I didn't...really know about it?" I shrug. Patrick glances back at the girls, who are all on their phones, and then back at me.

"Helen?" I venture. "I was messaging you."

"Oh, hey," she says, looking up and then back down. I suck at my teeth and look back to Patrick.

"Sorry, I thought one of them told you." He winces.

"It's all right. Go grab a seat. There's a free table over in the back." I nod over into the café and walk over to the girls, who are still milling around the door, and clear my throat.

I don't know if I would have wanted to go to breakfast anyway, not with him there.

Sophie looks up; the rest are still focused on their phones. She smirks at them and rolls her eyes, before enveloping me in one of her monster hugs, and this strange wave of relief washes over me. She smells like she just bounced around in a pile of tangerines, and the feeling that they've been ignoring me, distancing themselves from me, fades away a little. When she lets me go, she looks me right in the eyes.

"You okay?" Her green eyes flit over my shoulder, and I turn around to spot Patrick waiting on something in front of Dana at the coffee bar. Dana mimes putting poison in his drink, complete with her hands on her throat like she's dying, all while he stares at his phone, oblivious.

I snort out a laugh and turn back, Sophie giggling. She fusses with her glasses, oversize blue frames that pop out brilliantly against her red hair.

"I'll be okay." I shrug, nodding. "I think. Let's grab a drink and a table."

Sophie links her arm under mine and squeezes herself tightly against me, and we make our way over to Dana, who is still scowling as Patrick walks away. She turns to the two of us, a smile flashing across her face so quickly that it makes me laugh.

"And what can I get you two? The usual hot chocolate, Whit?"

"Yeah, and—" I turn around, but Helen and Andrea are still by the door, on their phones. I groan and nudge Sophie, who looks over at them and laughs.

"Hey!" she shouts across the café; a few people turn and

look at us. Helen looks up briefly, and then does a double take as if she just realized we're there and that she's here. She nudges Andrea with her elbow, who shoves her back without looking up. Helen swats her phone and Andrea finally glances at her and then over at us, a little smile lighting up on her face.

The two stroll over.

"You two good?" I ask, nodding at their phones.

"Yeah, it's nothing." Helen shrugs. "Just scrolling. So what's good here?"

"Everything," Dana says drily, crossing her arms.

"Okay," Andrea says, drawing out the word. "Just get us something sweet..." She looks back into the café, like she's searching for something. "We'll go grab a seat with Pat." She runs her fingers over my shoulder and flutters off, Helen following after, and I turn back to Sophie.

"Go ahead. I'll bring your drink over."

"You're the— Oh!" she exclaims, something behind me catching her attention. I turn around, and there's my dad, walking toward us. "Mr. Mitchell!" She grins and squeezes me again. "Come on, come say hi." I watch her hurry over to the table, where Patrick, Helen, and Andrea have all assembled, ignoring the monitors and various bits of tech in favor of chatting among themselves. My dad turns back at me and shrugs as he's dragged over to my friends.

"Those girls," I snort, shaking my head.

"FIREBALL!" shouts Lily, and I glance over just in time to see the professor spill his coffee all over himself from being startled. "All of you are terrible. ALL OF YOU ARE—"

"Lily!" I shout, and she stops midyell, her face turning into a grimace. She looks over at me.

"Sorry," she says, wincing.

"Thank you—"

"NO!" she shouts, briskly turning back around toward the table and her screen. "I wasn't talking to YOU. *You* should be sorry for that horrible last play." She digs back in, and the previously patient professor sighs loudly and gets up, moving to another table. I wince an "I'm sorry" his way, and he just softly smiles.

"No sitter today?" Dana asks, chuckling.

"Nah," I huff. "I thought Dad wasn't coming back until later tonight. Wish I knew he was going to be here earlier. Could have had breakfast with all of them." I'm not even sure why I'm saying that. I'd have rather just stayed home, maybe fired up *Mass Effect*. I've been meaning to replay the under-rated masterpiece that was *Andromeda*...

Adam. Adam got me thinking about those games again.

"Yeah..." Dana says, pausing. She picks up a mug and starts cleaning it out, a rag in her hand, digging inside. "You know, Whit, it's probably not my place, but as someone who is actually your friend... I gotta tell you, those girls are not."

"What?" I turn to her, surprised.

"They're not your friends."

"What do you mean?"

"Well..." She exhales. "Okay. It's just whenever they are here, they make a beeline to talk to your dad or grab a seat and ask for free shit. Just be careful. Money and success change people, particularly when it's not happening to them."

"Yeah..." I try not to scowl at her, while looking back toward the crew, all hanging at their usual table. My dad is sitting on the edge of a neighboring seat, and they're all talking about something. The café's gotten a little noisier, with the announcement from Blizzard no doubt almost here, but whatever it is, they're all smiles and warmth.

Dana doesn't know what she's talking about.

Right?

I try to push the brewing feelings down. This group that I've spent so much time with, my entire high school existence, really. I know they're all a bit self-absorbed and obsessed with their image, all of us and our matching jackets. But it's not that they don't care. They just miss things sometimes.

But I don't know. This past year, the way I sometimes heard people whisper about us, it made me wonder if having such a tight group was a mistake. Especially one where all we did was talk about other people, and never to each other.

I think this is the first time Sophie has ever really asked me how I was feeling, like, ever.

And I don't like how *that* feels.

I lean against the bar, sipping on my hot chocolate, watching them. Things are changing, but I think it's okay. Maybe the move to the new school will be good. Less time together, more to talk about. Or something.

"Hey, um, Whitney?"

I jump a little, and suddenly, there's Aaron from outside.

His face lights up, and I'm positive mine darkens.

"Customer!" Dana shouts in my ear. I turn around and send her my fiercest glare, which she catches and lobs back with a smile. Before I can look back to Aaron, I spot one of the soundproof booths opening up, and someone stepping out, carrying a VR headset. I reach out and grab Aaron's arm and

pull him along with me, hustling to the space before someone else steps in and claims it.

"Whoa!" Aaron says, a light laugh in his voice, and pulls his
arm away. "It's okay, Whit, you don't have to put me in one
of those." He keeps walking alongside me to the other end of
the café. "I know you're all swamped today. It's all right. I'll
keep it down." This kid. He's all carefree smiles and whole-
someness and it's a bit hard for me, a self-identifying hard dinner roll, to deal with him and his cinnamon-roll personality.

"No way," I grumble. "Aaron, you're sweet but I really
can't take listening to you and all your—" I gesture around
with my hand "—your babbling when you're here and on that
thing. Do you want some coffee before we get you set up in
the most soundproof room possible?"

"Oh, come on!" he laughs, clearly flustered. "It's not that
bad."

He pauses for a beat.

"Is it that bad?"

"Yes." I gesture for him to follow and he sighs, walking
after me. If I didn't want to keep an eye on her, I'd probably
put Lily in one of those booths so she could scream at *Magic*
players as loudly as she wants.

I know way more about this guy's love life than I should.
His girlfriend's name is Divya. That they have outstanding
virtual reality dates almost every other day. That she was
kinda famous online for a while. That they are currently
reading some book called *Virtually Yours* together, it's bright
pink cover under his arm. It's cute, but I really don't need to
hear him gushing over her in public, giggling with her during games or their book club.

It's not that I don't like that stuff, or that I'm against it, but I don't know. Me and Patrick aren't…well, weren't like that. All sweet nothings and pet names, reading books together or having "songs" or anything. It's fine for other people, but it's just not for me. I don't have the time.

I press a button on the side of one of the pods, big, almost office-like spaces in the back of the café reserved for private gaming, meetings, whatever you need. The glass door un-latches, a bit of suction whooshing as it swings, and he steps in. He turns back to me, looking at the rest of the café.

"Look, you really don't have to fuss. I'll be quiet and—"

I close the door, which shuts with a wildly satisfying snap as he continues to try to talk to me, his voice muffled be-hind the glass.

"I can't hear you," I mouth to him through the glass. He sits down in one of the big cozy chairs and reaches for his headset, and I catch a bit of my reflection in the thick glass separating us. Even in the weak reflection, I can see the bags under my eyes. My black hair a tangled mess. I pull my phone out to order a comped hot chocolate for Aaron, and maybe something for the professor—

Suddenly, my dad is right there, his reflection's arms crossed in the glass.

"Hey!" I shout, turning around to him.

"Hey," he says, a little smile on his face. "Pictures looked really good." He holds up his phone, nodding with approval, and there's just this blast of serotonin from it.

"Thanks." I feel myself beam. "Dad, do you have a minute to talk about the arcade situation a bit more—?"

"Are you okay?" he asks, looking back at his phone and then at me.

"Me?" I ask, trying not to deflate from him dismissing my attempt to talk about Adam's place again. I still don't think that situation is over. "Yeah, I'm fine, I—"

"Your crew told me about the breakup," he says, interrupting me. "Why didn't you tell me? Text or…I don't know, anything?"

"Oh." I'm a little stunned. I never even thought to tell him in the first place, and also, why are *they* telling him details of my personal life? "I just…you were busy and traveling. I didn't want to bother you. And there was the whole social media thing with the arcade, and there was a lot to take care of."

"Yeah, but…" He exhales through his nose. "Whit, this place will still be here if you take a minute to tell me about your day, okay?"

"Okay." I nod.

"With college coming—" he starts, trailing off for a second "—we should really start looking for someone to take over all this from you. I don't think you'll have the time to handle this place when you're at Penn or Drexel, and honestly, I'm not sure you have the time for it now."

"Sure I do!" I exclaim. "I've got this."

"All right," he says, and for a minute, I almost think he's about to hug me. There's a beat and he looks out toward the door, waving at someone, before glancing back at me. "I'll let you get back to it." He walks away toward the coffee bar, and I move to make my way over to the table where Patrick and…

I spot Patrick sitting at a table, alone.

"Hey," I say once I reach him, hot chocolate in hand. "Where'd everyone go?"

"Oh. They bailed?" He shrugs. "While you were talking to your dad. Sorry, Whit. You know they don't really get all the games and stuff."

"Yeah, but…" I sigh. "Never mind. I thought maybe they'd at least want to spend some time with me. Especially considering—" I point at him and me "—you know."

"I guess," he says, getting up from his chair. "I mean, Whit, you're fine." He looks at me, his warm eyes looking as tired as mine, but not the same. "You're always fine. Whenever anything happens, your parents last year, your move this year…" He pauses and swallows. "Us. You're fine."

"Doesn't mean I don't want…you know, people to ask me if I am," I grumble, crossing my arms.

"You almost always specifically say you don't want us doing that." He sighs and runs his hand through his hair. "Look, I… I miss you." He looks up at me and then back down. "It hasn't even been a week, and I miss you. But I know you don't miss me, and that's okay. I'm not fine. And it's okay to admit that you aren't, even if you feel like you are."

"How can you say that? Of course I miss—" I start.

"You don't." He shakes his head, a sad smile on his face. My phone buzzes and I glance down at my pocket. "Someone needs you."

"Patrick—"

"It's okay," he says and nods at me a little. "Text me later or something. Or don't. I don't know. This is hard." He glances toward the doors and back at me. "I'm gonna go."

I just nod at him. I don't know what to say.

He walks toward the exit, not looking back, and I make my way over to Dana.

"You okay?" she asks, reaching across the bar, grabbing my arm.

"Yeah…" I huff. "Yeah, I'll be fine."

I look back up toward the exit, Patrick on the other side, when Sophie pops up from behind one of the pillars blocking the view. She reaches a hand out, and my breath catches in my chest.

Patrick takes it.

I look back to Dana, who turns away from the door and whatever just unfolded, and she looks at me with the most devastating look of pity on her face.

Old City Pinball:
Preparations are underway for this week's Old City Winter Festival! What games of ours would you like to see outside? Weather permitting of course.

West Philly eSports:
Do you guys have Starcraft? Halo? Call of Duty?

West Philly eSports:
Maybe Rocket League?

West Philly eSports:
It's neat, in it the cars are basically playing soccer.

Old City Pinball:
Are you finished?

West Philly eSports:
Is your pinball arcade finished?

Old City Pinball:
Jesus Whitney I tried to be NICE to you.

West Philly eSports:
Whatever. I saw you like that reply yesterday.

Old City Pinball:
What are you even talking about?!

West Philly eSports:
You know EXACTLY what I'm talking about!

Smak Parlour:
Um. This is on main, you two.

Krumm's Boutique:
This feels like a phone call. Or a text. Or anything else other than being on here in public.—Mom.

Chris Makes Stuff:
What the hell.

Chris Makes Stuff:
Delete all of this. You two are ridiculous.

AKA Music:
I mean I think it's kinda funny.

Chris Makes Stuff:
Stop it Andres, I know that's you.

AKA Music:
LOL. Hi Chris.

Krumm's Boutique: Hey.—Mom

West Philly eSports: I know, I know. I'll stop. I'll take it offline

Krumm's Boutique: Right, yeah you will. I want you to swing by the arcade tomorrow with a few plants for Adam and his mom.—Mom

West Philly eSports: What? I'm not doing that.

Krumm's Boutique: Consider it your peace offering.—Mom

Krumm's Boutique: Otherwise, no cactus.—Mom

West Philly eSports: You're a monster. Also stop signing all of your messages, I know it's you.

Krumm's Boutique: Love you.

Krumm's Boutique:…

Krumm's Boutique:—Mom.

West Philly eSports: You are exhausting.

CHAPTER 7
Adam

"A good game of pinball isn't just about the score.
It's about the experience. The lights, the sounds, the
music…it brings it all together. The points don't
matter. You remember what happened while you
were playing, while you were there. And that's what
you should be thinking about, when considering your
player, and considering yourself. What will you carry,
when the lights are out, all is quiet, and the game is
over?"

–THE ART AND ZEN OF PINBALL REPAIR
BY JAMES WATTS

"*What* are you doing?" Chris shouts at me as I walk out of the
arcade, desperately trying to drag out the large tent we use
every year for the Old City Winter Festival. I glance up and
see him across the street, as flurries are pummeling my face,
though the snow isn't heavy yet. I'm still feeling hopeful things
will go on as planned tomorrow, and evidently, so is the rest

of the neighborhood. The small cobblestone side street that breaks off Second in front of our shop, Church Street, already has a few tents up and booths waiting. Throughout the rest of the year, the side street is generally lined with stands for a farmer's market, but is sadly empty in the winter months. Seeing it with the promise of life again fills my heart. I need this. The arcade needs this.

Whitney might be driving me up the wall lately, but at least the annual festival put together by her mom is something to look forward to. There's something about chilly weather, hot chocolate, and cobblestone streets at night, that gets people excited about playing pinball machines outside. It reminds folks that we are here, and there's always a small bump in visits come January and February. Until people forget about us again; but at least that's something.

"I'm trying to get this thing put up," I grumble, the end of one remaining pole stuck in the front door. I wiggle it around until it comes free, the door to the arcade shutting neatly behind it.

"You know that's not what I'm talking about!" he yells, and as a final car zips by, he darts across Second Street to reach me. "You and Whitney, bickering back and forth publicly online? What is that? How old are you two?"

"Brands fight on social media all the time." I wave her off.

"Yeah, in ways that are *funny*! You're not Taco Bell arguing about sauce…with…with an Arby's!"

"Is there even an Arby's in Philadelphia?"

"That is not the point!" he shouts before laughing. "Jesus, man, the two of you. What happened to moving on?"

I shrug, thinking of that long pause down the block from

her mom's plant shop, the snow and the streetlights…and everything it potentially held. There was absolutely a moment there, where I was standing with the same girl I knew five years ago.

"I tried." I bend down and grab one of the white pipes for the tent and toss it to him. "Come on, let's get this up."

It doesn't take long to get the large, thin tent up in the air, spanning the length of the arcade but just the width of the city sidewalk. The pinball machines don't quite work when they're placed on wobbly, uneven cobblestone streets, so year after year, we have the narrow tent to protect them over the bit of level sidewalk we've got out front.

It makes me think about the first big pinball festival Philly had. Out in Manayunk years ago, machines lining up and down the Schuylkill River, huge, billowing white tents all over Main Street, fabric battling with low-hanging trees.

As beautiful as the setting was, the river, the walk, the trees…it turns out hosting a pinball event in the most notoriously hilly neighborhood in Philadelphia is a bad idea because, you know, *gravity*, and a game involving steel balls. There's even a hill in that neighborhood that runners call "the wall." Dad was so mad about that first festival, he ended up just taking us to the Manayunk Brewing Company for fried chicken and deep-fried buffalo cauliflower. I heard they were thinking of having it again in King of Prussia, at the convention center, since buildings are decidedly more level than historic cobblestone streets.

"All right," I sigh, clapping my hands together. The tent rustles a little in the small gusts of wind, flurries dancing through the inside. "I guess the big question now is what machines don't we mind getting a bit of snow on this year?"

"Yeah, I'm a little worried about that," Chris huffs, looking up at the sky. It's dark gray and ominous, but the weather report keeps saying we won't get the heaviest blast of snow until after the festival. And by then, we'll be closed for the rest of the holiday season until the New Year. "Do we have any good tarps to cover the machines?"

"The ones from last year are still okay, I think." I shrug. "Come on, we'll get the hot chocolate stand out, too."

We duck inside the arcade, hit with a blast of warmth. I hold the door for Chris, whose glasses immediately fog up. He pulls them off, wiping them on his T-shirt, a black tee that says "don't get eaten," with the outline of a dragon on it.

"Is that a *Game of Thrones* thing?" I ask, nodding at his shirt, surveying the arcade.

"Le Guin," he replies. "One day I'll get you to read *Earthsea*."

"One day." I smirk at him and look back toward the machines. With the potential of a snowstorm and the fact that the machines go outside during all this, I want to make sure we're picking ones we won't be upset over getting a little wet or dinged up. Especially dinged up. Every year people have a little too much fun, end up getting a bit too rough with the games. It's how we lost *The Phantom Menace* machine years ago, when Dad was still here. Some sci-fi author on a book tour got way too excited and basically fell on top of the thing, knocking it over.

"I say we take out—" Chris stands next to me, hands on his hips "—the *Indiana Jones* game, the *Lost in Space* one, and maybe…*Doctor Who*?" He looks at me and I shrug.

"All just pop culture ones?" I ask. Something about that stings a little. While Dad understood the appeal of them, he loved the machines that were just the products of some designer's imagination. *Medieval Madness*, *White Water*, or *Funhouse*, games that had no real story or touch point in movies or comic books. They were exactly what their titles said.

They were original. They took risks. He liked making sure people tried them out.

"I mean, we're not exactly getting the pinball enthusiasts who want to play one of your vintage games," he laughs. I wince, but he doesn't catch it. "I say go with the pop culture games, so people take lots of pictures. The more people saying 'Oooh, *Doctor Who*!' and posting it to their Instagram, the better."

"Yeah, I guess you're right." I keep looking around. "Maybe a fourth one, too, maybe *Goldeneye*? There's a new James Bond movie out and about."

"Yes!" he exclaims. "Awesome, okay." He pauses for a beat. "How do we get these out of here ourselves?"

We manage to slowly get the four machines out of the arcade with some help from the booksellers at the comic book shop down the block, Brave New Worlds, both still wildly happy with us giving them the broken *Flash Gordon* machine. It could have gone faster if the two of them didn't chat about Ursula K. Le Guin with Chris nonstop, and didn't take a break to argue about why we should have the *Battlefield Earth* machine out for pictures. There's absolutely no way I'm putting that disaster on display. I'd rather put it outside to go in the trash.

I hand the two of them ten dollars in quarters each, and they close their comic bookstore for the morning to play some games. I take a picture of them in the arcade, playing one of the *Jurassic Park* games while waving at me and my phone, and post it.

Old City Pinball:
Shout out to Brian and Rob at Brave New Worlds, for helping us get our machines out on the sidewalk for the Old City Winter Festival! Stop by our arcade tomorrow for free games and hot chocolate!

I head back into the office and fumble around the cabinets, looking for the tarps to drape over the machines. Every year they get buried under more and more stuff, and every year I tell myself I'm going to remember to put them someplace else to make it easier. And as I'm wrestling them out of a box, it hits me that if Whitney's dad does buy the arcade, this could be the last year this happens.

The last year of wrestling out tarps, of fighting with that horrible tent, of freezing on the sidewalk with Chris, praying someone doesn't have one too many outdoor spiked apple ciders and break a machine. All stuff that is, I'll admit, horrible. But I would miss every second of it.

I try to shake that off as I subsequently shake off the tarps, bits of dirt and cobwebs fluttering about. I drag the tarps outside, when my phone buzzes.

West Philly eSports: Hey, I saw you posting.

West Philly eSports: Are you at the arcade right now?

I can't help but squint at the screen. Why is Whitney talking to me, never mind even *asking* me anything? I shove my phone back in my pocket and walk out the door, looking around for any sign of her. Chris is there on the sidewalk, using some old bike lock chains to attach the machines together, and lock them to the iron bars of our windows out front.

Not that I can imagine anyone actually stealing these things, even wildly late at night in Old City. I mean, how? Would you throw it into the back of a pickup truck? In a van? And even then, you'd need a few people to lift it up that high. Honestly, if someone did manage to do that, I think they deserve to have the game. They earned it.

"Here we go," I say, handing one of the tarps to Chris. I bend down and tug on the bike locks. "Looks good."

"It's not that hard." He shrugs. "Connect to machine, connect to wall." He unfurls his tarp, and starts to awkwardly nudge the thing over one of the machines on the end of the row, and I start doing the same. There are companies out there who make actual pinball machine covers, but we've been using these old motorcycle covers for years, ever since Dad got sent a bundle from an old biker club in South Philly as a gift for hosting a retirement party here. The other ones aren't exactly made for leaving pinball machines outside, as... well, no one leaves pinball machines outside.

I make my way to the last game and flap the cover over my head, opening it up. I push it over the machine, *Doctor Who*, which will likely be the most popular cabinet during the festival.

The machine always felt like such a missed opportunity, to just completely lean in and make the thing look like a TARDIS. Instead, it's just shaped like a regular pinball machine. The big draw on our cabinet is the little Dalek on top of the back box, that moves around back and forth when the machine is talking.

They only made the first one hundred with that little feature, and I'm sure a lot of people will line up to get videos of that little thing.

"Hey, um…Adam?" Chris ventures, while I'm getting the final bit of the cover over the side. I tuck it under the legs of the machine, and clip it tightly around it.

"What's up?" I ask, standing up. He's staring straight ahead, and I turn around.

It's Whitney.

She's walking down the block, a potted plant in her hands. The pot looks dark gray with little bands of gold trickling through it, like cracks that have been filled. Pretty sure I remember seeing pottery like that at the Philadelphia Museum of Art. Something about repairing a broken vase with gold makes what was once broken more beautiful? She's got on that white jean jacket of hers, even though it's absolutely freezing out, and her cheeks are red from the cold. There's a scowl on her face as she strolls toward us.

What is she doing here, and why is she carrying that plant?

"Are you two…friends again, finally?" he asks, whispering.

"I don't think so?" I whisper back, shrugging. There's a crinkling sound and I turn around to spot Chris handing me a bag of Swedish Fish, and I swat it away.

Whitney slows down at the tent, looking at the setup, and picks her pace back up to reach us.

"Looks like you guys are ready to go for tomorrow," she says, her eyes not quite meeting mine and looking around at just about everything else. She shivers a little, the plant shaking in her hands.

"Just about." I shrug. I can't quite bring myself to look at her, either. The other day, in her mom's plant shop, was the first time we'd been so close in so long. The photograph in my dad's workshop flashes to mind and I think... I think I've missed her.

"All right, well, I'm gonna go get the table for the hot chocolate," Chris says, and before I turn around to tell him to wait, he's practically down the street. I catch him turn around as he gets close to The Book Trader, and he bends down to look in the giveaway bins...but he's clearly staring at the two of us. He winks and gets up to keep going.

Goddammit.

I glance back at Whitney, who promptly looks away. Her cheeks are an even more bright red now, the freckles on her face dark, like little pinpricks against the rosy blush. The last time we were standing this close to one another, save for the incident at the plant shop, was that August before freshman year, enjoying the last gasp of summer before high school. We played kick the can in South Philadelphia, drinking Arctic Splash iced tea on the curb as the sky got darker. We hadn't hung out in months, but mutual friends found us together for that game, talking about all the things we were afraid of, which hit particularly hard just a few months after losing Dad. Staying friends was one of them, in the vast expanse that high school would be. But we made whispered promises there in the dark, over sweet tea and the cheers of our neighborhood friends. Then school started and she had a new group of friends, and suddenly, I felt like a punchline in the hallway.

What happened?

And why does it feel so different now, here in the cold? This girl who looks so different now but feels so familiar. Whose freckled face and ice-blue eyes remind me of a home that doesn't exist anymore...but maybe could.

Plumes of cold air are puffing from her mouth, and I can see her gritting her teeth to stop from shaking.

I wonder if she can tell I'm doing the same.

Dad's R.E.M. jacket doesn't exactly keep the cold at bay, and as I inch it closer to me, I remember one of the reasons we drifted apart.

"Hey, do you um...want to come in?" I ask, looking at the arcade door, thinking of the blast of heat from earlier. She turns around, looking back up the street, and for a second I think I spot her mom standing on the opposite corner by Smak Parlour. Between her and the fact that Chris is probably lurking somewhere nearby spying, it feels like a lot of people are invested in whatever is happening here.

"Is that—"

"Yes." She groans, turning back. "She's not gonna let me go until you take this plant." She holds it out, quivering more than a little.

"All right, come on in." I nod and start walking toward the door. "We'll find a place for it, and warm you up."

She follows, and I hold the door open for her. She exhales loudly entering the arcade, and I turn and wave to her mom down the block. She waves back, before darting around the corner, likely back to her shop to set up some more for the festival.

"Nice, right?" I ask, walking by her, the heat already warming me up.

"I feel like I'm defrosting." She snorts out a laugh and makes her way over to the snack bar, placing the plant down on the counter. She hefts a black backpack off her shoulder, placing that right next to the pot. She unzips it and starts to unload a bunch of little plants. More of the air plants from the other day, like the kind she gave me in her mom's shop.

"So what is all this?" I ask, walking up next to her. The windows are pouring in a bit of the morning sun in the way that makes gaming early in the day almost impossible, casting a glare over everything. But in her case, with it shimmering in around her, it gives her an outline of gold and white, just beaming off that jacket of hers. I keep glancing up at her and looking away, as if staring straight ahead at the heat lamp and the basket we fill with chicken fingers is going to make me forget the weird way I'm feeling right now.

Though chicken fingers *are* an excellent way to eat your feelings.

"My mom. She saw...all the *online* stuff. Ugh, hold on," she grumbles, and slides out of her jean jacket, revealing a bright red T-shirt, which makes her blue eyes spark like a mint candy. Her eyes flit up to mine and then back down to the plants she's unpacking onto the counter.

I clear my throat and look away.

That shirt, though.

"I remember that day, you know," I say, trying to focus. She looks up, confused, and I nod at her then point. "The shirt? Melissa Etheridge and Sheryl Crow?"

She looks down at her T-shirt and back up at me, a little wave of realization washing over her face. She smirks and I shrug.

"That was a fun day," she says, before looking back to her plants.

Huge open field at the Mann Center. Lawn chairs. My dad screaming along to "I'm the Only One" and dancing with my mom, much to the disapproving looks of everyone sitting on the grass around us. Cheap, far away, but the music was close and rattling in my chest. I can still smell the wet grass.

The two of us, thirteen, sitting on the ground, our shoulders brushing. Awkward, quiet and airy laughs, nudging away from each other and slowly falling back. That confusing feeling when you think there's something more, but you're not sure, and no one can really tell you but yourself.

I think myself was onto something back then, but it's way too late now.

"It was." I nod, and the door to the arcade swings open. Chris is back, a bundle of supplies in bags. His eyes go wide seeing Whitney, a little smirk on his face. I give him my best "don't" look, and he ducks into my dad's workshop.

"Hey, Whitney," he says from somewhere in there.

"Chris," she says back, glancing at me. I hear him fussing with something back there, and he quickly walks back outside, waving at the two of us as he exits. Fleeing the scene. Whitney focuses back on her plants, and the arcade door closes with a light snap.

And then I squint, trying to listen.

Is the…stereo on?

A synthesizer and the plinking of a keyboard sound out over the arcade, and suddenly, Nancy and Ann Wilson are singing about ticking clocks, unanswered phone calls, and dark empty rooms, and Whitney is standing there, fussing with her plants. I look up and see Chris peering in through one of the large glass windows in the front of the arcade. He catches me catching him, and bolts away.

Goddammit, *he* put this on.

I should have changed the password to the arcade's Spotify account.

Heart booms into the chorus of "Alone." It's like everything in the arcade is moving in slow motion, Whitney lit up by the sun in the window.

Her eyes flit forward, settling on me, and I feel my breath go short.

She looks the way Melissa Etheridge sings.

Fierce and beautiful.

How did we even get here?

"Hey, Whit, I'm… I'm sorry about all the online stuff," I stammer out. She looks up at me, placing one of the plants on the counter with a loud *plink*. My mind reels, from the T-shirt she's wearing to the photos hanging in my dad's workshop. "I just…" I feel the waves of anxiety rolling around in my chest, like they're swimming from my neck and down into my spine and back up. "I wish I knew how to get back there."

"Where?" she asks, zippering her backpack shut. She places it off to the side, looking right at me.

"There." I nod at her shirt again. "Before…you know, my dad, and high school, and…you know, you and your new friends." She gives me a confused look. "Well, I mean, they're not new now, but back then they were. Sophie and them."

"What do *they* have to do with anything?" she scoffs, pulling out one of the seats. She squirms a little on top of it before standing again with a laugh. "These still aren't great, huh?"

"Nope." I grin, laughing a little. "Just like that bunch you hang out with."

"Ugh! You always do that," she says, slapping the counter.

"Do what?" I glare.

"That." She points. "You say something nice, *almost* nice... and then you bring it back around to...to...something else. Some passive-aggressive thing about something you want to say, but never do. You did it online when we were messaging, and you're doing it now. And I don't care how much my mom wants us to get along, or your little friend—" she gestures toward the door "—thinks putting some old romantic song on is gonna fix things."

She grabs her backpack and throws it over her shoulder, power walking toward the door.

"Wait, wait, I'm sorry!" I shout after her, pushing away from the snack bar. She slows down a little and turns around. "I'm sorry, I'm just...this week, and Dad, and you, and... I'm sorry, it just brings those first few months after that summer back and I... It's hard for me. Every year, every winter, it wears me down."

There's a little storm brewing behind my eyes; I can feel it.

"And this is maybe the last winter, and—"

My lip quivers and I bite it back.

"This festival, every year, even though it's your mom running it, I see you. I mean, you just left," I stammer out, sniffling. And I just can't hold it anymore. I'm crying, and there's this ugly heaving feeling in my chest. "You left, and I needed you. He was gone, and I *needed* you."

The rage on her face wavers a little and she walks toward me again, her face lit up and glimmering with red, blue, and orange from the different pinball machines. Her white jean jacket, slung over her shoulder, reflects a splash of purple.

"You were the one who started ignoring me," she says, though there's nothing angry about it. She's gentle, and her blue eyes are wide. "I kept trying, all those months to get to you, and you kept pushing me away. There's only so much pushing someone can take before they just…go in that direction. Then we came back from the summer and you were just…gone."

"I wasn't gone. You just didn't see me anymore." I exhale. "I remember that first week. You and the girls, against the lockers. Just…laughing at me when I walked by. Making fun of my jacket, my hair…"

"Laughing?" Her eyebrows furrow down. "I don't—"

"I do." I sniffle, trying to get it back together. "You, Sophie, Helen, Andrea. Every time I went by, it was you four. And I heard it, Whit. Chris did, too, the following year, when he was a freshman. The way I looked, the way I dressed. It wasn't okay."

"Oh." Whitney rolls her eyes a little, and it makes me grit my teeth. "That… Adam, come on. They were…they were just joking around because…" She gestures at me, and her face looks like it's at war with itself. Like she wants to say something but isn't sure how to. "I mean, you showed up with this whole new look, kept wearing all these old bands and that jacket—"

"It was my dad's jacket!" I shout. "His shirts!"

"Yeah I… I know," she sighs. "I think I knew that. I'm sorry, I… I do miss junior high sometimes. It was…simpler."

"Me, too." I mostly whisper.

There's a pause, this beat of silence, just the two of us in the pinball arcade, the soft blips of music and sound interrupting the air, blending with passing cars and what sounds like a SEPTA bus. And there are all these words, just bounding around in my head and my heart, that I want to fill that space with. That through all of it, all these years, I wanted to get this out. Find a way to get here.

"So I, um..." She walks back toward me and over to the snack bar, where all the plants are sitting. "I should probably tell you how to take care of these, since your mom probably isn't going to."

I laugh a little and join her, standing diagonal from her, at the corner of the bar. It feels like a start.

"Plants have always been my mom's way of trying to make things right, I think." She shrugs, sliding the bigger plant in the large container closer to us. "And she thought maybe you could use a little sprucing up in here, in this space." She looks back at the rest of the snack area and up at the shelves. "She also gives them away to businesses here to get people to visit the shop. Revolution House across the street has succulents on every dining table. So not totally selfless."

"That's smart." I nod. "Wish I could leave pinball machines everywhere."

She smirks, and waves me closer.

"This is java moss." And that's when I realize there's a glass case over the pot, and it's not just some plant, but a whole big terrarium. She reaches in and pulls out some soft, green, feathery-looking stuff between her fingers, and nods at it. "Go ahead."

I reach out and pluck it from her fingers.

"It's happy anywhere," she says, looking at the green in my hands. "Land. Water. It can adapt to just about anywhere you put it."

"Huh," I mutter. "Sounds like you."

"Oh?" She looks at me, surprised.

"I mean…it was like when we started high school," I press forward, trying to step carefully. "You had this whole new look almost right away, with you and the girls and your jackets." I glance at her jean jacket and back up at her, and she's looking at me quizzically. "I feel like you transitioned so well, blending with this new crew, and I just…didn't."

I laugh a little.

"What's the uh…startup word for all that?" She smirks as I search for the word. "Pivot. You pivoted."

"Ugh." She rolls her eyes. "I hate that kind of talk."

"Well, hey, all that tech world stuff is what made Chris want to get the arcade up on social media." I shrug. "That and he couldn't stand my pinball trivia, and wanted me to put it somewhere else. So thanks for that."

"I'm not sure if I should say you're welcome, considering the last few years with us on there." She shrugs.

"Yeah, well…" I huff. "Truce?"

She smirks and does that snort laugh she's been doing since we were kids.

"Truce."

"Are we…going to talk about your dad?" I ask. "Him and his plans?"

"I think that probably breaks the truce?" she says, her eyebrows quirked. "That's… I'm not part of any of that."

"Fair enough."

She holds out a hand, and I take it. When she lets go... I feel the loss of her hand in my chest. She puts her hands back on the counter, and I have this wild urge to reach out across the counter and hold her hand. But she goes back to work on one of the terrariums, and the moment, if there was one, is gone. I try to shake it off but...something is there. Maybe all this talk about Dad and the past has me feeling a bit stirred up. That...has to be it.

"Here." She takes one of the smaller plants and hands it to me. The container is about the size of a Mason jar cut in half, filled with black stones on the bottom, bits of driftwood, some of that moss, and two of those air plants. The little green plants are about the size of a quarter. "Right there."

She points at the shelves in back of the snack bar, lined with jars of coffee beans and loose-leaf tea. I take the little jar and place it in one of the empty cubes, and pull the white glittering string lights around it. The plants inside light up, little bits of white light bouncing of the rocks, turning the terrarium into a big lightbulb.

"There it is," she says in an exhale.

"Wow." I stand back, the one beaming bit in the middle of the dark boxes. I turn around to her. "How many more does your mom want you to make?"

"*You?*" she asks, as though the word is insulting. "Let's see how many *we* can make."

She pushes an empty terrarium at me across the coffee bar, and I reach for the sand at the same time she does. Her hand is on top of mine for a second too long, and I look up at her. She shirks it away, clearing her throat.

"Maybe we add like four more?" she asks, still looking at

the shelf. "Here and here, maybe." She points. "Ooh! And then we could put a big terrarium here on the counter." She looks back at me, her blue eyes all lit up. "We could totally do a water one, with like, marimo moss." She walks over next to me and joins me in leaning against the counter. "They're these little green fluffs from Japan and…" She tilts her head again, looking at me. "What?"

"Nothing." I shake my head. "You just talk about plants the way I talk about pinball, I guess." I sigh. "Look, I don't think we can afford that bigger thing." I gesture at the countertop. "We're not exactly doing well. I mean, you know."

She winces.

"Sorry. It's just…this stuff is *nice*." I turn around, looking at the shelving. Little illuminated terrariums dotting through-out, the white Christmas lights twinkling behind the plants and the coffee jars. "But the way things are going, I might be walking across the street to give these back to your mom."

"God, don't do that," she laughs. "She'll think this whole apology thing didn't work."

I lean against the bar, turning to look at her.

"Did it work?" I ask.

"I'm… I think so?" she ventures.

"Yeah, I'm… I'm glad we talked."

She pushes a bag of sand across the snack bar and nods at the Mason jar.

"All right, R.E.M." She snorts, pushing away from the bar. "Get to work."

"Where are you going?" I ask, pouring some sand in a jar.

"I, um…" she stammers out. "Have plans with the girls."

"Ah." I nod, looking back down at the jar. "Just... Whit, you know those girls, they're..."

"What?" she asks.

"Never mind," I sigh, not wanting to ruin whatever is happening here. "I'll see you at the festival?"

"Sure." She nods, her tone a little sharp. I hope I didn't mess this up by bringing up her friends again, but someone has got to tell her. I just don't know if that person is me. Especially not now, but I can't help but wonder if she has anyone willing to have those kind of talks with her.

The people you want to have a discussion about, aren't the ones who are going to have that discussion. Not ever.

"Great." I smile, but her face is wavering. She nods at me, turns, and walks toward the door.

Old City Pinball:
It's almost time for the festival! We've got our machines ready to go and are prepping the hot chocolate stand. Games will be free outside, and all games in the arcade will be discounted down to a quarter a play!

> **Krumm's Boutique:**
> I hope you liked the plants!—Mrs. Mitchell

> **Old City Pinball:**
> They're very nice Mrs. Mitchell, thank you.—Adam

> **Chris Makes Stuff:**
> Stop that.—Chris

> **Smak Parlour:**
> Yes everyone cut it out.—The Smak Girls

> **The Book Trader:**
> Adam your book is in.—Daniel

Old City Pinball:
Oh my God.

Krumm's Boutique:
You're welcome Adam! Tell your guests to use the code "pinball" at our shop for a 15% discount during the festival!

Old City Pinball:
I will!

West Philly eSports:
Mom you are shameless. Shameless.

Krumm's Boutique:
It's called business and partnering with your community!

Brave New Worlds:
Jill you've never dropped off any plants here.

Krumm's Boutique:
You watered the last succulent terrarium with a cup of coffee.

Krumm's Boutique:
You're still on probation.

CHAPTER 8
Whitney

I put my phone down and take a long sip of my strawberry crème soda, fizzy bubbles tickling my nose.

The Franklin Fountain is always a bustling place in Old City, but I'm here early enough on a Tuesday that I don't think any of the off-for-the-holidays-so-let's-do-brunch crowd is ready to descend on it just yet, tipsy on mimosas and wanting something sweet before napping the rest of the day away. And besides, it's the winter, and the ice cream rush isn't what it usually is. Designed to look like an old-timey fountain soda and ice cream shop, a large, polished, wooden bar runs the length of place, massive silver-and-brass machines behind workers, aka "soda jerks," wearing bow ties and rocking curly mustaches.

I check the time. Again. And my notifications. Again. I keep telling myself that they are just a little late, that they're coming, but…between what Dana said at my dad's café and what Adam was muttering at the arcade, I'm wondering if I've been missing something all this time. I'll admit, my girl gang, all of us once inseparable, changed in the past few months. Hell, in the past few days, even, with Patrick breaking things off. Did he somehow get them in the breakup, even though I had them first?

I don't like the word *popular*, but that's what our little crew was. Is? Was. I'm not sure. The way they flounced out when they were done talking to my dad, how I thought I saw Sophie holding Patrick's hand... I'm not sure what to think.

I poke at a little planter in the middle of the table. It's a small terra-cotta pot, the size of a coffee mug, with a sizable chunky succulent in the middle, with spiny leaves in shades of green and reddish purple. Little white dots speckle the surface, and I tap one of the pointed leaves, sharp, but not enough to do damage.

"Zebra plant, right?" a deep familiar voice asks.

I glance up to see Neil, one of the regulars who works here at the Fountain, nodding at me, his eyes settling on the plant.

"Mom?" I ask.

"She's got good taste." He shrugs. I'm unsurprised. My mom enjoys handing out plants to every shop and restaurant in Old City. It's a mix of the kindness of her heart and a brilliant piece of advertising. Someone sees one of these on a table, and it's all *oh, I've been meaning to get some plants for the... why, there's a plant boutique across the street!* Part of me wonders if the whole apology thing to Adam was really just her trying to do a little advertising there, what with the festival coming, and the amount of traffic the arcade is probably going to get.

"Do you need another?" Neil asks.

I snort out a laugh.

"No, I've got a bunch at home and at the—" He waves a glass Mason jar in the air. "Oh!" I laugh again. "Yeah, sure. Keep 'em coming, Neil," I say, trying out my best 1930s accent.

He points at me and flips the Mason jar around in his hand before doing whatever magic he does back there. While most of the guys on staff are clean-shaven with a big ol' twirly mustache, Neil is one of the few with a gigantic lumberjack beard, and I have no idea how that thing doesn't get dipped into the ice cream floats he makes. And considering his work as an artist around Philly, creating wheat-paste stencils on the sides of brick buildings, it makes me question it even more. How his beard doesn't end up painting everything around him with whipped cream or white paint, I'll never know.

I check my phone again, and after a beat Neil slides another strawberry crème soda across the vintage table in front of me, the glass coasting across the surface with a satisfying *whoosh*. There's a massive dollop of whipped cream on it, and I glance back to him, staring intently at his beard.

He's got a gift.

I flip to the camera on my phone and snap a photo of the drink, all pink and white and beautiful. I go to share the photo on my personal page, and notice my notifications are lit up. Well, the café's notifications, not mine. Mine are quiet, although...there's a new follower on my personal Instagram.

I squint at the little photo of whoever it is that's following me and...

I laugh. Adam Stillwater.

I can't help myself. I look through his photo stream. It's mostly photos of pinball machines, all bright lights and lens flares from creative angles. Some weird circuit boards and piles of electric parts that I don't really understand or recognize. A couple pictures with Chris and shots of old vinyl records. It's exactly what I would expect, I suppose.

I swipe down some more, scrolling through, and stop when I realize what I'm doing.

Oh, my God.

Why am I looking for a photo of him with a girl, like I would while lurking on the profile of someone I want to… maybe talk to…?

I shake my head and follow him back before tapping to check the café's feed.

Old City Pinball:
We're ready for you, Old City! We've got our machines outside and ready to play. Which games? You'll have to drop by and find out. And check out our new decorations in the snack bar, and again, thanks to Krumm's Boutique and West Philly eSports. Looking good, right?

Krumm's Boutique:
Beautiful!

Krumm's Boutique:
I hope you enjoy them, Adam.—Mrs. Mitchell.

Smak Parlour:
Ya'll are cool now? I can't keep up.

Krumm's Boutique:
Remember, "pinball" for 15% off!

Meritage Coffee:
West Philly eSports? Have you been hacked?

Brave New Worlds:
Blink twice if you need someone to save you Adam.

I snort out a laugh.

I wonder if this means the more playful side of our little social media battles are going to fade away? It hasn't always been so... I don't know, intense and real. Adam's definitely left funny comments on promotions, and vice versa. Jokes and cracks that made me smile in that wistful sort of way, remembering how things were, before brushing it aside. There are a few other businesses in the area that like to bust each other's chops, the local boutiques, competing pizza places and cheesesteak joints, a local water ice company that snaps at an Italian ice shop in Jersey. I'd say water ice and Italian ice are the same thing, but I'm not *that* brave.

I enjoyed that stuff. And it's starting to hit me why I loved it so much. It felt like...it felt like I had my old friend back.

And it kinda feels that way now.

I wonder if that's one of the other reasons I've kept handling Dad's social media. These small moments, here and gone in seconds, that left me feeling the impact of something from years ago. Something deep down I missed.

I look toward the large windows in the front of the shop bordering the door, peering out into the Old City winter. The snow is coming down a bit heavier now, those mutterings of a big snowstorm hitting during the festival feeling less like whispers and more like shouts. But the looming blanket of white doesn't stop the handful of tourists bustling their way along the auburn brick sidewalks, ducking low against the wind, scarfs fluttering.

Neil's got some ill-advised plants in little old-fashioned test-tube holders and containers lining the sill, and up on the shelves close to the window. It looks like he's trying to propagate a few, in the dead of winter, in a window that's freezing. I can see Mom's shop across the street from where I'm sitting, and I don't know how she doesn't storm over here and fix them out of sheer principal. I make a mental note to say something to him about those, and maybe bring it up with her. I mean, some of them look like sticks he picked up off the sidewalk outside. And it's not going to help Mom's business having succulents on these tables, but a bunch of dead plants on display on the way out.

Sigh.

My phone buzzes again, and there are a string of more messages from folks commenting on Adam's post. It's nice, and I just want to sit here in Franklin Fountain, have some carbonated bubbles tickle my cheeks, and forget about all the pressure weighing down on me.

The brass bell above the Franklin Fountain's frosted glass door chimes loudly, and a family strolls in, a little kid with bright, wide eyes and a big smile. He runs in and grabs the counter, his tiny hands barely reaching it, and one of his parents leans down to scoop him up, a peal of laughter echoing through the soda shop.

Handling all the social, hanging out around his cafés, it's my one big way to stay in my dad's orbit. I see his universe getting bigger and bigger with each conference he goes to, and I feel like I'm just drifting away. I want to be a moon in my family's galaxy.

Not a comet burning bright and disappearing far, far away, screaming for attention.

"Whit!"

I look away from the kid to spot Andrea, Sophie, and Helen

breezing into the shop, a collection of bags hanging from their arms, a mix of purses and shopping totes from the boutiques in the area. Smak Parlour. Vagabond. Scarlett Alley. The three of them sparkle and glitter almost as much as the sequins on their bags, and I try not to let it bother me that they clearly went shopping before meeting up with me here. I've been in Old City all afternoon; they could have just texted me.

I shake it off and smile, anyway.

My girls.

"Hey!" I shout, standing up and motioning them over. I grab an extra empty chair from a table next to me, and the three of them sit down, their assorted bags crinkling and bopping into one another under the seats. Their wooden chairs squeak against the old tile floor of the shop as they all inch in around the table, and all their phones plop down in near unison. Andrea grabs one of those wireless chargers and puts it down, their phones all nestled against it.

"It's been forever!" Helen says, leaning onto the table. "Tell me everything."

"What?" I snort. "You were literally just at my dad's place a few days ago. And Patrick's party?"

"Oh yeah!" Helen laughs, looking at Andrea, who rolls her eyes. "What's good here?"

"I mean, everything," I laugh. How could she forget we just saw each other? I look over at Neil, who is leaning on the countertop expectantly. He shrugs, his hands out, and I smile. "Neil, just three more of these." I shake my Mason jar and he nods, and I turn back to the girls, the sound of glass clinking and pop machines churning in the background. I make a mental note to order an extra one on my way out, since Lily is playing across the street at Mom's shop while I play catchup and make amends with Adam. Definitely gonna owe her. Should probably just order a few for Mom and Ali while I'm at it.

"Trust me, this one is delicious." I tap a nail on my glass. "It's my second—"

"So why did you want to meet here?" Andrea asks, looking around, her eyes narrowed, eyebrows darting down like everything here offends her. "I mean, couldn't we have just met in one of your dad's places?"

"Andrea—" Sophie starts, and Andrea looks back at her, shrugging her shoulders.

"What?" she grumbles. "I mean, they *are* everywhere, right?" She leans back in her chair, shaking her head. "God, you guys must be loaded now."

"I mean, I'm paying for your soda if that's what you're asking," I snort, resisting the urge to roll my eyes, and trying to ignore the feeling brewing in my chest. Trying to steer the conversation away from where I already feel it is heading, where Dana said it was going, and I just don't want to believe it. "And no, not really. There's the one in West Philly, the other out in Camden by Rutgers. Remember the launch party for that one last year?"

"Oh, my God, it was so wild," Sophie says, laughing and swatting at me. "I still can't believe your dad got The Early November to play."

"Right?" I laugh. "I kept begging and I think he only did it for us."

"Yeah, that was cool," Andrea says, looking down at her phone, and then over at Helen. She nods at her, and then

Helen nods at her, and there's something unspoken going on here, and I'm not sure what this dance is, but it feels familiar.

I might not know the moves, but I can feel the rhythm.

I exhale. I see Dana in my head, I see Adam in that hallway, the girls laughing at him, me joining in, and my heart breaks. All the time they've spent in my dad's cafés, since they took off a little over two years ago, peppering me with questions. Never about how I was doing, but about opportunities. How our friendship took a swift turn into more about what I could do for them, like so many acquaintances at school.

The pause. The silence. It's saying a lot. And I've had it.

"All right, out with it," I scoff, just as Neil drops off the sodas. The three glasses coast onto the table, each of them finished off with a heavy dollop of their made-in-house whipped cream. Before I can even think of saying anything about mine missing some, he drops a large spoonful on my already half-drained glass. I look up at him and smile, and he just nods his head, walking back to the soda bar.

Helen dips one of her long fingernails into the whipped cream and scoops a bit out, placing it in her mouth.

"Wow, this *is* good," she says. "Do they make this here, the cream? So...how long have you been coming to—"

"I don't want to keep playing this game." I slide my chair out and cross my arms. I've been through this enough at school, over the entire course of my dad's startup career, and I've humored it enough. Parents who brought their kids over for playdates with Lily, only to hang back to "pick his brain" instead of leaving, while Lily and whatever kid sat staring at tablets or the television.

I used to be able to see it coming from a mile away.

From a fake smile away.

But for some reason I've been blind to this the whole time. To them. And only since Adam came stumbling back into my life in this strange way, that I've started seeing through it all. Sometimes it takes something genuine to spot the fake.

"What do you *want*?"

Helen looks at the other two, and Andrea sighs loudly. Sophie just shakes her head.

"Look," Andrea starts, huffing again. "It's just…senior year is half over, and none of us landed an internship yet and…" She looks at the other two again, looking like she wants support or something.

"You're on your own here," Sophie scoffs at Andrea, and then looks right at me. "I hate this idea. I didn't want anything to do with this."

"Ugh, fine," Andrea grumbles. "We were all just hoping you could put in a good word with your dad, maybe?"

"You two were," Sophie presses. "Not me."

"Oh, like you're innocent in all this," Andrea snaps, and Sophie deflates a little. I glance over at her, and she looks away.

"Come on, you guys," Helen says, seemingly trying to soothe whatever is happening right now. "Look, his cafés are all over the place now, right? How many are there in town, five? He's got to have *something*."

"Pretty sure I *just* said he only had—" I start.

"It looks so good on college applications," Andrea huffs before I can bring up the fact that there are two. Just two. Again. How are they unaware of this? They've been there for the first one taking off and were *literally* there when the second one opened. "The whole high school internship thing, especially with Drexel, and we just didn't—"

"And what is it—" I reach out and grab my soda, pausing for a long sip, for drama; let them be uncomfortable "—you think you're qualified to do?"

Andrea and Helen look to one another.

"Well, I mean, I want to major in marketing, so…maybe something with social media? Like you! You're so good at it!" Helen ventures, reaching for her phone. "I shoot a lot of video and—"

"You couldn't even be bothered to respond to my DMs the other day," I huff, inching my chair back in and glaring at her from across the table. "How would you possibly handle what I manage to handle? That entire blowup with the arcade? Pissed-off customers sending me messages in all caps like I ruined their life when their coffee order got mixed up? People furious that we don't serve dinner or that we dare to close at a reasonable time?

"All I get is attacked by people. On all sides. All day."

And that's all they do.

And that's all…we did.

At school, making snarky comments about other kids.

And I hate this. These realizations washing over me, how I've gone along with it for so long, and I'm stuck with a shitty group of friends that I don't even want to hang out with anymore, a family at home that only sees me when I work hard enough to earn it, and old friends so distant that I missed how much they grew up without me.

"It's just…with Patrick and—" Helen stammers out, her eyes flitting to Sophie.

"Oh, my God, you two," Sophie interjects, groaning, putting her head in her hands.

"Whit, I'm sorry," Andrea says, reaching out across the table.

"No, don't *Whit* me," I snap, swatting her hand away. "What possible excuse could you have for all this? And *Patrick*? Really? Do you have any idea how many people ask me about this kind of stuff, especially over the last year when the new place opened? At school? People I don't even know, asking for part-time jobs or internships or whatever. Our *history teacher* asked me if I could get him an interview the other day."

"Mr. Perdue?" Helen laughs, as though we're going to joke around about it.

"Yes, *Helen*." I glare at her, and her smile fades. "I can't... I can't believe the two of you would..." I grit my teeth. "And after *Patrick*, just show up with..." I shake my head. "You even went to Smak Parlour without me. That's *my* place. I introduced all of you to that shop."

Sophie looks down at the backs of the chairs, bags hanging, and grimaces.

"It was just...on the way..." she stammers.

"It's across the street!" I slap the table and point at the window, the pink shop clearly in view, right next to my mom's place. The glass Mason jars clink around from the force, a little bit of soda spilling onto the surface. The few people in the shop glance over at our table and I exhale. I fold my hands, like I'm in a meeting, which is basically what this is now. They want business? Let's do business. "Is there anything else you wanted to talk about?"

"I... We..." Helen stammers, looking to the other girls,

and then digs around in one of her bags. She pulls out a little white paper bag with gold leaf stamped on the front of it,
bits of fluffy tissue paper billowing over the sides. She nudges
it cautiously across the table. "I remembered how much you
like them."

A smile twinges at the corner of my mouth and I push it
back down. I can tell from the calligraphy-scripted gold K
that it's from my mom's shop. They must have stopped there
on the way over. I wonder if they said hi to Lily.

I gently pull the tissue paper out, and there, tucked inside
all of it, is a very dead, very brown, air plant. Like, crisp to
the point I wonder if someone set it on fire. It's the kind of
plant that should normally be all shades of dark greens and
blues, maybe a bit of purple. Not the color of burnt toast.

I glance up at the girls.

"It was on sale?" Helen ventures, shrugging and wincing.

I grab the little plant and throw it away from the table, but
any attempts at a dramatic gesture are ruined by the fact that
it weighs nothing, and just falls to the old-fashioned black-
and-white tile floor, landing barely a few feet away from me.
I know where she got it. From my mom's discard bin that she
leaves outside the store by the door, much like how the used
bookstore down the block has withered cardboard boxes of
out-of-date textbooks and computer software guides as give-
aways out front.

This dead plant is the used bookstore Windows 95 User
Guide of plants.

"Hey!" Helen shouts. "Jesus, Whit. What do you want
from us?"

"How about *how are you*, Whitney? How have things been?

Are you still upset after the breakup? Yes, by the way!" I feel a warmth prickling over my skin and it's taking everything in me not to cry right now.

"Oh…" Helen's expression sinks. "I… Hey, I didn't know it was bothering you that much." She looks over at Sophie, who turns away. "If I'd known—"

"I told you! I told all of you!"

"Well, maybe I would have—"

"Have come here *without* some kind of agenda?" I snap. I get up from the table and grab my soda and start gathering my things.

"Whit, hey, come on, you don't have to leave—" Sophie starts.

"Oh no. I do. I really, *really* do." The words crack out of me, but I feel the entirety of my mouth shaking like I'm about to start sobbing, and I'm not going to let them see that happen. "I feel like part of me expected this from these two, but you, Soph?" As I get my favorite white jean jacket on, which is *from* Smak Parlour, the same place we all got our matching jackets from, I notice the growlers on the shelf across from where Neil makes his drinks. Big, dark amber-colored glass bottles meant to fill with like, a gallon of cold brew coffee, artisan beer, and—

Helen scoops some more whipped cream with her finger, and Sophie glares at her.

"What?" Helen asks, smacking her lips.

I grab my glass jar off the table, and I take one of the growlers off the shelf, where it sits with soda-making supplies and fancy books and tools for making ice cream, floats, old-timey candy, and the like. I set it down on the table a little too hard, pop it open, the rubber stopper making a satisfying *plunk* as it comes uncorked.

"What are you—" Helen starts.

I take my glass jar and start pouring the soda in, and promptly take the three sodas away from the girls, the jars clinking against the tall glass growler.

"Hey—" Sophie moves to protest, and I just glare at her. There's a pause, a beat. "Whit, we're still your friends. I'm still your friend."

I think about what I saw, her taking Patrick's hand outside my dad's café. That flash of...something, that I'm still not quite sure I witnessed. I push it away; there's just no way she would have done that to me, but I still don't want to be here with any one of them.

I fill the growler up, one by one, as the girls squirm in their seats. It's not a fast process. It's tedious. I have to pour each one fairly carefully in a little stream, and even then, some soda spills out due to the whipped cream blocking the pour, leaving the surface of our table pink and white and probably sticky. I can feel the eyes of other people in here on me, and I don't care.

This place is mine. The pop. The glass tables. The tiled floor.

"You don't deserve this place," I say through gritted teeth. But I know what I really mean, even if they don't. They don't deserve *me*.

I seal the growler and turn around to Neil at the counter, who is staring at me with the most bemused expression on his face, his tight-lipped grin disappearing into his beard.

I set it down in front of him.

"Sorry for the mess." I pull a couple bills out of my wallet and place them on the counter.

"No, no, that was hilarious," he says.

"Hey!" Helen shouts from the table.

"You ain't paying," Neil snips back at her, and grins at me. "Get going. Tell your mom I said hi. I'll take care of the table. And the uh, *mess* over there." He says it in a way that I know he's talking about the girls, not the soda, and it gets a smirk out of me.

I put the growler under my arm and can feel it sticking to the fabric of my jacket, and make my way to the door... but stop to scoop up the dried-up air plant, tucking it gently into my jacket pocket. Maybe I can save it, but if Mom had it in her bin, the chances are unlikely. I turn around once I get to the exit. The girls are muttering amongst themselves, taking out their phones, as Neil flips a rag over his shoulder. He looks up at me.

The girls don't.

I walk out into the Philadelphia winter, cold and alone. I see Mom's boutique across the street, next to Smak Parlour and other shops. I did promise Lily a soda, so I guess a growler full of three of them will work, even if there is whipped cream mixed up inside. The dog park, lined in old bricks and black iron fences, that kicks off right at the edge of the stores, is empty, snow starting to pile up. I see Lily dash by Krumm's storefront window, and I imagine Ali is getting pretty tired from chasing her in there. I make my way across the street, a growler of strawberry crème soda under my arm and a dead plant in my pocket. I hope they have cups in the stock room.

I catch a reflection in the large plate-glass window of the

shop, the large K glimmering gold, and turn around to spot Patrick walking into the Franklin Fountain.

I grit my teeth and power walk back across the street, my shoes slipping a little as I do, the road getting slightly slushy. I swing the door to the Franklin Fountain open, just in time to spot Patrick giving Sophie a quick kiss hello before pulling out the seat I was just in, and sitting down across from her. He glances down at the table, all the soda spilled and whipped cream floating in it and looks a bit puzzled. Neil is making his way over with the rag.

Patrick looks up at me and I swear, all the color drains from his face.

"Whitney." He gets up, his wood chair squeaking loudly against the floor.

All three girls turn in their seats to look at me. Sophie looks like someone just punched her in the stomach.

I'm not sure what jars me more. The fact that *all* of them have been hiding this from me, or the fact that this has clearly been going on for way longer than just now. That handhold outside my dad's was…two days after we broke up? Was he texting with her, all those times he was hiding his phone from me? Outside his house, when he dumped me? Now here they are, kissing in one of my places, one of our places, barely a week later.

Sophie starts to stand up, and I hold a hand out, shaking my head.

"You're not worth it," I stammer out. I glance up at Neil, who looks at me with a devastated face. I sniffle, shaking my hair, and exhale.

I'm out.

CHAPTER 9
Adam

"The game of pinball, just like a relationship, evolves.
And has evolved. From the original wooden sets that
barely did a thing to the massive electronic machines
we see today. The difference? Moving parts. Things
that churn. Originally, it was mostly up to us to move
them. But as the machines got more sophisticated,
they moved along with us. Everyone, and everything,
has the potential to move and change."

–THE ART AND ZEN OF PINBALL REPAIR
BY JAMES WATTS

I lost track of how many times I walked by the plant boutique
yesterday. I wasn't sure if I was looking for Whitney to be in
the shop, or for her not to be there. One moment I was peeking in through the glass window to see if she was inside, to
convince her to come back to the arcade, to talk some more,
and the next I was running away because I didn't want to be

spotted by her mom or her partner. Why do I want to both
see someone and avoid them completely at the same time?

All of it, that whole morning and afternoon, her in the arcade, fussing with the plants, us talking about that summer…

For the first time in a while, I'm feeling the way a Tom
Petty song sounds. Light and full of hope.

The Old City Winter Festival is this week, in just another
day, and it's one more chance to see Whitney, to talk some
more, and… I can barely see outside.

I slide one of the Heart albums out of the wood crates
in my room, alongside Dad's collection. *Bad Animals*, with
that "Alone" song on it. I suck through my teeth and shake
my head, sliding it back in, and despite myself, laugh a little.
Freaking Chris.

I peek between the blinds in my room to our tiny yard,
which is absolutely filling with snow. The storm is just about
here, and it's wild to think that it *isn't* here yet, and this is
just a sampling of what's going to hit, especially with the festival kicking off, and the whole neighborhood gearing up to
get things ready.

If anyone can even *get* to the arcade after the snow. Philly
isn't exactly a master of clearing its narrow historic streets
during snowstorms. I check social media, and it seems that
every boutique and restaurant is still pushing full speed ahead
with festival prep, no matter the weather.

Old City Winter Fest:
Stay strong, Old City! We're still on! While a few shops are canceling
in preparation for the storm, almost everyone is staying open and
hitting the snow-covered streets this Thursday! Dress warm! We will.

Revolution House:

The festival is upon us! Don't worry, we're planning to bring our heat lamps down from our rooftop dining area and are sharing them with our community! Let's do this! We'll see you on Thursday!

National Mechanics:

Thanks for that, friends! We'll be out, serving our trademarked popcorn chicken and fried mac and cheese balls.

Kale Yeah!:

And we'll be there with a healthy alternative! To-go salads in biodegradable cups will be available, with forks you can plant in the springtime

National Mechanics:

Technically all forks are forks you can plant.

Kale Yeah!:

These ones are compostable and have seeds inside!

National Mechanics:

It was…a joke… I'll see you there Britt.

I laugh and roll my eyes at the battling restaurants while digging through my dresser.

I pick out some clothes that feel like they'll be at least reasonably comfortable while darting in and out of the arcade, getting everything set up with Chris, from the bitter cold to the warmth inside. An REO Speedwagon sweatshirt, jeans, my boots… Dad's jacket. I know, I know, the leather jacket in a snowstorm isn't sensible, but I don't know. It doesn't feel right wearing anything else today.

I toss another sweatshirt into my backpack, as well as a few pairs of socks just in case, and make my way down the stairs.

Mom is in the kitchen, sipping on a cup of coffee, dressed in her sweatpants and a hoodie.

"Well, well," she says, putting the mug down. "Seems like you and a certain childhood friend are on the up and up again." She grins and holds her phone up. She's on the arcade's feed and I roll my eyes. "What happened?"

She puts her elbows on the table and puts her head in her hands, tilting it to the side, like she's ready to get the best gossip ever. Like one of those women in those reality shows she loves so much.

"We just...talked." I shrug, making my way into the kitchen. I dig around in the cabinets and snatch a Pop Tart, stuffing it into my jacket. "I don't know, I think we're good? I think."

"That's good." She nods. "It'll make the festival a lot less weird, for once."

"Whatever," I scoff.

She looks down into her coffee cup and then at her phone, and sighs a little.

"What is it?" I ask, nodding.

"Nothing. We'll um...we'll talk about it later." She looks up and smiles, but I keep staring. "It's nothing. Are you heading to the arcade?"

"Yeah, me and Chris are going to do some last-minute prep, dust off the tent and the machines." I shrug, trying not to let the whole *we'll talk later* comment work at my anxiety. That's the worst kind of response. It's one of those "I'm not upset, I'm just disappointed" bits of Mom dialogue, only this one usually has some kind of devastating surprise at the end of it.

"Good, good." She nods. "Make sure you hit up the bank and get a lot of quarters, in case the snow gets too intense? I don't want us leaving the panels on the machines open for free play, and end up with them full of snow, in the event the bank doesn't open the day of the festival." She smiles and sighs. "I'll be up there a little later. I've got some meetings."

"Meetings?" I ask. "Isn't school out?"

"Yeah, it's just…" She waves it off. "Don't worry about it. I'll see you there. Oh! Wait."

She gets up and walks into the living room, returning with a few small boxes. She has a confused look on her face as she hands them to me, but I can't help but smile.

"And what are these?" my mom asks, nudging them before sitting back down. "They showed up this morning in the mail."

I peel the tape off the boxes, popping them open. One has a bundle of LED lights inside, the other a ton of batteries and magnets. I dig around the LEDs, flipping them about, see what colors came in the miscellaneous bunch of lights that I ordered online. Turns out if you order in bulk, you can get nearly 500 of these little bulbs for ten bucks. The batteries were a bit more expensive, but if it'll make the inside of the arcade look cool when we get back from the winter hiatus, it'll be worth it.

"I learned something new at the makerspace with Chris." I start putting one of the LED throwies together, attaching a little bulb to the battery. I look around for some tape, and dig some out of a drawer in the kitchen.

"What are you doing—?"

"Hold on, almost there," I say, walking back. The tape

wraps around the bulb, battery, and magnet, and blinks on. I hold it out to my mom and turn around, tossing it onto the refrigerator. It hits the steel with a satisfying *plink*, sticking there, and I turn back, shrugging.

"Figure it might look nice, a few of these on the ceiling in the arcade."

"You're going to Drexel," she says, reaching out and messing with my hair. I shirk away, laughing. "You and your circuits and electronics…your dad woulda loved that."

"I don't think these are gonna get me a scholarship, but we'll see." I get up and awkwardly give her a hug. "Love you, see you later."

I hustle toward the door, unloading all the bulbs and batteries and magnets into a tote bag, when she shouts after me.

"Wear a warmer jacket!"

I turn around and see her grinning at me.

We both know that's not gonna happen.

CHAPTER 10
Whitney

Growing up, every once in a while, before he had any kind of success and when we had the money to spare, my dad would take the whole family to this bowling alley in Northern Liberties. North Bowl, they called it. The entire interior was lightly themed around *The Big Lebowski*, a movie my dad made me and Nick watch, insisting anything by the Coen Brothers was a masterpiece.

He wasn't wrong, but that's not the point.

I remembered picking up our shoes and dropping them back off, and how the hip-looking people behind the rental counter would spray them down with some mysterious disinfectant, while still appearing impossibly cool with their tattoos, dyed hair, piercings, and rebellious T-shirts. This was Northern Liberties, after all. A neighborhood where looking hip was a requirement. Part of your lease, I think.

I can't help but think about that while spraying down the keyboards and computer mice in my dad's café right now, taking them over to a space behind the register, giving them a good once-over. I take a few Clorox cloths and wipe them down, all around, being careful not to get any of the exposed electronics. The ports and all that.

I put them up on the counter and watch as someone who works for my dad, some college kid named Michael with short curly hair who seems absolutely miserable to be here, scoops them up one by one, taking his sweet time back to the tables to place them on their stands. Like each one is a boulder and he's Sisyphus or something.

I smell like Lemon Pledge and look nothing like the people I grew up sighing over at that bowling alley. And no one is looking at me with that kind of awe here.

With the last mouse wiped down, I take it myself over to one of the tables. I catch my dad walking out of his office, and he turns and smiles at me, waving. I give him a nod. There's this twisting feeling in my chest, being here now. After Sophie, Helen, Andrea, Patrick…

It's like, this place is who I am to them.

And I'm more. I know it.

And it feels so wildly lonely.

It's the day before the Old City Winter Festival, Mom's big crowning achievement every year. I can't wait to get down there, and… I can't stop thinking about the plants at Adam's arcade. I wonder if he's taking care of them, or if they are just withering up in the growing cold. If he'll take them home with him over the holiday closures. Mom does that every year, when she wraps up for the holidays, bringing home the most fragile blooms. It's silly; it's just been a few days and I know they are the toughest plants out there but…

I don't know. Even the tough ones need love.

And what if he just lets them die?

Just, forgets about them.

Me?

I put the mouse down on one of the charging stands and hear a spritzing noise. I glance up to see Michael spraying one of the headsets on the table, the mist clearly getting all over the plants I have tucked into the grooves and cracks of that particular one. I bolt over and snatch it out of his hand.

"Hey!" he shouts, glaring at me.

"We clean the headsets *in the back*," I grumble, taking the headset off the stand. "If you spray out here, you can get it in people's drinks, or mess with the plants."

"The plants? Who cares?" he snaps, grabbing for the headset.

"Excuse me?" I shout, jerking it away. "I care. You're fired."

I'm not going to let anyone step all over, or just spray all over, what I care about. It's not just about the plants. Carelessly poisoning them is poisoning *me*.

"What?" He scoffs out a laugh and looks over to the other side of the café. I look over my shoulder and spot my dad walking over.

"What's, um…what's going on?" he asks, nodding at me and Michael. I cross my arms, the headset dangling from one of my hands.

"She said I'm fired because I sprayed the plants," Michael grumbles. He sounds like a child.

"Whitney, come on," my dad sighs. "Michael, go take care of some of the tables in the back there." He mutters something under his breath and walks away. "How are things going with—" he looks off, like he's searching for something, and then snaps his fingers "—Adam? The kid at the arcade that you're always fighting with online."

"We're not really fighting anymore?" I shrug.

"Oh." He smiles, scratching his chin. "Well, that's nice. That's good to know."

"Why?" I scoff.

"I just...want you two getting along again." He shrugs. "I remember the two of you, thick as thieves."

"I wouldn't go that far," I snort.

"I don't know, I would." He smiles. "The old house in South Philly, climbing the trees in FDR Park? When are you heading down to help with your mother's...thing?" He asks this like the words themselves taste bad. "The snow is getting pretty bad outside. Little worried about getting a rideshare or the subway."

"Soon... Could you, not talk about it like that?" I ask.

"Oh, come on, Whit, I'm just—"

"Being unfair," I interrupt, and he glowers at me. "I'm gonna head down in a little while. Do you think you'll come to the festival this year?"

"Probably, yeah." He shrugs. "I've got some meetings down that way later. Want me to pick you up?"

"Sure. And I'll make sure to post some photos and updates from there, showing our support." Meetings. How is he having meetings on a day like today, with all the snow piling up outside? Who still wants to chat with him?

He gives me a look and shakes his head.

"You know, a few of your friends applied for internships here," he says, his eyes darting around like he's searching for something. "Helen, I think? I'm surprised you didn't tell me they were interested. Aren't they your best friends? If you put a good word in, I'm happy to try to find something for that bunch."

"Well, not really." I shrug. "Not anymore."

"Oh?" He grabs a seat and sits down. "What happened?"

He's looking up at me with this…genuine concern on his face, and all it does is make me feel heated and angry.

"Do you…really care?" I ask.

"Of course I do!" he exclaims. "How could you ask—?"

"Dad, you…" I sigh. "I mean, I do all this work for this place. All this work. I pour my heart into all our online stuff, stress myself to death over bits of drama, and it barely registers on your radar. *I* barely register. And I just thought…" I grit my teeth and shake my head, not wanting him to see me cry in all this. "I just thought if I made enough noise you'd notice."

"Hm?" my dad mutters out, and I blink back some oncoming tears, shaking my head, only to see him on his phone. "I'm sorry, what was that, sweetheart?"

Fuck.

"Nothing," I turn away and mutter out, and take the long way around the café to get to the front door, arching around the entire space to avoid him seeing my face.

"Whit?" he shouts across the café.

"I'll see you in Old City." I pull my jacket off a hook at the front door, threading my arms through, and make my way out.

I only think I'm going to die once or twice on the rideshare from West Philadelphia all the way down to Old City. The streets are coated white the entire way, even at the roundabout that circles City Hall in Center City, the snow crunching under the car's tires. The people walking throughout the city are dressed in a mix of thick, massive coats and jeans and T-shirts, as though they were outside and the snow just dropped, an absolute surprise.

Old City looks like a slice of winter magic.

A huge "Old City Winter Festival" banner hangs over Market Street near Third, the entire area closed off. It's honestly a shock every year that my mom is able to finagle this with the Old City District, shutting down the intersection of one of the biggest streets in Philadelphia. But I think the business and the local government administration types need this, more than anyone needs to hop onto Columbus Boulevard for an easier route to hit the IKEA.

There are people milling about the street, the road coated in snow and footprints, multicolored scarves and peacoats dotting the snow-covered landscape. I hop out of the car and make my way toward Mom's shop. White twinkle lights are already on and beaming, shimmering from streetlamps and off various buildings. It's going to look gorgeous when the sun is completely gone, and the festival kicks off.

Some of the larger restaurants and boutiques are already getting their festival tables and tents ready to go. A few even have heat lamps out, chained up to iron gates or the bars on nearby windows. A seafood joint a few doors down from my mom's boutique has a sign promising five-dollar "crab claw fingers," and I'm completely unsure of what that might be. Chicken fingers, but crab? Some of the girls who work at Smak Parlour are out in front of their shop, working on their trademarked Fashion Truck, a food truck that's been converted into a mini clothing boutique. They're loading outfits in and out, and I see a few people from the Omoi Zaka shop, a Japanese stationery and lifestyle boutique, helping them out. Every single time I'm in their store, it takes everything in me not to purchase an enormous Pusheen plushie and this might be the year I finally give in.

I catch Mom and Ali fussing with a large wooden table under a bright green tent, right in front of their shop. As I get closer, my mom stops what she's doing and smirks at me.

"Seems like the moss worked?" my mom asks, crossing her arms as I get closer.

"Stop it," I snort and make my way under their tent. It's surprisingly warm, and I spot a portable heater at the back. "How's setup going?"

"Not bad," Ali says, looking down at the table, hands on her hips. "Couple people even swung by to buy a few terrariums early. I'm getting really worried about the snow, though."

"It doesn't seem *that* bad." I look out over the street, the snow coming down a bit harder.

"It's pretty bad," my mom retorts. "Are you…gonna go say hi?"

"To…" It takes me a second. "Oh." I smile, struggling to hide it. "Yeah, yeah, I'm gonna head over in a bit. I wanted to see how you two were doing first."

If I was being completely honest with the two of them, which I think they'd enjoy a bit too much, I'm trying to delay it. There's something here, in all of this. In this renewed connection. Is it something real? Am I just latching on to it, in the wake of me and Patrick and everything with the girls?

Am I opening myself up to get hurt all over again, from someone I've unintentionally spent time hurting, and vice versa?

It's a lot to process, and I'd rather sit here with the plants for a minute longer.

"Well, we're fine," Ali says, shrugging. "Ah, hold on a second." She darts around the table and I peek out of the tent to catch her heading into the shop. There's someone in there behind the register, probably a hire just for the festival week, and Ali quickly hurries back, something bundled up in her arms.

"Just a little something, for being brave," she says, grinning. I look at her and to Mom, who shrugs, and take the package. It's one of the Krumm's bags, white with a gold K, and I peek inside to spot one of those silver dollar cacti I was swooning over just the other day.

"Oh no," I say, shaking my head. "No way. These are too expensive." I try pushing the bag back, but my mom reaches out and joins Ali in pressing it toward my chest. "You guys," I groan. "You know Nick or Lily will just end up killing it at home or something."

"Well, we'll see." My mom shrugs, patting the bag. "If those two cause trouble, you can just keep it at the house in Manayunk. See it on the weekends. Or you could keep it at your dad's café."

I think about Michael and his renegade sprayer.

"Yeah, I don't think so," I snort, taking the bag. "Thank you. I'll take good care of her."

"Hey," my mom says, reaching out and grabbing my shoulders. "It's time you start taking good care of you, okay?"

I smile, if only to hide the wince of pain that's nibbling away at my heart. I know. I know I should start being a little more selfish, but in the good way. The way that prioritizes me, instead of what other people are telling me is a priority. Like how Dad pushes his café and the events and all of that ahead of anything we're doing. And that maybe it's okay to want to be seen for more than what I can do for people.

"I'm trying to learn how," I manage to get out.

I reach out and give Ali a hug in addition to my mom, and duck out of the tent, strolling down the brick sidewalk toward Old City Pinball. The sun has definitely dipped a bit more, the sky above Penn's Landing turning hues of purples and maroon, the twinkle lights on the streetlights all the more arresting.

I take my phone out and snap a few pictures.

West Philly eSports:
Ducked out of West Philadelphia to help friends get set up at Old City Winter Festival. Hi everyone!

> **Krumm's Boutique:**
> It was nice seeing you!—Mom.

> **Old City Pinball:**
> Hi!

Old City Pinball: You're here? Whitney?

West Philly eSports: Hi. Mind if I stop by?

Old City Pinball: You'd better.

Old City Pinball: ☺

Oh, my God.

Is he…flirting with me? Is this flirting? When we were

younger and friends would tease me, when Nick or my parents would joke about us, I always dismissed it. There was no way. Adam Stillwater? He's my best friend, not possible.

And then suddenly he wasn't my best friend.

And now suddenly he's…this.

And suddenly…it's possible.

I clutch my phone to my chest and look ahead toward Second Street.

I'm coming.

I hustle down the sidewalk, weaving between curious tourists making their way up toward the tents, a bit too early for the real thing. The dog park, which used to host an ice-skating rink in previous years, is just packed full of snow, a bundle of kids waging war in the bricked-in square space. I wonder if they had to cancel bringing in the temporary rink due to the snow, or what. It usually got set up way in advance of the festival, so I'm guessing no ice-skating this year.

For all the people moving up and down Second, stopping at the shops there and then shuffling up Market toward the booths, there are a sizable amount descending into the SEPTA station, off to take the train to whatever neighborhoods they live in. The snow *is* getting heavier, and I wonder if all of these people got out of work early or something, heading home before the trains and buses inevitably slow down. Or, since this is Philly, stop completely.

The brick wall that the Old City Pinball mural is painted on is dusted with snow, bits of white settling into the cracks and bumps. It makes the multicolored map of Philadelphia, with all the pinball kitsch, look like the surface of a Christmas playset. I press my hand against the freezing cold wall, flecks of snow coming off as I trail along toward the entrance, and watch as patches fall off in large chunks, revealing the mural once more.

There's a tent closer toward the door, and what I'm guessing are pinball machines, covered up by large tarps, underneath it. Some kind of small table setup is at the end. I pass the table and the protected cabinets and peer into the arcade. It's a sharp contrast to the outside in there, cold and fading light outside, and the warm light of video games and house lights in there. I think I can make out some people in the back, over by the snack bar.

I grab the handle to the door and tug, but it's not opening.

I look back in, and back at the door, and…just completely lose my nerve.

What am I even doing here?

I'm just gonna mess all this up, the way I did with Patrick, focusing on the wrong thing instead of the right person. Or at least, who I thought was the right person. I move to grab the door handle one more time, stop, and turn away, walking under the tent to avoid the gusts of wind and snowdrifts.

I wonder how long I'll have to wait to grab a rideshare, or the SEPTA, back across town. I pull out my phone, request a Lyft, and it's going to take nearly half an hour to get here. I groan out loud and debate heading back to Mom's shop, but I really don't want to get roasted for not going to the arcade, and going inside the arcade… Oh, my God, I hate all of this.

I glance over at one of the covered pinball games and flip the tarp up a little, to get a look at what's underneath. I can't really make out much, some weird alien-looking things and a spaceship, I think. My phone buzzes, and hopefully, another driver has taken over, and will get me home faster, where I can be alone with all these feelings.

But instead, it's a message from Twitter coming through.

Old City Pinball: You ARE here.

I gasp and turn around to spot Adam, grinning with his phone in his hand. He's got some... I don't know, wires and lights or something in his other hand, which he promptly crams in his pockets. Part of me wants to...hug him? I think? I even feel myself move forward a little bit, but I shirk back, and just smile and laugh at him. He strolls over, smirking.

"Hey." I grin and give him a little fake punch in the shoulder. Oh, God.

I just want the arcade to collapse, and the walls to fall on top of me.

"Hey yourself," he says, smiling still. He's wearing some thick, vintage sweatshirt that...hasn't aged well. It's gray in a way that tells me it *maybe* used to be black, with the name REO Speedwagon on it. I'm guessing it's a band, but I'm not sure I want to ask. "Ah, I see you've met the worst game in the arcade." He laughs, stepping around me. He unfurls the tarp, revealing the whole machine. The spaceship and aliens that I spotted on the corner is really just the start, and the odd sci-fi art sprawls up the length of it, in shades of blue, green, and black. It almost hurts my eyes.

And then on the top, a familiar actor holding some kind of weird gun, and...his hair in locs? With some kind of metal headdress on?

"What is this?" I snort, not quite over John Travolta looking like...that.

"First, let's get inside," he says, flapping the tarp back over it, and securing it to the bottom of the machine. "It's way too cold." I follow him into the arcade, and it's just an absolute blast of warmth inside, just as cozy as it looked from behind the front door.

"Can I take your jacket?" he asks, holding out a hand.

"It's okay. It's part of my look," I laugh, pulling it closer. "I should have worn something warmer, but I spend so much time inside my dad's place, I almost never bother."

"Yeah, I feel you," he says. "I wore my leather jacket here."

"I am unsurprised."

He smiles for a beat, and then looks back into the arcade. "Can I show you around? I mean, it's been a while since you've really been in here."

"Christine Loy's birthday party." It comes at me in a flash. The bucket of quarters on the snack bar, his dad dishing out a seemingly unlimited amount of chicken fingers and slightly-too-squishy French fries. Everyone huddled around the *Stranger Things* machine, talking about the show.

"I remember," he says, digging his foot into the floor a little. "It was the last big event with most of our class before... well, before things changed. Here, with Dad, with you, too, I guess. What was that, in November?"

"Yeah." I nod, agreeing with more than just the month.

"Well..." Adam clears his throat after a beat. "You already saw the entrance, I suppose. So, um..." He laughs. "It's hard because I see this place every day and don't really think about it. But a lot of the newer games line the front of the arcade. We keep the older, fancier ones in the back here. The last thing we wanted was for a fight to tumble in from one of the Old City bars and lose a rare machine close to the door."

"And what's the story with that one?" I nod back at the door. "Outside."

"I hate it," he scoffs. "So much. But it gets a lot of gawkers, and the guys from the comic shop were insisting we bring it out. So we keep it up here with a lot of the other games released in the '90s and early 2000s. My dad found it at a flea market, if you can believe that, and made me and Mom watch the movie on a bad movie night. It doesn't even work, but people take so many photos of it." He waves me over, and we walk along the machines that line the wall. I run my hand over the glass surfaces of the games that aren't surrounded by people, and watch the various lights illuminating the side of his face, casting different hues against his tan skin. A flash of purple, a bit of blue, a splash of pink.

"Which one is your favorite?" I ask, stopping at the *Stranger Things* cabinet that's a little farther from the door than the rest. I take a picture of it and snap a few more of the machines around the space. Memories from that party float back, and I have this vague memory of his dad giving us this talk about it, how there were only a few hundred? He made such a big deal over it, and Adam's mom came over and dragged his dad away, back to get everyone fried snacks.

Adam looks around the arcade, like he's considering carefully, and then turns to me, a little smile on his face.

"Come on."

We walk by a few more machines, heading back toward the entrance; there's a *Die Hard* one and a *Matrix* machine, all bright green and black, and we reach a beaten-up red door at the end of the building. He tugs on it a lot before taking a step back, his hands on his hips.

"What is it?" I ask.

"Eh, it's the cold," he grumbles, walking across the arcade to the snack bar. He ducks behind there and pops back up after a loud clang echoes through the space. He's got a crowbar in his hand. "Some of the doors in this place swell up from the cold and get stuck." He wedges it into a spot on the door that looks practically banged up.

"I see this happens often."

"You wouldn't believe it." He wiggles the bar around and gives it a good pry, and the door swings open, hitting the wall opposite us with a bang, a small dark room in front of us. He pats the wall inside and flicks something, and bright fluorescent lights illuminate the small room with a pop, flickering a little before beaming. I blink my eyes to adjust to them, coming in from the dimly lit arcade to this space, as he drops the crowbar on the floor.

"Whoa," I whisper.

It's some kind of workshop, a bit of a disaster of electronics, metal pieces, lightbulbs, and circuitry. There's a big workshop table covered in wires and scraps, drawers upon drawers that are overflowing with things I don't recognize. There are some of those lights he packed in his pockets, scattered about and mixed in with tape and batteries.

I've never seen this space before. I don't even think I knew it was here, back when we were kids.

"*This* is my favorite." He nods at an incomplete-looking machine on the right. Much like the workshop, it's got parts all over it. There's no glass surface, only a few lights, but it's packed full of Philadelphia...kitsch, maybe? I don't know what the word is, but there's a lot of silly nods to the town on it, like you'd see on a Starbucks coffee mug in a Philly shop.

Pretzels, water ice containers, a big Liberty Bell, mixed in with tools scattered on the surface.

"What is it?" I ask, leaning forward to peek in a bit more. He bends down a little next to me, that scent of cedar and vanilla washing over me, and my heart pounds in my chest.

"Here." He reaches in, nudging a few parts away from the center, revealing more of the art on the surface. "My dad wanted to make a Philadelphia pinball machine that was all about our home. Maybe shop it around someday. There *is* a Philly-themed machine already. Kinda. It's called the *Liberty Bell* and it's from the '70s or '80s and…"

He stops, looking at me.

"What?" I ask.

"No, nothing, it's just…" He laughs. "You're like, actually listening to my rambles about old pinball machines and I'm not exactly used to that. Chris made me get on social media to share all that stuff. Him and my mom were getting a bit tired of it."

"I mean, you listened to me when I rambled about my plants." I shrug. "It's interesting."

"Thanks." He smiles. "But…uh, yeah. So he's got a bunch of landmarks in here, some art here on the back glass. That's where the like, big art for most games are, and the interactive lights and messages. Hoping one day it'll be done, and I can put it out there for people to try."

"Do you fix other machines in here?" I take a step toward the workshop table, rubbing my hand over the surface. I pluck a little, I think it's a resistor—I learned that much from science fair experiments as a kid—up and look at it between my fingertips. I can't help but feel… I don't know, sad, over the idea that his favorite game in here is an unfinished broken one he can't even play, left behind by his dad. Something about that feels devastating, and it doesn't seem like he even realizes it.

"I mean, I try to," he huffs, walking over and leaning against the table. He brushes a few bits of electronics off to the side, placing them in a little box, and slides it against the wall. "It gets tricky sometimes. Some of these games, they're twenty, thirty years old. Sometimes they're older than some of the people who come in to play them. And the parts, especially when it's something that isn't universal, like a lightbulb or one of these..."

He reaches out and plucks the resistor from between my fingertips, the tips of his fingers brushing against mine. A tiny jolt of static electricity zaps between us, and we both jump back, shouting our own little yelps. I laugh and he looks up at me, as though he's fighting some kind of a blush.

"You, uh...you can end up with a problem you just can't fix."

"Are...we an unfixable problem?" I ask.

He stares at me for a beat.

"I think we're working on that."

There's an awkward pause, and I glance back out the workshop. Something catches my eye on a board near the door, and I take a step toward it—

"Whoa, wait," Adam says, moving.

"What are these?" I ask, eyeing up the odd blueprints on the wall. They look a lot like some of the things in the pinball game. "Are these designs from your dad?"

"No, they're...mine, actually."

"What?" I snort, unpinning one and placing it on the worktable. "Really? What's it for?"

"Well..." He smooths out the paper, tilting his head. "This

one is for a flipper I was designing. But see here, along the edges?" He glances up at me and back down. "The idea is that there would be a solenoid in the side that would come out during bonus games and…" He stops and shakes his head. "This is not interesting."

"I mean, I don't know what a lot of that means, but…you build these?"

"Kind of." He shrugs. "I have help, up at the makerspace. You know NextFab? Up across town? If I go to college, I think this is the plan."

"Electronics?"

"Yup." He smiles. "Engineering, it's slowly been becoming more a thing for me…but maybe not all about pinball. I don't know. Come on, let's go try out a few games." he says, pushing himself off the workshop table. "We haven't really gotten any new ones since that *Stranger Things* one, but I bet I can find one you like."

"Okay." I smile and walk out ahead of him. I fish out my phone, posting some of the photos from inside the arcade while he leads me along some of the machines.

West Philly eSports:
Hi from Old City Pinball! Games are just a quarter, come say hello during the festival this week! They'll even have games outside!

"As you can see—" he starts as we stroll by the snack bar "—your plants are doing quite well."

I look up at the shelving, all the little plants sitting comfortably in their containers, the big moss terrarium looking lovely.

"And this is where we stop." He grins, hands on his hips. There's a *Star Trek: The Next Generation* game in front of him, images from the sci-fi show all over it. I glance up and spot a tiny plaque next to it and walk alongside the machine to read it.

"What's this about?" I ask, tapping the plaque. There are a bundle of high scores and some initials next to them, but most look the same, and it's all from a few years ago. Nothing new.

"Ah." He walks up behind me and reaches out, tapping the little bronze bars. "Those are all my dad. This one here is me, but the rest are him."

I squint at the plaque and the initials.

"Even the initials ASS?" I laugh.

"He was so embarrassing sometimes." Adam shakes his head.

"So he…gave himself a plaque for his own high scores?" I snort.

"Yeah, he was silly like that." He laughs. "People have since beaten his scores, but we don't update that thing. And won't. Makes a lot of newcomers irritated, but oh well. This machine here was *his* favorite."

He digs in his pockets and pulls out a few quarters, handing me some.

"Oh, I don't really know anything about *Star Trek*?" I start.

"It's not going to *quiz* you." He grins. "It's one of the most popular pinball machines ever made, next to *The Addams Family* one, which literally is the best-selling pinball game of all time. Tons of fun interactive bits, lots of voices and effects. It's a marvel." He slides a quarter in, and a pinball pops out the side into the long stretch of space that leads into the game. "Go ahead."

I lean against the machine and pull the plunger. The ball soars up into the game, across a ramp, and *bings* against a few things, making music and laser sounds, before plummeting immediately down the middle.

"Argh," I grumble, tapping the buttons to make the little flippers go. "I don't think I'm gonna be any good at this. I don't think I was any good at pinball the last time I tried it, for that matter." I remember lots of whatever-the-pinball-equivalent-of-a-gutter-ball is, while Adam and our friends bounded around the space.

"Here," he says, coming up next to me. He reaches his arms around, places his hands on mine against the flipper buttons. "Is this...okay?" he asks, tilting his head and looking at me.

"Yes," I whisper out.

"See, the trick when you're playing a serious game of pinball isn't to pull the plunger here all the way back." He takes my hand and places it on it. "If you give it a lighter tap, sometimes you can control where it goes. All the way back, and sure, it soars up and over through the ramp, maybe hits a few things. But if you're strategic about it, maybe it only gets *half-way* up that ramp."

He points at the middle of the machine, at some little piece of plastic up and near the ramp that takes the pinball into the game. It breaks off and leads somewhere else.

"Little details like that make a game special. It's not just about hitting the flippers. It's about making the ball go where you want and navigating the story. All games have a story."

He pulls the plunger back, holding my hand, and lets go, sending the pinball...not quite soaring the way I've done, but just coasting a little, and onto the ramp, where it slows down, and sure enough, breaks off from the route and tumbles down into some lights and noises. His score racks up.

"See?" he says, leaning over the machine, getting ready to hit the flippers. "Another entrance to the game, tucked away there."

He gently taps my fingers with his hands, controlling the game a bit. The points soar up, lights go up, sounds go wild. I have no idea what's happening, or who any of these characters really are, save for Patrick Stewart, but I can't stop laughing and grinning. It feels like…it feels like we're those awkward eighth graders again. Before my dad's success, before Adam lost his, before everything got so complicated.

The lights on the machine dance on his face, lighting up in flashes of gold and white. His face gets a little close to mine and—

My phone buzzes, vibrating through my pocket and rattling the machine. I jerk back and bump against Adam.

"That's weird," he says, pulling his phone out, too. "Did our phones go off at the same time?"

"Yeah…" I swallow, feeling a little breathless. He's looking down at his phone, rubbing the back of his neck, his eyes flitting between me and the screen, an awkward little smile on his face. I glance down at my own glowing screen, and one of those Emergency Alert notifications is there.

Emergency Alert
Winter blizzard warning for the
Greater Philadelphia County.
Dangerously high winds and snowfall
up to one foot expected overnight.
Seek shelter, stay inside.

My heart goes from thumping hard to pounding, and I look up at Adam, concerned.

He glances over at the large windows lining the arcade and bites his lip.

"Did it really get that much worse?" he asks in a way that feels like he's not only talking to me. His eyes flit over to me, and I nod toward the door.

Gusts of snow are billowing wildly outside the windows, in thick curls of white, swirling against the white twinkle lights and the streetlamps lining the street. I press my hands against the thick glass of the front windows, and my palms feel ice-cold, like they might just freeze to the clear surface. Another blast of wind vibrates the windows, and I dart back.

Adam catches me as my back thumps against his chest, his chin dipping over my shoulder just a little. Our phones buzz a bunch of times, and he pulls his out same as me.

MOM

Oh my God, where are you right now?

MOM

Are you still in Old City? Did you get the alert?

MOM

I'm trying to call but not getting through.

ME

Yes, I'm fine. I'm at the arcade, I'll head home soon.

MOM

We already left! I wish you'd have come with us!

ME

I'll be fine.

I glance over at Adam and nod at his phone.

"Your mom, too?" I ask.

"Yeah." He holds his phone up, and it's just a series of "hurry home!" texts. "What about you? Are you okay?" he asks, not quite pushing me away yet, and me, not exactly stepping forward. I look out the window and see a flash of... something, across the street.

"Yeah, yeah, I'm fine." I step away from him and lean in toward the window.

"What is it?" he asks, walking up next to me.

A little shadow darts around, moving back and forth in the bricked-off park square.

"I can't quite—" I start.

"Oh no." He exhales, and hurries away. I follow him across the arcade and have to hurry, as he just bounds toward the front door, grabbing his leather jacket off the register countertop. He spins it over his shoulders and threads his arms through in a practiced, fluid motion, and reaches for the door.

"Adam!" I shout. "What are you doing?"

"It's Coco," he says as though that even means anything, and tugs the front door open with a loud grunt. "She's out of the bookstore. I gotta get her." He looks out toward the wild snow and back at me, breathing heavy. "I'll be right back."

And just like that he's gone.

I hurry myself toward the door, grabbing my jean jacket that's still pretty damp, and run my arms through it, the cold of the melted snow chilling my arms. I press my shoulder against the front door and dart out into the white. There are still a handful of folks making their way around the corner down the block, coming up from the SEPTA station from the latest train, I suppose, but otherwise, most of the street looks empty.

I see Adam's figure pressing up against Church Street across the way. With all the snow piling up and the lack of cars down Second Street, no people on the sidewalks in that direction and buildings coated in white, he looks like an extra who got lost during the making of *The Road*.

I hurry toward him, my useless-for-snow shoes leaving my feet wildly cold as they fill with ice.

"Adam!" I shout. He looks over his shoulder, and I can catch the surprise on his face despite the gusting of snow.

"Go back inside!" he shouts, and points at the little park that sits parallel from the arcade. "I'll be right there."

That little shadow that was flitting around from the window is clearer now.

It's a small dog, leaping about joyfully in the snow. It's a little white fluffy thing, and I honestly have no idea how Adam even noticed it out here. The pup looks like it's actually made of the snow it's running in, and I'm not sure if I'm looking at fur or snow.

Adam makes his way into the park, and despite his ask, I push forward. I'm not leaving him out here by himself. I stand at the edge of the park, the snowdrifts way too high in there, for my jeans and fabric sneakers. Adam bounds about the deep snow, the little dog popping up and down in the small hills of white like a porpoise in the sea.

"She looks happy in there!" I shout over the wind.

"She's the bookstore dog from next door!" he shouts back, taking a dive at the dog and missing, disappearing into a fluff of snow. He scrambles to his feet and makes another dive, this time catching the little dog, who squirms about in his arms before licking his face.

He hustles toward me, the dog bundled up against his chest.

"Come on," he says, his teeth chattering a little.

I follow him, my arms tight against my chest, and he takes a surprising right away from the arcade, skipping the chance to dart under the big white tent that protects the pinball machines. He stops in front of the used bookstore next door, The Book Trader, looking into the windows and then the door.

The glass on the door is shattered.

"Fuck!" he shouts, and I get up next to him.

"What is it?" I ask, my teeth definitely chattering. He peers inside the shop, his feet crunching against the snow and the glass on the ground, and then back at me.

"No one's here. Snow is filling up the store and Coco must have run out." He glances back across the street and at me. "All right, let's get back inside." He steps toward me, holding his arm out, and loops his arm through mine, a wriggling dog pressed against his chest.

CHAPTER 11
Adam

"When played correctly, pinball shouldn't be a short game. It should last. There are goals to accomplish, in each game. Pieces of the playfield to conquer. It's a long con, not a short one, so consider every move carefully."

–THE ART AND ZEN OF PINBALL REPAIR
BY JAMES WATTS

Whitney's arm is looped in mine as we make our way back down the street toward the rapidly emptying neighborhood. Coco squirms against me, a ball of drenched energy despite the mayhem happening around us. The snow is really coming down now, and there are barely any people left on Market. I have to battle with the front door, gusts of wind slamming against me. Whitney barrels in, and I push it closed against the storm, take a deep breath, and survey the arcade.

It's empty, though I don't know why I expected anything different. I put down Coco, and she scampers off toward the back of the arcade.

"I'll make some coffee or something," I say, shrugging my leather jacket off, completely useless against the cold. I can feel my feet squishing in my boots, hear them, too, despite the fact that they are supposed to be fairly waterproof. I look down and watch myself leaving a trail of water. I know I'm just gonna have to slip into all of that again in a minute. With the bookstore's front door smashed in, snow is just gonna flutter inside and mess up all the stock at the front of the shop. I can't let that happen to them. I'll have to cover it somehow. I sigh and duck behind the snack bar, and instinctively look around for Chris. I shake my head and laugh, and pull the Keurig out from under the counter.

"Chris really hates this thing," I say, digging around through the makeshift drawers under the snack bar for pods. Each drawer is basically filled with what you'd find in a junk drawer in anyone's kitchen, various wires and batteries we couldn't get rid of, slips of paper for who knows what, condiment packets, and…

"Got it," I say, holding a pod up. "Have you seen those pour overs he makes? With the glass and everything?" I pop a pod in and hit brew, the machine whirring to life while I grab a mug and position it inside. "I'm not sure if you follow him on Instagram, but—"

"Adam," Whitney says, her voice close.

I look up and she's standing right at the snack bar, shivering wildly.

"Oh no," I gasp and look at the brewing coffee as though that will somehow fix everything. "Um…" I reach out and grab her arms as she sits down on the floor, folding into herself a little. "Hold on."

I rush across the arcade and battle with the red, impossibly closed door of the workshop, which has once again swelled up against the wood. Coco is abruptly next to me, jumping on my leg as I wrestle with the door. I try to nudge her away, but she persists, and it's adorably annoying. I look around for the crowbar and curse, realizing I left it inside the workshop. I scoop up my leather jacket and I run to Mom's office, and thankfully, find another first-aid kit against the back of her mercifully open door. There's also a ratty hoodie on the floor, one of Mom's from when she goes to the nearby gym, and I snatch it up, too.

"Hey," I say, tossing the hoodie around Whitney, who makes a bit of a face. "I know, useless, just a second."

I dig around in the kit and pull out an emergency blanket, which is folded up into an impossibly small square, and pluck out two hand warmers. I unfurl the emergency blanket, which looks like a gigantic sheet of foil on one side, bright orange on the other, and flutter it down on her. I activate the hand warmers and tuck them under the sheet.

"Are you okay?" I ask, kneeling down.

She looks up at me, her cheeks impossibly red.

"I think so," she chatters. "I should…have worn…a better jacket."

"Me, too," I laugh, and reach out, tucking some of her hair behind her ear. It's hard to move, and that's when I realize her hair is a little frozen. "Jesus. Let me get your coffee."

"I, um…" Whitney says as I hand her the steaming mug. "Adam, I have to get out of these clothes. The blanket is great, but I'm soaked and frozen and this hoodie smells like a gym bag."

Oh.

"*Oh...*" I swallow. "Um...okay, um..."

Whatever frozen ice or snow that was still stuck to my skin has absolutely melted. I feel like a cartoon character, and I'm convinced if I flapped my T-shirt, a little steam would float out. I peek in my mom's office, but the windows are rattling from the cold and the snow, to the point that I'm pretty sure I can see frost on the desk. I'm gonna have to get the workshop door open; at least there's gonna be heat in there.

I move to close the door to my mom's office when I spot some of the spare pinball machine parts on the ground, underneath some of the machines we've left back there. I grab a machine leg off the floor, and it slides across the cold concrete of the office with a scratching noise.

Okay.

I run over to the workshop and wedge the pinball machine leg in the space that I usually cram the crowbar on cold days like this, and push and pry until the door swings open again. I toss the leg down and grab the crowbar from the inside, placing it outside the workshop. Not making that mistake again.

"All right." I walk back over to Whitney, still wrapped in the silver blanket, help her get up, and head over to the room, letting her in. She sits on the floor, kicking off her soaking-wet shoes and peeling off her socks, which hit the dirty concrete floor with a wet slap. I look back into the arcade for Coco, and she's already snuggled up in Mom's old hoodie. I huff, fiercely jealous of how she gets to unwind, like nothing troublesome is happening at all.

I turn back to Whitney, who is looking up at me, expectantly.

"Everything okay?" I ask.

"You should probably shut the door." She smirks.

"Yeah, oh, God, yeah…" I start to close it and stop. "Do you need me to get you anything?" I talk into the crack between the door and wall, willing my eyes to stare straight ahead at the arcade.

"I think I'll be fine," she says, still chattering a bit. "Just… knock."

She snorts out a laugh and I close the door, but I don't press it shut. I don't need it getting stuck again. I run my hand over the red wood and remember all the other boutiques and vendors who were setting up outside just…what, under an hour ago. It hasn't been that long.

I pull out my phone to see if anyone out there is still posting anything.

The last tweet from Smak Parlour was just five minutes ago.

Maybe they're still at the shop.

I rush over to the snack bar and dig around underneath the counter, pulling out a bundle of garbage bags and an absolutely ancient roll of duct tape. The cardboard circle it's on is warped into a barely passible oval shape, but when I pull at the edge of the tape, it's still sticky.

Good, good. I dart back over to the workshop.

"Hey." I shout through the door, tapping on it. "I'll be right back."

The snow hurts this time as I press against it, stinging across my wet cheeks and neck, like little pinpricks in the darkness. I wince as I walk through it, Dad's mural along the arcade almost entirely covered, and get to The Book Trader. The inside closest to the door has a pile of snow pooling, and I can see sheets of it smattered here and there around books by the windows. As much as I'd like to hop in there and scoop out that snow, there's no real time, and this will help just as well.

I flatten a bunch of the trash bags as best I can against the door, ripping little holes in them, and tape the fluttering plastic around the door handle and pipes near the edges of the door. The black bags billow out like a giant balloon, and I hope it'll do the trick.

I take my phone out, my hands trembling in the cold, and snap a few photos for the owner. Maybe it'll help with insurance? I don't know. I'll tweet it their way, along with a picture of Coco snoozing in the arcade.

And then I set my eyes on the corner down the block.

The walk from the arcade to the corner of Second and Market should take mere seconds. It's right there. I can see it. I feel as though I should be able to just run to it and up around the corner. But as the gusts of wind and snow press against me, I find myself physically pushing to take any steps, each lunge forward digging me into the snow around my feet.

The snow is piling up, midway up my calves, and is filling my boots and soaking my jeans.

I get to the corner, and there are a bundle of people hiding underneath the SEPTA station overhang that leads into the subway, fussing with their phones and shivering. Someone shouts into their cell, and a woman takes off walking down Market toward Columbus, clearly irritated. I make out somebody grumbling about rideshares, just as a few people come up from inside the station, also on their phones.

Fuck.

If the trains aren't running and rideshares can't make it through…how are we supposed to get home? The stroll to home from Old City isn't terribly far; I do it all the time when I have something on my mind and just need to walk it out… but three miles in this? I would never make it. Not in jeans and a leather jacket.

I grit my teeth and keep pushing, the bright pink exterior of Smak Parlour sticking out amongst the splashes of snow stuck to the walls of the building. Nothing is shoveled out yet along the brick sidewalks, and just as I reach the boutique, the lights inside snap off.

"No!" I shout, and trudge through to the front door. A few shadows are moving around in there, and I pound on the door. "It's Adam from the arcade! Come on! I know you're in there!"

I see the light from a cell phone, and then another, start moving from the back of the store and over to me. Janet, one of the women who works at the shop, peeks out at me from the storefront's glass window, and opens the front door.

"Jesus, Adam," She gasps, pulling me inside. "What are you doing?"

"I need some clothes," I stammer out, shivering. "One of my…friends is back at the arcade, and was soaked through everything."

"Yeah, okay, but so are you." She crosses her arms and nods at me, and I glance down at my jeans, which are now drenched up to my knees in snow.

"I'll be fine." I shake my head. "She was wearing a jean jacket and like, a red T-shirt."

"In this?" she practically shouts. "All right." She glances back in the store. "Nena, are you back there?"

"Tell whoever it is we're closed!" a voice shouts.

"Just a second," Janet says, starting to walk off and then turns to me. "Wait, what size is she?"

"Uh…" I try to picture Whitney but immediately feel flustered. "I, um…medium?" I attempt.

"Oh, God." Janet slaps her forehead. "Like me? More like your mom?" I try not to scowl, and she must see the look on my face. "All right, like me. Be right back."

She darts to the back of the shop. It's weird being in here with all the lights off. The entire boutique smells sweet, like I just stepped inside a pastry. The interior is normally full of wild pinks and bright splashes of white, bits of gold and silver everywhere, fashion jewelry accompanying all the high-end outfits. And I can't help but wonder if this is what it'll be like when the lights in the arcade really go out, for the final time. All the splashes of color and joyful sounds, quieted.

Like they were never really there.

Like I was never really there.

What's going to be left?

"We're going to find something warm!" Janet shouts from the back of the shop. "I hope she isn't picky!"

"It's fine!" I shout back, turning to look out the window. All the shops along Market are closed; lights are out. A bunch of tents that had been set up outside Fork and Mac's Pub are collapsed under the weight of the snow, and there's a table halfway into the street, its legs sticking up out of the snow like a dead animal.

This is…really bad.

A gust of wind howls just as a hand touches my shoulder, and I spin around.

"Hey, sorry," Janet says, the other woman working there, Nena, I think, right next to her. "We only had a few sweatshirts and jeans back in clearance there."

"Oh, awesome, thank you." I reach out and take them, whatever they've picked all tucked into a bright pink paper bag the size of a large suitcase. There's more than one outfit in here. I glance up at her, puzzled.

"How much—"

"Just bring back whatever doesn't work," Janet says, waving her hand around. "Are you gonna head out?"

"What do you mean?" I ask, lowering the bag.

"Adam, it's a disaster outside," she presses. "Nena has her truck parked in the lot over on Church Street. Why don't you all pile in and we'll drive you home."

"It's okay. I gotta get the machines inside," I say, though something is poking at the back of my mind, telling me this is a good idea, and I should get the hell out of Old City.

"Are you sure?"

"Yeah, totally."

I'm not.

Janet glances over at Nena, who shrugs.

"All right," Nena says, pulling some keys from her pocket and nodding at the front door. "Good luck, kid."

CHAPTER 12
Whitney

After what feels like an agonizing few minutes, my phone's screen blinks on. The battery is near dead, but thankfully, there's a charger and cord in Adam's workshop. My power banks are in my backpack in the arcade, and I am...in no condition to sneak out there and grab it. Adam could pop back in at any minute, and this fluttery emergency blanket isn't exactly weighted. I open up my rideshare app, and...the surge pricing is trying to charge something like two hundred dollars for a trip from Old City to West Philly, which, in any other circumstance, I could just spend an hour walking across the town.

Whatever, Dad has the money. He'll be fine. All the worrying and fretting I've done for the past year has been for nothing.

I request a car. It gives me something like an hour wait before one can even get here.

I lean against the wall closest to the workshop door, despite the cold gusts coming in between the crack between the door and the wall, and wait.

★ ★ ★

There's a little knock at the door.

"Adam?" I ask.

It cracks open a little bit, and I spot some fingers pop out in the crack between the wall. They wiggle.

"It's me," he says. "I got you something. Can I open this a little more?"

"Sure," I snort, pulling the emergency blanket closer to me. It's almost too warm in here now, and a bright pink paper bag crunches its way through to me, crinkling up between the door and wall. I reach up and grab it, and a T-shirt falls out. I dig in, and there's a pair of jeans inside, too, along with some other shirts and bright pink sweatpants.

"Adam, you didn't…" I start, flapping out the shirt. It's bright red, like the one I had with me, with "Philly" written in rhinestones. I slide it on and slip into the jeans, which surprisingly fit well. "How did you manage this?"

The door cracks open a little more.

"I just fought through the snow," he says through the gap. "Some of the women who work there were basically on their way out. We got lucky."

"I'll say." I shake my shoulders, the fabric already warming me up, and reach out for my wallet and phone, shoving them in the pockets. A strange pattern brushes against my fingers, and I look down to spot a soft pretzel pattern on the pocket. It makes me snort out a laugh; it's the same kind of Philly pretzels that confuse the hell out of my friends who aren't from the area, or didn't grow up here, thinking pretzels are shaped with those two big loops. Everyone knows real pretzels, properly made in Philly, are basically a chunky braid.

"Did you actually pick these out?" I ask.

"Oh no," he says, sounding almost disappointed. "The girls did. All the lights were out and they were just wrangling up what they could."

"Well, they did okay." I shrug. "You did okay." Everything but my socks are completely dry at this point, and even if things were still freezing cold, I don't think I could have asked Adam to find me a new bra.

I've seen the way he gets flustered. I think that request would have killed him.

"Are you—" he stammers out "—um, decent?"

Yeah, definitely would have killed him.

I nudge the door open and he's standing there, shivering a bit himself. I glance down at his trademarked combat boots and jeans, which are drenched, and back up at him. He shrugs.

"Tables have turned?" I ask.

He shrugs with a smirk.

"I have, um…backup outfits in the workshop." He points at the door behind me, and I step aside, letting him duck in. He closes the door over, and I hear a bit of ruckus, things moving around and getting dragged, and the flop of his leather jacket against the ground.

"You know, you could have just let me wear like, your backup jeans and a shirt," I say, leaning against the door. He lets out a curse behind the door, under his breath, but I still hear it and laugh.

He pops back out, looking much the same as before.

"So," he says, looking about the arcade and back at me.

"So." I shrug.

"Any luck finding a ride?" he asks, nodding at the phone in

my hand. I swipe it on and the wait for a rideshare went from an hour to two hours. I groan and cancel it. "That's a no."

"The wait is looking like hours." I walk over to the front door and peer out the window. "How did the SEPTA station look?"

Adam laughs, and he doesn't need to say much more than that.

"Dammit," I huff.

"Well, look," Adam says, walking over. "That storm isn't letting up anytime soon, so why don't we play a couple of games while we wait for it to calm down?" He walks around the counter at the front of the arcade, and pops open the register, scooping out a bunch of coins. They fall back into the tray, clinking musically, and he jingles a few around in his hand, wiggling his fingers like a pirate showing off some treasure.

I can't help but smile.

"All right." I nod, reaching out. He drops a bunch of change in my hand, and hops around the counter. "Where should we start?"

"Let's go."

He walks in a straight line to a machine he seems to have his eyes set on, but I look around at some of the others a little more closely, games I didn't see on his little tour earlier, when we got distracted and ducked into that workshop. Some look like they're tied into old movies or television shows, some I recognize, like *Jurassic Park*, and others don't make much sense…there's one called *The Avengers*, but it looks like a bunch of British people with umbrellas, no Robert Downey, Jr. to be seen.

"Here we are," he says, tapping the sides of the machine.

He rubs his hands together. The little bookstore dog is snoozing in that smelly hoodie near the snack bar, and I take a step toward her, squatting down. She is out.

"Do you remember Coco?" Adam asks. I get up and turn around.

"No, should I?" I shrug.

"Eh, maybe not." He shrugs back. "She's been the bookstore dog at The Book Trader since we were kids. She's probably old enough to be a sophomore at Central, but still acts like a puppy."

He smiles, nodding at the machine.

"You ready?"

The front of the machine, where he drops in a quarter, has a bunch of white-and-black spirals, and the whole actual game is full of odd images. Rocket ships and astronauts, pyramids with eyes and a weird gumball-looking thing. The board on the back, whatever it's called, reads *The Twilight Zone*, with some guy stepping out a lit-up door.

"I'm guessing this isn't the Jordan Peele one." I nod at the machine as he steadies himself in front of it, the machine roaring to life with the coin.

"Hah!" he laughs. "Nope, this game is older than us. 1993. Long before any streaming service was around." He pulls the stick on the end of the machine, sending the silver ball inside soaring up and into the game, a series of loud *chunk-chunk* noises rattling from the game, lights and sounds flicking and chiming. The scoreboard racks up impossible numbers in the tens of hundreds of thousands for like, doing five or six things, and I'm really not sure I understand how that system works. Words flicker across the orange screen, numbers flit by, but

Adam stays focused, looking down at the game, making the flippers control the ball.

"Aren't you…missing the messages and stuff?" I look up at the orange pixelated board, stuff from what I'm guessing is the show fluttering by. Something about a triple score… I don't know.

"Nah." He shrugs. "That's just gonna distract me from the mission at hand. Get as many points as I can and ah—" The ball goes straight down the middle and he smacks the side of the cabinet.

"Oops, sorry," I mutter.

"It's okay." He turns around and smiles, leaning against the machine. "Your turn. What do you want to try?"

I look around at all the different machines, and then back at Adam.

"All of them?"

His smile beams.

CHAPTER 13
Adam

"One thing people seem to forget about pinball, is that
it's also a game about honesty. You can shake a
machine, to try to get your way with this movement
or that…but you'll get caught. The machine will tilt,
sometimes not physically, effectively ending the entire
time. Pinball forces you to face your truth."

–THE ART AND ZEN OF PINBALL REPAIR
BY JAMES WATTS

Whitney is playing *The Addams Family* pinball machine, the
telltale sounds of the characters' voices ringing out through
the empty arcade, as I stare out the window outside. The snow
is showing no sign of stopping, and I can see another tent has
fallen down up Church Street, but at this point I can't even
make out whose it was. All the tables and booths are coated
in white, and my phone keeps buzzing.

MOM

Adam. When are you coming home?

MOM

It's getting so much worse out there.

ME

We're just waiting for things to calm down, we literally can't leave yet.

ME

Don't worry, we're safe and warm.

MOM

We?

I wince and put my phone back in my pocket.

I try to catch a glimpse of our tent from inside, but all I can see is the inside of it, and it's hard to tell if it's wilting or ready to fall. I walk the length of the arcade, but it's no use. For now it's doing what it needs to...stopping an avalanche of snow from covering the machines. Sure, they've got those tarps over them, but just a quick glance down at the street tells me they aren't doing much. There's already a few inches piled up around the machines.

I look at the machine closest to the door. It's the *Lost in Space* one. It's a rare machine, and I remember Dad really liking that one. And if Whitney's father really is going to buy this place, there are a few cabinets I'd like to save. Maybe bring home. I'm sure we could find a way to fit a few in the basement, right?

I inch closer to the door. Maybe Whitney could help me get it in here.

"Hey, Whit?" I venture.

"Yeah?" she shouts across the arcade, and I laugh, turning around. She's focused on *The Addams Family* game, and it warms my heart. She hits a few buttons and lets out a frustrated groan before turning around to look at me. "You owe me a game."

"Deal." I grin. "Can you help me with something really quick?"

"So what's the game plan here?" Whitney asks, lingering in the door frame while I unclip the tarp around the machine. The wind flaps against the tent and tarps madly, whipping them around loudly. The covers do an awesome job covering them up, sure. But you can't exactly grab anything to move them with those things on. Snow immediately starts dusting the *Lost in Space* machine, and I unlock the bike locks from the legs.

"I figure, you grab one side, I get the other, and we lift?"

"All right..." she ventures, stepping into the cold. "If I get drenched again, you're gonna have to break into that boutique. Or give me your outfit."

The warmth that spreads to my neck could melt the snow.

"Okay, ready..." I count down, and we lift.

Without the guys from the comic bookshop helping us, I feel like I'm going to die. The machine teeters back and forth as we awkwardly try to lug it inside, weighing more than the combined weight of the two of us.

"Oh, my God, I'm dying," I groan, gritting my teeth as Whitney walks onto the small step leading through the door, the weight of the machine pressing downward on me. The tent squiggles a little as a gust of wind pushes against my back, and as Whitney hoists the machine up a little bit more, my foot flips.

I try to keep my grip on the machine, and slide more, kicking out one of the tent poles…and a swell of snow pours down onto me. I can't hold on to the machine and I fall into the snow, pressed down face-first as the pinball cabinet crashes against the building and steps. I hear the bookstore dog go wild.

I push myself up, shaking off the snow, and look ahead. Whitney is already trying to push the machine back up, but I can see the damage is done, and Coco is hopping up and down by her legs.

"You okay?" Whitney asks, gently nudging the dog away.

"I'm fine, let's…get the game," I groan, walking over toward her. There's a sharp pain in my leg that makes me limp. I look over at *Lost in Space*, the playfield facing away. But I can see the shards of glass splayed out in the snow, looking like pieces of ice.

"Let's be careful here, come on," I say, climbing up onto the stair with Whitney. We both grab the back of the machine and pull it inside, the slicked wet metal squeaking against the hardwood floors. It sits there, on its side near the door and register, and I push the front door shut as tight as I can, snow squeezing in between the cracks.

"Well, that sucked," I groan, pulling my jean leg up. My shin is scratched to all hell and there's already a bruise purpling, but I'm more or less okay. I turn back to the machine. The glass is definitely broken, and the sides look a bit dented in, but it doesn't feel like a total loss. The pieces on the playfield are still looking fine. This feels like one I could easily fix. New glass, hammer out the dents…not a big deal.

The sound of tiny toenails clicking against the hardwood floor snaps me away from the machine, and I watch Coco snuggle up in Mom's hoodie. The drama is over.

"I guess it's my turn to break out the first aid?" Whitney suggests, making her way to Dad's workshop. I watch her as she strolls over, and glance back down at my leg. It's not that bad. Just some scratches. I pull my phone out, a bundle of text messages waiting.

MOM

Adam. Who is the we? Who are you with?

MOM

Do they have a car, can they drive you home?

CHRIS

Hey bud. You okay? Your mom is texting me asking me where you are.

CHRIS

She thinks I'm at the arcade with you?

CHRIS

What are you even still doing there?

There's a pause, the wind roaring outside, as I try to think of an answer...even though I know what it is. And strangely, I don't think the answer has anything to do with the actual arcade.

I look up at the workshop.

"Whitney?" I shout. "Did you find it?"

I wait for a beat, but she doesn't answer.

"Whit?"

I get up, groaning, my leg stinging as I make my way across to the workshop. She's standing by the door, staring ahead at something next to it.

"What are you—" I start. But then she looks at me, and I know exactly what she's staring at. "Oh."

I walk up next to her in the workshop, and turn to the bulletin board my dad kept in there. Where the various tickets from shows we went to, flyers, and photos, all stay tacked up. Like a flattened time capsule that stopped collecting memories a few years ago. The photo of me, Mom, Dad, and Whitney at that concert...the nearly ripped corner with Whitney, is unfolded.

"Was this..." She looks at me, her eyes sad. "Your dad? He kept all these?"

"Yeah." I nod.

"Just your dad?" She smirks.

I set my eyes on the board, and exhale.

I reach up and nudge some of the tickets around on the bulletin board, shifting the little rectangular pieces of paper this way and that, like little fragile Tetris pieces. Splashes of color appear from behind a bundle of them, and I grab a thumbtack in the middle of it all, and pluck a large flyer for a Kings of Leon concert off it. A group that Dad loved bringing up, how he knew who they were before they "got all popular." There was a lot of music like that, for him, like how he saw Jason Mraz perform in a coffee shop one time.

As the flyer comes down, Whitney gasps.

And all the photos show themselves.

There's the nearly torn one from that concert with my family, Whitney in that American Hi-Fi T-shirt, but then, there's all the rest. All of us at a Train and Lifehouse concert, seeing Wilson Phillips, where my mom and dad sang loudly to their cover of a Fleetwood Mac song, an R.E.M. show where my dad cried…and Whitney, next to me, in every single photo.

She reaches out and brushes her fingers against a picture of herself, wearing a Goo Goo Dolls T-shirt, and she laughs a little before looking at me.

"I don't even remember this concert," she says, turning back. "Or that shirt."

"Or the rubber bands?" I ask, pointing at her smile, bright pink dots in her mouth. She swats at my hand.

"I'll have you know, rubber bands help adjust your bite." She gives me a look and turns back to the photos. "Pink ones work better. It's just science."

"Sure." I grin.

"I can't believe he kept all these," she sighs, pausing. "That you kept all these."

"Well," I huff. "I have a hard time letting go."

"Is that what this is about?" she asks, stepping back into the arcade. She crosses her arms, nodding at the space. "Holding on?"

"Yeah." I step out of the workshop, patting the door frame.

"I'm…fairly aware of that." And there's just this…awful stirring in my chest, from seeing those photos to looking at the arcade to Whitney being here and pointing all that out. There's definitely something rattling around in there, and I clear my throat and shake my head.

"Whit, look, I—"

"All right, some big feelings here," Whitney says and walks across the arcade. She turns to look at me, smiling and shrugging, before turning back around. She hops behind the snack bar and returns, a little smile on her face. I sputter out a laugh, wiping at my face as she flaps a bag of Swedish Fish candies at me.

"I think you earned one." She smiles, plucking one out and handing it to me.

"Where did you get these?" I ask, making my way toward her. I step around Coco, who lets out a little snore and kicks her small legs. I make a mental note to tweet something to the bookstore later.

"Eat your candy first." She grins.

"You sound like Chris," I grumble, popping the fish in my mouth, chewing as the cherry flavor bursts over my tongue.

"Outside my mom's shop," she says, tilting her head. "The day you came by and deleted your post. Were you…going to do this there?"

"I'd thought about it." I shrug. "I remember Chris's dads doing the whole Swedish Fish thing with you and everybody else when we were kids, and I thought maybe you'd remember."

"How could I forget?" she laughs, and there's a beat of silence between us, the wind thundering against the windows. "What are you going to do now?" she asks me.

"I'm not sure I know?" I sigh.

She looks at me, I mean right at me, those blue-mint eyes.

I reach out, my hand shaking a little, and tuck a wayward strand of her hair behind her ear, her windswept hair no longer frozen against her scalp. I step back and look at the Swedish Fish bag in her hand and reach in, pulling one out. I hand it over, and she takes it in her delicate hands.

"Whitney," I start. "I'm sorry. For all of it."

She looks at the candy, handing it back.

"Me, too."

"If I could, I'd—" I start.

She holds a hand up, staring down at the little bag. She jostles it around a bit, pulling a candy out, and holds it between her fingertips as though she's considering it. Her eyes flit to mine, and then back to the candy.

"There's this fantasy author I like a lot who always talks about falling in love when the world is ending, and how it sometimes doesn't feel real," she starts, spinning the piece of candy between her fingers.

"You still read fantasy novels?" I ask and immediately realize I'm asking the wrong question as she just said *falling in love*. But I can't help but remember all those Holly Black and Fran Wilde and Leigh Bardugo books in her room, the paperbacks beaten up beyond recognition. "I kinda figured you stopped when…" I shake my head.

"No, go ahead," she says, walking over to the snack bar. She grabs a seat, the same chair she was in when we were working on those plants, and pats the one next to it. I smile and go to join her, plucking a candy out of the bag.

"This isn't how it's supposed to go," I say, holding the candy. "You're supposed to get all your feelings out, and then we take turns."

"I feel like the last few days have been all about breaking old habits," she says, exhaling.

"Fair enough," I reply. "I just…you and the girls. I figured maybe you stopped, you know, being a geek like me."

"Adam, I feel like *you* stopped being a geek like you, that spring, that entire summer when we didn't really see each other," she says, pulling out another piece of candy. "You turned into…this." She nods at me and then reaches out, twisting her fingers around the long curl that drops from the middle of my head. "You used to wear dorky T-shirts, sure, but they weren't all just old bands. They were weird movies and television shows no one knew, instead of just bands no one knew."

"Excuse me, people know who REO Speedwagon is," I stress. She gives me a look. "Well, fine, but you turned into *this*." I pluck out a candy, and gesture at her. "But this isn't fair. I can't point at those things. You don't have your white jacket, your girl gang, your social media to manage, all of that right now. It's just you."

"It's just me," she says, twirling that piece of candy. "But that fantasy author…whenever I think about that, about the idea of love when the world is ending, you're supposed to be able to cling to it, right? It's what keeps you going in those kinds of stories. That hope of someone."

She exhales.

"My mom left my dad when things were starting to get better, business-wise. The cafés and all that were taking off. But he forgot about her. About me, too, really. And being here, in this arcade—" she looks around, her eyes still startlingly blue in the fading light, plumes of her frozen breath floating in front of her, our heater trying its best but failing as the storm gets worse "—spending these few days with you. I think I unraveled something. That maybe I haven't been handling all of my father's internet stuff and keeping that café in order because it's the only way to make him see me. That if I wasn't there, present in that way, he might forget about me."

She sighs, her lip quivering a little.

"I think my dad's cafés are *my* arcade." She looks up at me, her eyes a little glassy. "A way to hold on to him, not the other way around. I think I get it now. All this. I can't stop thinking about it. How a bit of my world has been ending for years, and I didn't have time for just...well, *anything* else." She reaches out and hands me the Swedish Fish. "You should know that when...me and the girls were laughing, and we stopped hanging out... I was just in another headspace. And this year, the way they've been acting, it's made me rethink a lot of things."

"I know," I whisper out and toss the Swedish Fish into my mouth.

"Anyhow, I hope after all this we could...start over." She exhales again. "Whew. Okay, I'm done. Did I do it right?"

"Yeah." I nod. "Yeah, you did."

I stare at the bag and the few candies in front of me, the few in front of her.

"I guess it's my turn, right?"

"If you want."

"I just..." I sigh. "Look, I feel like I said a lot of it earlier. When you came here with the plants and just..." I shake my head and grit my teeth a little. "Okay, okay."

I slide the Swedish Fish over to her, but instead of grabbing it, she takes my hand.

"Go ahead," she says.

"Whitney, when we lost my dad that summer, before school—" I exhale. "I don't know, him, growing up in this arcade, it was my whole world. I had you, Chris, our other various neighborhood friends to run around with. Playing manhunt, kick the can, all that...but when that happened, I just felt like I..." I squint, trying to find the words. "It was like I grew up overnight. I felt older. Like I do right now, here in this place, trying to let go of it all."

I shake my head.

"Hey," Whitney says, leaning across the bar. "You have the right to walk away. You know that, right?" She clears her throat. "You can walk away from a place, you can go your own way, and still hold on to the memories that made it special. Because at the end of the day, it isn't about the place. It's about who you shared it with."

I swallow, and I'm not even sure what to say.

"Can I ask you something difficult?"

I wince.

"Do I have a choice?" I ask. She slides a Swedish Fish across the counter to me. "I guess not?"

"Would your dad have wanted this for you?" she asks. Her eyes flit up from the candy to me, and somehow, my entire throat goes dry. "It's funny. I don't think my dad wants all the work I do for him, for me. But at the same time, I think that's the only reason he sees me. Your dad, he saw you for more. Not just for what you could do for him."

"Whit, I'm not sure your dad really thinks that." I shake my head, wiping at the tears on my cheeks. "Maybe he's just lost in his work."

"Maybe you are, too," she says. "Don't ignore what's really important, in favor of what you think other people want."

"I'm trying. I've just...been sad for such a long time. And not living like I'm, you know, not actually an adult. Mourning does that, I think. It ages you. And it doesn't matter if you find joy later. There's no getting younger. That's not how time works."

"So this?" Whitney reaches out, swatting at my T-shirt. I glance down, not even realizing I was wearing a Pearl Jam shirt under that hoodie. "What's this, then?"

"My dad's shirts? His jacket?" I sigh. "My time machine, maybe."

"Does it work?"

"No," I huff. "No, it doesn't." I look up at her and she's smirking. "If you're expecting me to rip this shirt off in some dramatic fashion because of that statement, you're mistaken."

She nips a piece of candy off the bar, and pops it into her mouth.

"We'll see about that shirt." She smirks and bites her lip, and I feel like I'm going to pass out. What...what did she mean by that? "I'm gonna go try out some more games. You coming?"

"But wait, don't you have to... I don't know, get a rideshare home or something?"

My heart is pounding in my chest, to the point I feel like it's
going to burst out and bounce around the arcade like a pinball.

"I do."

She smirks.

"But I'm not gonna."

CHAPTER 14
Whitney

I'm running my hand over the surface of these pinball games that I have vague, flashy memories of from when I was a kid, but nothing I can really latch on to. Just their shape, their sounds, their lights…but not much else. Not their names or their stories, what they're all about.

In a lot of ways, that's how it feels when I think about Adam.

I remember the way he looked when we were younger, the way he looks now, but I missed out on the details all these years. And hearing all these stories unspooling at once, here in this arcade and around Old City and in my social media messages… I've been playing the fastest game of catchup ever.

And now I'm flirting.

I'm flirting with Adam Fucking Stillwater.

CHAPTER 15
Adam

"How do you reinvent something? Something that you've known for so long? That's the question a lot of pinball creators find themselves in. The trick is to remember what you've always loved about it in the first place."

–THE ART AND ZEN OF PINBALL REPAIR
BY JAMES WATTS

Whitney is on her third game of the night, and keeps smirking at me as I stand and squirm. I don't... I don't know what to do here. How to navigate this. I've never been on anything resembling a date before, and now here I am, alone in my arcade, surrounded by snow and the Philadelphia evening, and everything is screaming "romantic" at me.

"The dinosaur ate my balls!" Whitney shouts, and I glance up. She's in front of the *Jurassic Park* cabinet, laughing. She turns and looks at me, her blue eyes sparkling. "That was hilarious. I'm maybe starting to get it." She looks to the left and right, like she's crossing the street, and I hear her humming, making a decision.

My phone buzzes.

MOM

Adam? Can I get an update?

Oh shoot. I completely forgot, and it's nearly 9:00 p.m.

ME

Hey, sorry. Still killing time until the snow dies down.

MOM

Whew. Okay good. I didn't want you trying to take the train back or trudging across downtown.

MOM

Although I hear the surge pricing is outrageous? If you have to put it on my credit card, just do it. Having you home safe is more important.

MOM

Keep me posted. Love you.

ME

Love you too. I will.

"Adam!"

I glance up and Whitney is in front of the Super Mario Bros. pinball game, beckoning me to come over.

"Why don't you hit one flipper and I'll hit the other?" she asks, standing off to the side. "It could be fun!"

I can't stop the smile on my face and look back down at my phone.

I walk toward Whitney and flick a quarter her way. She reaches out, snatching it out of the air with the most wildly satisfying chime.

Rideshares can wait.

The storm outside stands no chance against the one brewing inside my chest.

As I make my way over, her phone buzzes on the pinball machine. She does a double take before abandoning the game, and looks up at me, eyes wide, a smile on her face.

"I got one!" she shouts.

"Got...what?" I ask, now next to her, the glow of the phone lighting up her face.

"A rideshare." She hurries over to the snack bar, grabbing her backpack, and hustles toward the workshop. She darts in and out and starts cramming a bundle of her clothes into her pack, before slowing down and looking up at me.

"Well?" she says, gesturing around. "Get your stuff!"

"Oh!" I exclaim and gather my things. There's some movement in front of the arcade, the first I've seen in what feels like an hour, and a car's headlights illuminate the still-snowy evening.

"That's them!" she says, and rushes toward the front door. She pulls at it.

And pulls.

And pulls.

"Adam!" she calls me over and I join her in wrestling

against the door. But it absolutely isn't moving. I glance through the window at the snow piled up in front, but it's not even that much. "What is going on?" She rattles the door, but it holds firm.

I look back at the workshop door, left ajar, and curse under my breath.

"I think maybe we're stuck in here." I go to grab my crowbar from the workshop and look at the edges of the door, but there's just nowhere to get that thing in.

"Stuck," she says. "As in trapped."

The rideshare blares their horn, and Whitney calls them.

"Hey, we're here, just a minute."

She fights with the door some more, and I join her, but absolutely nothing is happening. The rideshare beeps again, flashing their lights, and calls Whitney back.

"The door out here to our building is stuck. Can you hop out and pull? Hello? Hello?"

The sound of tires fighting against snow fills my ears as the rideshare driver outside takes off, his lights disappearing down the block.

"Fuck!" Whitney yells. "I would have left a huge tip, you asshole!" she yells at the window, and I have to fight to not laugh. She spins around and sees my face. "Something about this funny?"

"I mean…" I grin and shrug. "That was some real 'don't you know who I am' energy right there, Whit."

She glares at me, and a smile creeps over her face.

And then the power goes out.

"Oh no," I sigh, turning on my phone's flashlight. Whitney does the same, and we're waving them around. "Look at the street."

A few emergency lights on the streetlamps flicker on, but the entire neighborhood looks washed in darkness. Snow keeps falling through the bright white emergency lights, making the whole thing look like some kind of black-and-white movie that I just don't want to be in right now.

"What do we do?" Whitney groans. She starts swiping at something on her phone and then shakes it. "Rideshares aren't operating in the area anymore. Period."

"Do we…call 911?" I ask.

"For a stuck door?" Whitney scoffs. "No one is coming to get us out of here with a stuck door."

"I mean, you could just tell them who you are," I suggest.

"Oh, my God, Adam, I hate you." She swats at me and sits down on the floor a few feet away from the door, digging in her bag. I aim my phone's light at her, and she digs out a couple black square bricks, cords dangling from them. She gives them a shake, little LEDs on them lighting up green in small bars.

"What's all that?" I ask, sitting down near her.

"Portable batteries for my phone," she huffs. "I carry them around for the work with my dad, in case my phone dies, which it does all the time. I've got three full charges here, and all of these can charge a phone fully at least two or three times." She holds one out to me, the USB wire hanging from it. I take it.

"What now?" I ask.

"You tell me." She shrugs, her eyes looking around in the dark. "Have any candles? Flashlights? Lanterns?"

I laugh and shake my head before an idea strikes me, and I fumble my way into the workshop. I come back out with a headlamp on, which I've used a few times to look at parts and pieces of machines while they were still inside the machine, where it's fairly dark.

"What do you think?" I shrug, grinning.

"Maybe...put it on your arm so you don't look like a miner, and so you aren't blasting a halogen light in my face."

"Fair enough." I nod, stepping back into the arcade. I shine the light over on Coco, who is snoozing nice and cozy in Mom's hoodie still. "All right, I don't think The Book Trader folks are coming back tonight." I take out my phone and swipe over to Twitter. "I better let them know that..."

I squint at the screen. At the timeline.

No way.

"What is it?" Whitney asks, fumbling for her own phone. "Is everything... What?"

She darts by me and presses her hands against the glass of the arcade's front windows. I walk toward her, looking through the timeline.

Brave New Worlds:
So, uh...is anyone else stuck here? I'm sure as hell not walking home to Fishtown in this.

National Mechanics:
Oh, wow someone else is here? I thought it was just us and the Meritage crew.

Meritage:
Hey Brave New Worlds!

Revolution House:
Hey! Some of us are still here too.

Kale Yeah:
Us too!

National Mechanics:
Booooo.

Kale Yeah:
Shut up.

National Mechanics:
If you're in Old City, the VIP Old City Festival begins tonight! Right now! We're dragging our heat lamps into the middle of Market Street between Second and Third. Join us, Brave New Worlds, Meritage, Revolution House, and… Kale Yeah.

Kale Yeah:
Goddammit Jon.

"This is amazing," I say, glancing over at her. She's squinting through the frosted glass, and I wipe away at the condensation on our side. The snow's stopped a little, there's still a lot of flurries, but it doesn't really look like a terrible storm anymore.

And I can see them, down the block, a bunch of people dragging huge heat lamps out into the road.

"Is there another way to get out of here?" Whitney asks, looking at the frozen-shut front door.

"Maybe." I glance back at Mom's office. "Come on."

I push open Mom's office door, and the crappy, warped wooden windows are still rattling a little from the wind outside. I push Dad's old desk against the wall, the metal feet squealing against the floor. Whitney hurries over and helps with the final shove, and I climb up on it, and battle with the painted-over lock above the window frame.

I grit my teeth and strain until the little metal latch snaps to the side with a crack, paint chips scattering down to the sill. I hop down and wrestle with the window, lifting from one side to the other, shifting it back and forth, a little bit at a time.

Until it opens with a loud snap.

Sending bits of glass and splintered wood everywhere.

"Oh fuck!" Whitney laughs, jumping back. Wind rushes into the office, and I wince against it. I search my hands, thankfully shardless, and use the sleeve of my jacket to brush bits of glass and wood off the desk and from off the sill.

"Well," I huff. "I guess we've got our way out?"

"Wait," Whitney says, and darts back into the arcade. I hop off the desk and shove it to the side and move some of my mom's papers from off it and into the drawers. If snow and wind are gonna rush in here, I don't want anything getting ruined. Everything else is in containers and plastic folders and looks pretty safe.

After a lot of clattering around, she comes back, some plastic bags in her hands. They look like freezer bags from the...

"Are those the fries and chicken fingers from under the snack bar?" I laugh, pointing at her.

"Listen, your freezer is out, and apparently—" she waves her phone at me "—the National Mechanics crew are planning to bring a grill outside."

"Well." I nod. "No sense letting them go to waste."

"Agreed." She walks over toward the window and looks back at me, smiling with a playful little glint in her eye. "This is going to be terrible."

CHAPTER 16
Whitney

I've got a freezer bag full of fried snacks slung over my shoulder like a burglar lugging a sack full of cash in a cartoon, my former best friend turned social media nemesis turned friend again turned…into something…following me, and there's a trash can on fire in the middle of Market Street.

Not quite how I planned the evening to run its course, but here we are.

"Adam!" shouts someone next to the big metal trash can, as they throw a bundle of newspaper inside. It goes up with a whoosh, sending flaming bits of paper into the sky, little embers fluttering around in the flurry-filled evening. There is a good dozen or so people out here, with three wildly warm heat lamps surrounding the outskirts of the little crowd. Something tells me they can't be terribly close to the barrel on fire.

Might be the propane tanks.

"Hey, Brian!" Adam shouts, walking right up to the flaming barrel. He holds his hands out, warming them by the fire, and I inch my way closer to him. "This is Whitney."

Brian, a slightly older bearded guy wearing a thick pea-coat, sizes me up really quick and squints at me before turning back to Adam.

"Is that—?"

"Be nice," Adam interrupts, and Brian crosses his arms, frowning at me.

"I brought chicken fingers!" I exclaim, holding out the bag. "Also fries!"

Brian stares at me as though considering whether or not this will gain me entry into this exclusive club of people setting newspaper on fire in the middle of a normally busy but currently snowed over downtown street. He ducks behind the barrel for a moment and pops back up with a grate, and plops it over the thing, sending a few more embers up into the night.

"All right, Philly eSports," he says, a little grin cracking his tough face. I let out a snort of a laugh and roll my eyes. "You can stay."

"I brought lights!" someone shouts, and I turn to spot some women stringing twinkle lights around the heat lamps, attaching them to all three, surrounding us in a triangle of lovely, but wildly unsafe, warm light. I feel like you're not even supposed to lean against or touch those heat lamps you see outside restaurants, never mind string plastic lights from them?

I glance at Adam, who is staring at them with a similar expression of both shock and horror. He catches me looking and shrugs.

"We won't be out here long," he says.

"No kidding," I scoff. "It's probably gonna explode."

A few more people make their way over to the...well, whatever this is. Street bonfire? Mini festival? I feel like I vaguely recognize a handful of people from social media and the neighborhood, and Adam's face just lights up with every new person who pops by. Someone starts passing around a massive growler full of something that smells sharply of whiskey, filling up plastic cups and palmed hands.

I take a few photos, the flames from the can casting a soft orange glow across the snow and into the evening, the warm twinkle lights looking like fireflies.

MOM

Still doing all right? I really wish we would have taken you home with us.

ME

It's okay! We're fine, there's food and a fire.

MOM

A fire?

I laugh and send her some of the photos before she has a total meltdown and move to post a few on social media... when I realize broadcasting the neighborhood has a fire in the middle of the street might be a bad look for everyone here. Including my mom. This is her festival and all.

"Anyone have some music?" someone shouts. I think about the Bluetooth speakers I'd left at Patrick's and wonder for a moment what he'll do with them. I wonder if Carlos held on to them. It sure would be nice to have one of them here. I look at Adam, who has his hands buried in his pockets now.

"You don't have any—" I point at his jacket "—you know, *you* music?"

"They would not appreciate those tunes." He grins. "Not as much as you do, you know."

I laugh and bend down to rip open the bags of chicken, and shake them down on top of the grate covering the barrel. They clatter and bang against the metal, like I'm dropping rocks on the thing, and I laugh as I turn to Adam, who just shrugs.

"What are you feeding people down there?" I nudge them around on top of the grate, and Brian takes over with a nod, a pair of tongs in his hand seemingly out of nowhere. A few more pieces of food get thrown onto the grate. Burgers. Sausages. There are some buns he starts placing gently along the edge.

The wind whips and smells like snow and a campfire, roasting meat and whiskey.

I take a step back from the fire as smoke wisps in front of my eyes, and an arm reaches out around me.

I look sharply to my side, and it's Adam. A can of Dr. Pepper in his hand. He smiles and squeezes me close, handing the can to me. I take a sip and the soda is so cold it feels like it's freezing as I swallow it. But my chest feels so warm.

"Where'd you even get that?" I ask, leaning my head on his shoulder, watching the fire in the barrel.

"Someone from that coworking space up the street brought a backpack full of soda and huge container of coffee." I hand the can back to him, and he toasts it at someone across from us. "Thanks, Alex!"

"You're welcome!"

Music abruptly booms, startling me more than a bit, and

I laugh, leaning back into Adam. It's some Imagine Dragons song, eliciting groans from some and cheers from others, and it almost feels like Patrick's house again. It's funny that my mind keeps wandering there, but happily settling right back here. From a party I thought I belonged at, to a person I...

Feel I belong with.

"Whoa," Adam says, looking up. "Whoa, whoa, whoa..."

I look out to where he's focusing, and a pair of beaming headlights are pushing through the snow.

"Car," Adam says, and then gets a little more frantic. "Car!"

The crowd around the lights and heat lamps scatters a bit as the headlights get closer and thankfully, peel off to the side, pulling up along the setup. It's a pretty sizable SUV, and when the driver's door swings open, everyone around us cheers.

"Dev!" an array of voices shouts, and a woman steps out, her eyes wide and concerned. She looks around at everyone.

"What are you idiots doing?" she scoffs, looking at the lamps and lights. "Jesus, you're all gonna get yourself caught on fire." She sets her eyes down the block, and then looks at everyone again. "Anyone have a decent flashlight? I have to get my dog."

Dog.

Dog!

"Adam, is that the bookseller?" I ask, nudging his jacket.

"Yes!" he says, rubbing his hands together, the two of us walking back toward the lamps and the fire. "Dev!" he shouts, motioning her over. "Don't worry, I've got Coco. She's in the arcade. Your door broke and we took her in out of the snow."

"My door what?" she snaps. "Goddammit." And then suddenly its like she's seeing the two of us for the first time.

"What are you kids doing out here? Jesus. Adam, where's your mother? Who is this?"

"Don't worry, she knows we're here. We're gonna call a rideshare any minute. Snow's died down."

"A rideshare, right," Dev scoffs. "You think I would have driven to the hardware depot in South Philly for snow supplies if I could have gotten a rideshare? After I salt my sidewalk, I'll drive you home. Let's go get Coco."

She powers ahead of us through the snow, and we both follow after her. The warmth from the fire and the heat lamps the second we get more than a few feet away is just so noticeably gone, and I'm struck by just how horribly cold it really is out here. More wind picks up, sending frozen clumps of snow against my neck and cheeks and face. It's terrible.

And then something grabs me.

I shirk away a little, and then realize it's Adam.

Holding my hand.

"Sorry," he mutters, letting go. "I, um…don't want you to fall…" He trails off.

I reach back out and grab his hand. He looks at me, his face contorting to hold back a smile. The arcade quickly comes into view, but really not quick enough in this cold, and we duck down an alley near the SEPTA stop with Dev.

"Wait, don't you want to check on the bookstore?" Adam says, slowing down.

"My baby first," Dev says, walking ahead. Adam nods, and we keep going.

The broken window looms ahead, and Adam jumps right up the wall and through it. I hear Coco barking, growing louder and louder as he gets closer to us, and he peers out, handing Coco over, bundled up in that hoodie.

"Just drop off the hoodie whenever," Adam says from the window. Dev scowls at it.

"Are you sure I shouldn't just burn it on my way out?" she asks, looking up the alley. Her dog is squirming around, nuzzling her face. "I mean, they have a barrel on fire."

"Kind of you, but it's my mom's," Adam laughs.

"Right." Dev nods. "All right, well, come on. Let's go."

Adam pauses for a minute, looking back into the arcade, and then back at the two of us.

"You know," Adam says, wringing his hands, rubbing them together, "with the window broken, and the front door frozen..." He shakes his head. "Honestly, I think I'm just gonna stay here tonight."

"What?" Dev scoffs. "You'll freeze."

"I have blankets," he says, and I wonder if he's lying. "Don't worry." He looks down at the bundle of dog, and back up at Dev. "Don't you want to hang back, maybe take care of the bookstore?"

"Psh." She waves her hand. "Most of the stuff in the front are quarter paperbacks that no one is going to buy, anyway. I can take care of it tomorrow." She bobs her dog up and down in her arms. "It's not the place that matters. It's who you share it with. And I got my number one right here."

There's a pause, a little beat in the air. I could swear Adam mutters a "huh" as the dog licks Dev's face.

"But you know," Adam says, clearing his throat and turning toward me, "if you're heading up toward West Philadelphia, maybe you could take—"

"I'm staying, too."

The words just rush out of my mouth before I can get them

back in. What am I doing? There's a ride. I can get home, out of the cold. Out of this jean jacket that's doing nothing for me.

But there's this boy. Who...is doing something for me?

Oh no.

Whitney. What are you doing?

It's dark.

It's getting late.

And there's only the one emergency blanket.

Of course.

Part of me wonders if people who put those first-aid kits together read too many of those hilarious Christina Lauren rom-com novels, just hoping for this level of awkwardness. That the blanket was just a wink, compressed into blanket form. I suppose the makers of the kits couldn't have known that I'd get stuck here at the arcade, but still. Somehow. Somehow, they did this.

And I guess I'm really crashing here.

I fire off a quick text to both Dad and Mom, to let them know I'm staying and that we're fine, following Adam's lead. Dad doesn't respond, but Mom chimes in almost immediately.

MOM

I'd say keep the door open, but there's a snowstorm outside.

Jesus, Mom.

MOM

So what's the plan? Now that the snow is calming down?

I stare at the message for a beat, and then up at Adam. I worry at my lip a little with my teeth, chapped and dried from the cold and the wind. Getting home would be nice. It would be warm, and if Mom somehow figured out how to get me and whisk me off to Manayunk, she's got that hot tub in the yard. I feel my back relax just at the thought of it.

But I want to be here. I want to see this through. And if she thinks I'm staying here solo with Adam, it's not going to happen. Her or Dad will find a way.

ME

We're staying with Chris.

ME

He's just over in Queen Village, we're gonna walk there together.

MOM

Hmm, okay, be careful and text me updates.

Perfect.

I smile and glance up, looking at the snack bar. The little cactus is out of my backpack, sitting there nice and cozy. Adam is fussing with something on the other side of the arcade and glances over, smiling at me with a little wave. He grabs one of the portable batteries and checks the charge, a little white light lighting up his face.

I'll be stunned if Old City has power tomorrow.

There's a little nook over by the workshop space, where the red door meets the edge of another wall, that looks like it could be potentially cozy.

I dig around in my backpack. My clothes, still pretty damp, are in there, and I roll them up into a ball for a pillow. Everything else inside, paperbacks and various gadgets, aren't really going to work, no matter how much I fluff the backpack full of tools. I get myself settled into the corner and pull the blanket up over me, a tent of silver all around me. My phone's flashlight reflects it right back into my eyes, so I shut it off.

I wonder about Mom, up in Manayunk, that wildly hill-filled neighborhood that would be an absolute joy coated in snow. Dad's probably hired someone to dig out his house by now, or discovered some ridiculous new startup company making snow-powered robots that'll clear the walkway only to stop functioning because there's no more snow.

I pull out my phone, lighting up the space inside the poncho. Still zero texts from Dad, despite all my attempts at messaging him.

MOM

If you need to burn the cactus for warmth, please do.

MOM

Okay but don't. Find something else.

MOM

I'm so worried.

MOM

About both of you.

MOM

The cactus and you. Adam'll be fine.

MOM

Okay I need to stop.

I smile and let her know I'm fine, but really, my chest is a knot of stress. No messages from Dad. At least the sitter has been responsive.

LEANDRA

Hey, any idea when your dad is coming back?

LEANDRA

I'm fine staying here and watching Lily, I mean, I can't go anywhere.

LEANDRA

But it's gonna cost extra. And your dad is being a real dick not messaging me back. Your brother's here but won't watch Lily, says I'm being paid so I might as well stay. I'm...not sure how much more I can take of this guy.

I snort out a laugh at the mention of Nick, because yes, not a surprise. But Dad should at least be messaging her back. I hope she charges him extra.

Where is he, and what's so important that he's ignoring all of us during a damn blizzard?

"Hey."

I jump a little, dropping my phone and fluttering my orange blanket tent. A shadow looms over the outside, and I peek through.

Adam tilts his head, peering at me back, a bemused look on his face. He's wearing that jacket again, and is shivering a little bit, puffs of cold air floating out with each breath.

"You okay in there?" he asks, smirking.

"Are you okay in there?" I ask, laughing at the jacket.

"Shut up," he laughs. "It'll do."

"I'm fine." I grab my jean jacket, covering myself a little bit, but it does absolutely nothing. The cold air hasn't done much for drying out anything that got soaked from the snow, and it's still damp. "It's just cold—"

"Here, let me, um…" He slides his leather jacket off and hands it to me. "You should take it."

He grits his teeth, and I can tell he's trying his best not to start shivering. He's got that sweatshirt back on, covered in grime and oil from moving more of those machines around, and it still looks pretty wet from the snow and sweat.

"You know, you're really gonna have to explain to me who that is," I say, nodding at his shirt.

"What?" he asks, his teeth chattering a little. Yup. Definitely cold. "Oh. Yeah, here…take my jacket—"

"Nope, first your shirt."

He looks down at his shirt and laughs.

"You really don't know who REO Speedwagon is?" he scoffs. "I can't fight this feeling anymore."

My heart quickens.

"W-what?" I ask.

"It's a song," he says.

Oh.

"My dad loved them, but it was really my uncle Tom who was *obsessed*. They sing that song 'Keep on Loving You…'"

He reaches into his pocket, slinging his coat over his shoulder. "Here..." He pulls out his phone and fusses a bit with it, his body shaking from the cold. He holds it out, some music playing from the weak speakers.

I look up at him and shrug.

"I don't know who—" I start.

"Here, hold on." He takes a step toward me and holds it up, but it still isn't quite clear. "Do you hear—?"

"Just...get in here," I grumble, lifting up the blanket, a gust of cold billowing in.

"Oh, um, yeah, okay," he stammers out and sits down next to me. I pull the blanket back up and over us. He's gone dark, his face lit up a little by his phone, the silver of the interior glinting like a metal awning in the sun. Both him and his shirt smell like cedar and oil and sweat, and he skootches closer to me, his phone out. He must see me scowl at it because he laughs. "Yes, I know, it's like eight years old but I don't really use it for anything other than texts and music."

"And snarky social media posts," I add.

"I've changed." He smiles.

"Sure you have," I snort.

"You don't just give up on something 'cause it's old and out-of-date, you know?" He shrugs, flipping through the music. "My parents gave me this in...wow, seventh grade, I think? Feels like a part of me."

I stare at him for a beat, trying to figure him out.

"What?" he asks, catching me.

"Nothing." I shrug. "It's sweet. Weird. But sweet."

"All right, plant girl." He smirks. "I'm surprised that cactus isn't in here, getting a good snuggle." He hits Play, the song playing through the tinny speakers of the aging smart-phone. Some guy with a high voice and a piano plinks in the background, and I'm starting to think that every band Adam likes has some kind of keyboard or synthesizer in the beginning of every song.

I glance at his shirt.

"All right, so REO Speedwagon." I nod.

"Yep."

"Why is it every band from that era is some kind of a vehicle?" I ask, looking up at him. His eyebrows quirk up, surprised, and he looks over at me, his face lit up by the screen of the phone. "Is every band you listen to potentially some sort of boat?"

"What?" he laughs. "What are you talking—?"

"I mean, I don't know many of them, but aren't there like ten bands with Starship in the name? Or Jefferson something?"

He barks out a laugh.

"Jefferson Starship, Jefferson Airplane, Starship…" He chuckles. "Yeah, it's a bit confusing. My dad swore off Starship in here. I think there was a pinball game named after them, too, but it just kept playing that 'We Built This City' song again and again—"

"Wait, I know that song! It's awful!" I laugh. "It's in that *Rock of Ages* movie. Or musical. Whichever."

"Wow, you've actually seen that?" he asks, awed. "That was like, *the* movie for my dad. My mom hated it, but anytime it was on, he had to watch it."

He shakes his head and looks down in his lap, the phone

clutched in his hands, and even though he's staring down...
it looks like he's staring far away.

"You know, I'm actually reading this book that's a terrible,
terrible play on words when it comes to that band and song."
He sighs, shaking his head.

"Oh?"

We Built This Gritty?" he says, wincing. "It's this entre-
preneurial book about starting and running a small business,
and it's interesting and the guy lives here, but... I don't know.
Something about it isn't hitting the way I think it should."

"Did something change?" I ask. He nudges a little closer
to me, and a bit of heat rises to my cheeks.

"Maybe." He exhales. "But like... I'm thinking about the
bookshop owner and that dog now." He looks at me before
biting his lip and looking down into his hands. "She said it's
not the place, but who you share it with." His eyes are looking at something...not here. He's got this faraway look on his
face. "You said the same thing, and it's really sticking with
me. Like the snow outside, in your hair."

He glances back at me.

"Does that sound...ridiculous?"

"No, not at all." I shake my head. "Though, I really wish
I had one of Chris's Swedish Fish right now." I laugh a little,
and so does he. "I think they're across the arcade and it's...
pretty warm in here."

"Yeah." He smiles, shifting his phone light around. There's
a bit of quiet in the air now, and it feels like he's done talking
about the arcade and how he feels about maybe not having it
be in his life. I don't want to keep pushing it.

"It's...it sure is dark in here. No chance of emergency
night-lights or something in that workshop of yours?" I ask.

Adam sits up, turns at me, smiling.

"Just a second." He beams and scurries out from under the blanket. I peer out and watch him disappear into his workshop. When the door opens back up with a loud groan, his hands are covered in small lights. Just...rainbows of color, beaming from his hands. He looks up at me, the light reflecting off his skin, smiling like wild.

"What is that?" I ask, baffled.

"They're called throwies." He sits back down next to me and dumps a bundle in my unsuspecting hands. I grab a bunch, a few others scattering into my lap. "Just watch."

He grabs one and throws it up at the ceiling, and with a *plink*, it sticks up there.

"Rare-earth magnets, plus LED bulbs with batteries... equals night-lights." He nudged against me, his shoulder brushing mine. "Go ahead."

"How will you get them down?" I ask.

"That's for me to worry about in the New Year." He laughs, throwing another. A green one. *Plink.*

I start throwing mine. Red. Yellow. Blue. Green. Purple.

Plink.

Plink.

Plink.

Plink.

Plink.

By the time we're done, the ceiling above us is coated in the small multicolored lights, like small stars. The sort you'd have in your room as a really little kid, only in this case, they're battery powered, and a dozen different colors.

The moment is like a bag of Skittles. Colorful, and just as sweet.

He looks up, just as the screen on his phone blinks out, his face going from being washed in the pale glow of the smartphone to being gently lit by the orange hue of the blanket and the rainbow of lights above us, and whatever bit of light is still pulsing in from the emergency lights in the street. He looks back to me, his mouth opens just a little, like he wants to say something, but isn't sure what.

"What is it?" I ask.

"I just…" He swallows and bites at his lip. "I've never…" he huffs. "Whatever is happening here or was happening—" he points at me and then to himself, shaking his head "—with us. That's what I want. *This* is what I want."

"Adam—" I start.

"You," he presses, moving closer to me, inching across the floor, the orange blanket around us, his jacket in my lap. "In the middle of the snowstorm, sitting here in the dark. You're what I want. It's the people. The person. Not the place." He lifts up his hand toward my face and moves to place it on my cheek, but hesitates, jerking his hand back. "Can…can I?"

"Yes," I exhale out.

His hand is back on my face, cupping my cheek, and I reach out and grab his free one, and he moves toward me. His eyes shut, but I can feel him shaking.

"Are you…?" I stop him. "Are you cold? Do you want—?"

"I've never done this before," he whispers out, looking away.

"Never done—"

"I've never kissed anyone." He looks down at our intertwined hands, now grabbing my lone hand with both of his. He squeezes. "I…never really dated. I've always been so busy with school and this place and…" He sighs, but then it turns into something more. His lip quivers and he inhales sharply. "You're right. You're right about me."

He looks right at me, and even in the fading light, I can see those light brown eyes of his are glassy with tears.

"I've never made time for what I really want."

"Adam—"

"I want to change that," he says, clearing his throat, sniffling. "I want to make time for what I want. For who I want."

"Shh," I whisper, and reach my hands up to his face. I touch his cheeks with my fingertips, his skin wet with tears. "We'll make that time. You and me. Together."

And I kiss him.

Old City Pinball:

Hey all! We're closed, but some of us are er...stuck in here weathering out the storm? So, stick with us for some fun videos and photos of our rarest machines.

> **West Philly eSports:**
> We're here too! It's a big party!

> **SmakParlour:**
> Wait what?! Are you snowed in, in Old City? Are you both still inside the arcade? You should have let us drive you home!

> **Franklin Fountain:**
> Stay safe.

> **AKA Music:**
> Who is this posting? Is this Chris? Adam?

> **Old City Pinball:**
> We are! We're okay. We'll keep posting. We've got blankets and heat and chargers galore to keep our phones going.

Old City Pinball:
We're running a special! All games are free! Come on down! LOL. You can't! There's no power. Stay inside.

Krumm's Boutique:
Why are you still there?

Krumm's Boutique:
I'm seeing all the photos of you two in the arcade. I thought you were staying at Chris's house.

Krumm's Boutique:
Adam. What is going on.

Franklin Fountain:
(pulls up a seat, eats popcorn)

Brave New Worlds:
Please pass the popcorn.

Krumm's Boutique:
Shut up, both of you.

Philly WHYY: Hey there, Old City Pinball. Can we post some of your photos and videos here, to our readership online? We'll make sure we credit you.

Old City Pinball: If you Venmo me a few dollars so we can rent some movies on our phones, you've got a deal.

Philly WHYY: Heh. That can be arranged. What's your username?

Chris Makes Stuff: Your MOM won't stop texting and DM-ing why did you pull me into this mess?

CHAPTER 17
Adam

"Depending on when you're reading this, the pinball industry is in an interesting state these days. There are fewer and fewer manufacturers; a lot of the industry is relying on the pop culture tie-in of movies and television shows. I'm not sure where it's going, or where it'll be. But like all passion projects, if you want it to thrive, you need to support it. Remember. Show up for what you love. For *who* you love. Or no one else will."

–THE ART AND ZEN OF PINBALL REPAIR
BY JAMES WATTS

I wake up with a start, and an arm around me that isn't my own.
Oh, my God.

Whitney nestles into my neck, leaning over my chest. We're snuggled up inside the bright orange poncho she unfurled from the workshop's first-aid kit, using our jackets as comforters. It's almost *too* hot inside here, and I...do not smell great. I lean my head a little closer to hers, and she still smells of vanilla and strawberries and oh, my God. I kissed a girl last night.

We kissed a lot.

I pat around on the ground and around us, feeling for my phone, and finally find the little rectangle off to the side a bit. A few of the throwies are scattered about us, tiny little lights glimmering, and up on the ceiling, most of them remain. I grab my phone, flick it on. The battery is pretty low, but thanks to all the chargers and cords Whitney had in her bag, I'm not terribly worried. The notifications are all over the place, including some calls and texts from Mom.

MOM

Hey, morning. I need an update please.

MOM

Are you and everyone else doing okay? I've been so worried.

MOM

Is Chris there with you? Is it just you?

MOM

Adam?

MOM

EXCUSE ME WHITNEY IS THERE?

MOM

WHITNEY'S MOM JUST CALLED ME.

MOM

JUST YOU TWO ALONE OVER NIGHT IN THE
ARCADE?

MOM

ADAM ANSWER ME.

Oh no.

I look at the time and the timestamp from my mom's messages, and she definitely sent that last one an hour ago. I slept in a little longer than usual. It's not like I have to open this place or come do repairs or any of the other things Chris and I would be doing over the holidays. Or what I'd be doing here with Dad during that time.

I glance over at Whitney, who lets out a little snore that sounds awfully a lot like the snorting laugh she has. I smile, a warmth pulsing through my chest, and tuck a strand of her thick, curly black hair behind her ear. She moans a little, her eyes tightening, and falls right back into the deep sleep she was in.

ME

Hey, we're okay! Sorry, was sleeping.

ME

Yeah Whitney just crashed in the arcade.

ME

Should be home later.

ME

What's going on over there?

MOM

Nice try burying the lede. We're going to have a conversation.

MOM

Is it JUST you and Whitney?

I feel like I'm about to start sweating.

ME

Yes?

MOM

ADAM.

"Are you texting your other girlfriend?"

I drop my phone on my face, the plastic brick clattering against my nose and teeth.

"I'm just saying," Whitney says, rolling over onto her side to look at me. "If you've got someone else in another emergency-blanket-tent, jacket-for-a-sleeping-bag, you should be honest with me."

"No, just...telling my mom we're okay." I reach out again, fussing with her hair, the kind of thing I've seen in endless movies and television shows, in *Riverdale* like three dozen times, and thought about doing. "Your mom saw our social media posts and maybe called her? Perhaps we got a little... overeager last night."

"Sure did." She smirks.

"With our social media posts!" I sputter out.

"Oh psh," Whitney scoffs, waving me off. "My mom doesn't actually care."

But...

Girlfriend?

If I could blush, I think I would.

"So...are you two awake?"

A voice interrupts the two of us and Whitney jumps back. I flip the blanket down, and there's Chris, hands on his hips, grinning at the two of us.

"How did..." I stammer and look over at the door. I sit up straight, gasping.

Not only are there are a ton of people walking around on Second Street, but there's also a significant line forming outside the arcade. They're lined up by the collapsed tent, hanging near the tarped pinball machines. A couple of shovels are leaning against the window by the door, and some of those large metal picks I've seen people use to break ice up along sidewalks.

"Oh, my God." I laugh. Whitney slowly sits up, peering out from the blanket.

"Whitney," Chris says, nodding.

"Chris." Whitney nods back.

"So I'm guessing the snowstorm is really over?" I ask.

Chris barks out a laugh.

"Come on." He reaches down, and I grab his hand, him hoisting me up. I glance down at Whitney and help her up, and when she gets to her feet, I pull her into my arms. She lets out a little squeak and kisses my nose.

"Great," Chris grumbles, and then squints at the floor. He

bends down, picking up one of the throwies, and slowly looks up at all the little lights glowing on the ceiling.

"Goddammit." He glares at me. "*You* are figuring out how to get those down." He walks toward the front door and turns to look at me. "Dude, there's a line. Come on."

"Yeah, yeah." I nod, looking around the arcade. "Just a second."

I dart toward the back, where it just gets progressively colder the closer I get toward Mom's office. I pull the door open, which screeches against the floor, and it's not as bad I thought it might be. There's a bit of snow left, but it's mostly just wet in here. I wipe some puddles off the desk and scan the floor for broken glass and wood shards. I think last night made it feel way worse than it actually was, and I nudge a few broken window pieces against the wall with my foot.

All right. Not bad, not bad.

I shove the door closed. Whitney and Chris are standing by the front door together now, arms crossed, looking uncomfortable. Like they're trying to pretend each other isn't right there. And it hits me that things are…fine, I guess, with me and Whitney now. Whatever they are. Whatever this is. But that doesn't erase the years of me grumbling about her to him. I've spent a lot of time coloring in her pages. It's not like that's just going to disappear.

I'm going to have to repair all that, to make this work.

Whatever this is.

"All right." I hurry over toward them. "I guess…let's do this?"

I reach out to the switches along the wall by the front door, and wincing, give them a flip.

And the arcade roars to life.

"Yes!" Whitney shouts, and Chris stares at her, his eyebrows furrowed. "Hey, do you think our clothes are dry?"

"Oh!" I walk over to the workshop and pull the door open, mercifully still open a crack from last night. Her outfit from yesterday, as well as my jeans and our socks, are crinkled and cracked when I pick them up off the heater. All that dirty water and sweat did not do them any favors, and I put them back down, away from the grate.

"Let's just, um…" I look back at the workshop. "Let's get them later. We don't want to carry those around."

"You know, I'm not even gonna ask," Chris grumbles. "Let's go."

The three of us step outside, and all of Old City is in a blanket of white.

Despite the news reports that were promising the end of the world, it doesn't look that bad, and the Old City Winter Festival is absolutely still on. In fact, it weirdly seems bigger than ever, with families making their way up and down the streets, bundled up in huge coats, little kids dragging behind them in small sleds. There aren't as many booths or tables set up in the snow, but from what I can tell as we step away from the arcade, it looks like most of the restaurants and boutiques have their doors wide-open. Maybe they're doing something inside?

"Wow, what happened?" I ask, eyeing up the line outside the arcade. People are rubbing their hands together, chatting amongst themselves.

"Well, if someone woke up early enough or answered their phone," Chris starts and smirks at Whitney. "You'd have gotten all the texts and emails and phone calls about the festival being back on." He nods at the fallen part of the tent. "What happened here?"

"Ugh," I groan. "I wanted to bring *Lost in Space* into the arcade and we ended up breaking the thing."

"No way," Chris bemoans. "That's too bad. Wasn't that a rare machine?"

"It's okay," I huff. "I feel like it's nothing I can't fix, and we managed to drag it to the back of the arcade."

"All right, good. Let's get this tent up and then you two can go wander around," Chris grumbles. I glance down the line of people waiting for games, and their eyes all look eager as we fuss with the knocked-out poles at the front of the tent near the door, wrestling to get it back up. A bunch of snow dumps out of the sides of the tent; the excited pinball players jump out of the way, laughing. It doesn't take too long.

"Are you going to pick another game to bring out here?" Whitney asks. "I can help carry it out."

"Will it go as well as the *Lost in Space* situation?" Chris asks, crossing his arms.

"Come on, there was a storm and wind and it was night-time," Whitney snips back. "Do you want anything? Maybe on our way back over here, I can grab you a coffee at Meritage?"

"That sounds great," Chris says, seemingly taking the peace offering, giving me a look. I walk toward her, taking her hand, and we rush across the street, our feet crunching in the thick, iced-over patches of snow covering the cobblestones. Down the other side of Second Street, I can see a handful of other shops with tables out, like AKA Music and Brave New Worlds. I wonder if Brian is there, and how he slept last night inside the shop. The Book Trader has their door propped open, and we slow down, peeking inside.

"That was cool of you," Whitney says, looking down at the broken door. "Stopping to wrap it up like that."

"Oh, I don't know." I shrug. "She'd have done the same for us." I don't see any sign of Dev or Coco in the shop, but a few of the other booksellers are milling around, sipping hot drinks and talking to people who are already inside. We keep going down the street, rounding by the SEPTA station, which looks closed. I wonder if all these people walked here.

It's like the entirety of Old City turned out.

Some of the girls at Smak Parlour are busy shoveling out their sidewalk, and someone is clearing out a parking space in front of the shop in the street. Sometimes they have this food truck converted into a fashion truck setup, and I wonder if they're planning to have it set up here, and also, how? There are people walking up and down the streets, but the snow is still heavy and stuck to the ground. Driving on this would not be the best idea. I love that fashion truck, though. I wouldn't mind seeing it down here, especially if this…

If this is gonna be my last festival.

Not that I wouldn't come back to wander around. I love this thing. The community, the joy in the air like snow. But the last one with the arcade.

Mixed in with the sounds of shoveling and people chatting, there's the squealing of children, sliding up and down the road. Garbage can lids, huge black trash bags, the lids of sandboxes…it looks like people grabbed whatever they could from their respective tiny city yards, and are hurtling themselves down Market and up onto Columbus.

It's not exactly *Snowpiercer* out here.

"Hey."

I look at Whitney, who smiles, squeezing my hand.

"This is nice," she says, exhaling a cloud of cold air. "I don't even feel that cold."

She nuzzles into my neck, and with my arm around her side, I hug her close, my heart fluttering in my chest.

Goddamn.

What a snowstorm.

"Whitney. Eleanor. Mitchell." A voice sounds out over the snow.

"Oh no," Whitney groans.

There's Whitney's mom, power walking across the snow. She's bundled up properly, a thick winter coat that masks all her features, but everything about the way she's moving, the way she's speaking, says Angry Mother. There's no mistaking it.

"I can explain," Whitney starts.

Whitney's mom marches over and throws her arms around her, nudging me away.

"You're so grounded," she says, and then throws an arm out to the side, grasping for me. I take a step over, and she gets a grip on my jacket collar, pulling me in. She lets go and looks at the both of us, before gazing up and down the street, toward her shop and back to the arcade. "You're lucky I've always liked him." She gives me a little push, and I laugh.

"Mom," Whitney groans.

"We'll talk about this more later." She takes a step back and looks at the two of us, sucking at her teeth. "We're going shopping for another jacket, right now. Adam, I have half a mind to make you come."

I smile and shake my head, and look over at Whitney, who is looking down at her jacket, seriously. She quickly takes it off. It's dirty from our time in the arcade, nearly off-white from all the fumbling around in the dark and brushing it against the floors and walls and being used as a blanket. Same as mine, really.

"Let's go," she says. She leans over and kisses me on the cheek. "I'll be right back. Meet you at the arcade?"

"Sure." I reach out, taking her hands, squeezing them.

"Jesus." Whitney's mom let's out a snort laugh, the same she has. "Maybe I really had better talk to your mom. Let's go."

The two of them walk inside Smak Parlour, and I move to hurry back toward Chris, when I remember we promised him something hot. I make my way up the street, passing the Old City Business District's small office front, which is surprisingly completely clear of snow. They're putting together some kind of small platform, and I wonder if they've got a band or something coming in later.

It's almost business as usual here, just with snow all over the place.

I make my way across the snow-covered street, weaving around some sledders and people just standing about sipping coffee, and round the corner up Third toward the café Chris loves so much. There's an unsurprising line, considering the amount of people out here and coffees that seem to be in everyone's hands, so I pull out my phone to kill some time and see just what the hell is going on.

National Mechanics:
It's on! We're getting shoveled out now, but will have all kinds of

snacks, treats, and drinks to serve around 11AM! And thanks to everyone who joined us last night, to keep our spirits up.

Brave New Worlds:
I'm still recovering from those "spirits" thanks.

National Mechanics:
Hey, be cool.

Old City Winter Festival:
Come on down, Old City! The snow stopped, vendors are rushing to get set up, and coffee is flowing.

Franklin Fountain:
We'll be open, serving all kinds of delicious ice cream flavored coffees!

Brave New Worlds:
We're open. Come get your comics? Also, we'll have select graphic novels up to 50% off, and a limited edition, signed Jadzia Axelrod print for the first 50 purchases!

Old City PAWS:
We'll be there with our booth, just a little late! Come meet all the pups and cats we have up for adoption, including Gracie, Lola, Baxter, Auggie, and Diva, five snuggly senior dogs excited to get out of the snow and into your hearts!

The Book Trader:
Get your dollar paperbacks! We're having a "wet book" special. Is the book a little damp? Take it for free with a purchase. Or just take it, I don't know. Shout out to Old City Pinball for helping secure the shop during the storm, and for taking care of our most important bookseller, Coco!

Old City Pinball:
No problem. Give her a snuggle from me.

I can't stop smiling, and finish replying to a few posts just as I reach the front of the line at Meritage. I get an extra-large hot chocolate and start to make my way back toward Market. The owner of Omoi is outside, getting a table ready, and waves to me, a delightful pile of stationery already collected outside. Looks to be a few discounted books out there, too, and I make a note to come back here and pick up a few for Whitney.

The bars out here look pretty quiet, and I'm not sure if any of them are going to open for this thing. I walk along-side them, an Irish pub that's changed hands and names more times than I can remember, where my uncle Colin and Aunt Lisa met on their first date. There's the Malt and our Stars, an ice cream shop with a name way too close to a John Green novel, and there's sign of life inside. I wonder what they've got planned. Last year they handed out mini milkshake shots, and it was amazing. Chris and I took turns coming back, wearing different outfits, throughout the day, only for them to bust our chops on social media with a bunch of photos of us in different clothes.

Well played, malt shop. I go to look up what they might be up to, and spot something else at the top of my feed.

West Philly eSports:
Stay tuned, Old City Winter Festival! We'll be making an appearance with a special announcement shortly!

I squint at the tweet. Announcement? What's Whitney up to?

I reach the corner, and in the time I spent in line and on my phone, a few more tables have propped up along the sidewalk.

A popular pizza place and cheesesteak joint look like they've basically shoveled themselves out, and are getting something set up, which excites me more than I'd like to admit. The cheesesteak place makes some of the best mozzarella sticks downtown, which is weird to say considering there's a pizza place right there, but it is what it is. I'm already daydreaming of a paper cup with fried cheese inside, and sharing that bouquet with Whitney.

Does she even like mozzarella sticks?

Who doesn't?

I step off the curb and onto the snowed-over Market Street, and the roar of what sounds like a motorcycle nearly sends me to the ground. I manage to stop myself from falling over, and miraculously avoid spilling piping-hot hot chocolate all down my neck, and look around for the source, just as a snowmobile rockets down Market.

People hurry out of the way, and it stops just short of the Old City District building, and the little platform they've got set up. A few curious people make their way over there, and I realize there are two people on the snowmobile.

Who...who even has a snowmobile in Philadelphia? Where would you take it? Where would you drive it? I join the milling crowd and look around for Whitney and her mom, when the two people on the snowmobile get off and remove their helmets.

And while I don't see Whitney's mom anywhere.

I see mine.

And she's with Whitney's dad.

CHAPTER 18
Whitney

I follow my mom out of Smak Parlour, a new thick blue-and-white peacoat warming me all over, my white jacket crammed in my backpack…and I'm wildly confused at the scene unfolding.

What is Dad doing here, on a snowmobile?

Why is Adam's mom with him?

And what is he doing getting onto a makeshift stage in front of the business district's office?

"Mom?" I venture. "What's going on?"

"I'm as confused as you are, dear," she says, walking toward the stage. Adam's mom puts her helmet down on the stage, and her face is alight. Laughing. She turns and sees me and Mom walking toward her, and rushes over.

"Ah!" she shouts, her arms out, pulling us both into a hug. "Hey, you two. You setting up something special in the boutique? Where's…" She looks around. "Where's Adam?"

"He ran across the street to get Chris a hot chocolate…" I

start, unsure of what to say here. "What are you… What is all this?" I point at the snowmobile and at my dad, who is up on the platform now, talking to someone at the edge.

"Oh, your dad gave me a ride down." She laughs. "I've never been on one of those before. We had a meeting this morning and—"

"Hello? Hello?" My dad's voice booms over the crowd, and a squeal of feedback follows. "Argh, sorry." He's got a megaphone in his hand, and waves over the crowd. "Hi, everyone. A lot of you know me. I'm Randall Mitchell, owner of West Philly eSports, the premiere eSports café here in Philadelphia." He pauses, looking out over the crowd.

Is he waiting for people to clap?

"Anyway, I'm thrilled to be here to make an announcement and offer up a fun giveaway." He digs into his jacket and plucks out a whole bundle of what I think are gift cards. He starts tossing them into the crowd, the little bits of plastic not exactly sailing all that well and scattering to just a few people in front of him.

"Wait a minute," Adam's mom barely whispers out, but I hear her. She starts toward the stage. "Hey, wait, Randall."

"Just a second," he says, looking down at her. "Some of you in the area have likely heard the rumors that I've been trying to expand down here, and great news."

"Randall, hey, this isn't—" Adam's mom presses, getting up on the stage. "What are you doing?" I can hear her through the megaphone, even though it's not in front of her. "I didn't agree to this."

"Relax." My dad shrugs, smiling. "We'll be expanding.

Effective next year, we'll be purchasing Old City Pinball and creating a new eSports experience right here in Old City."

"Goddammit," Adam's mom mutters, hopping off the stage and storming toward us. "Your ex is a real piece of work."

"That's why he's an ex," my mom grumbles. "Are you really selling?"

"Yeah," Adam's mom huffs. "But I really wanted to chat with Adam about it first. Is he here? Is he at the arcade? Where is he?"

"I'm not sure. I think—" I start, when a hand grabs my shoulder.

"Whitney!" my dad exclaims. "Come on, come on up here."

"What?" I snap. "No, Dad, what are you doing—?"

"So much of the credit for this expansion…" My dad continues, talking into the megaphone as he makes his way back to the stage, people around him backing away. I follow a little but stay at the edge of the platform. I'm not getting up there. "So much of this beautiful opportunity, that will provide new jobs and internships and major events, I owe to Whitney here, my bold and brilliant daughter."

"What?" I step away from the platform.

He looks down at me, his hand out, and his face turns up in frustration when I slap it away.

"Old City Pinball has been a staple of this neighborhood for over two decades, when the Stillwater family opened it in the '80s. In fact, our families have been linked for nearly that entire time. My daughter and Adam Stillwater have been dear friends since childhood. And a bond like that deserves to be honored."

The hell is this? It's like he's just unraveling everything I've told him and spinning it into his own narrative.

"We imagine the relaunched space will respect the original vision, maintaining the old arcade look so many of you love, while embracing new concepts. VR headsets. Gaming PCs. We'll bring competitive gaming to Old City, ushering in modernity and—"

Suddenly, my dad jerks back, stumbling on the platform. The bullhorn clatters to the floor. He looks totally startled, and some people closer to him start laughing.

"Who did that?" he shouts, brushing snow off his jacket. Did someone throw a snowball? He moves to pick the bullhorn up when a snowball hits him smack in the face. He falls backward, landing on his back, on the stage, with a loud bang. The bullhorn skitters across the platform and hits the concrete sidewalk with a squawk of feedback.

My dad sits up, staring into the crowd, and I climb onto the stage.

"Are you all right?" I ask as he brushes snow off his face and out of his eye.

"I'll be fine…hey! HEY!" he shouts, pointing into the audience.

The crowd disperses, some folks stepping to the right, others to the left, and straight down the middle is Adam, balling up some more snow. He glares ahead at the two of us, his face fuming, and the ball of snow breaks apart in his shaking fist.

"Adam," I say, and the crowd has grown so quiet that I can hear myself over everything.

He turns and walks away.

No.

No, not after everything we've been through. Everything we've scrapped back.

I rush off the platform and through the crowd.

"Adam!" I shout, hurrying after him. He picks up his pace. "Adam, wait!"

"What?" he snaps, turning around to glare at me. His mouth is turned up in a thin line, quivering, and his eyes are glass, the way someone gets when they're angry to the point of sobbing. "How could you? How could you?"

"Please, Adam, come on, I had no idea—"

"Have you just been telling him everything these last few days?" he sputters out, sniffling. "I thought you changed. I thought you didn't want—" he points back at the crowd and my dad "—all that anymore."

"I don't!" I shout. "And I have."

"I'm just a joke to you," he says, shaking his head. "Me. My family. My grief. It was all to just report back to your dad so he could make whatever move this was. It's like that first day of freshman year, all over again. Only instead of laughing at me in the hall, you're laughing at me here."

"No, that's not it," I snap back. "I can't believe you'd think that about me. After all this. After all we've shared."

"Shared?" he scoffs. "You're just someone who takes. Just like your father." He turns away.

I ball my fists up and grit my teeth. I'm not going to sit here and plead with him.

I walk back over to my father and his crappy little stage. There's a bruise purpling his cheek, and he's sitting on the edge of the platform, talking to some people who have their phones out. Reporters maybe? I don't know.

I stroll over. Adam's mom is gone, and my mom is standing in front of her shop, leaning against the door. She makes eye contact with me as I reach Dad, and motions for me to walk her way. I shake my head, and sit on the stage next to Dad.

This is where I'm supposed to be.

It's where I belong.

CHAPTER 19
Adam

"There's an ongoing trend in pinball, where the price of a game keeps going up. What used to be a quarter, now costs fifty cents, sometimes a dollar depending on where you are. But the games remain the same. Same amount of time, same amount of plays. If you're going to raise the prices for your players, don't leave the stakes the same. It's unfair to them, and unfair to your game."

–*The ART AND ZEN OF PINBALL REPAIR*
BY JAMES WATTS

"Hey," Chris says from across the arcade.

I keep sweeping, bits of glass still smattered about near the front of the place, from the fallen *Lost in Space* machine. Little splinters of it make their way across the floor, from the door to the other side, like little bits of sand that will hurt like hell if someone presses their hand to the ground.

"Man, you can ignore Whitney all you want. And your

mom, too, I guess. But not me," he presses. I glance up, and he's cleaning a cup at the snack bar. He looks up, makes eye contact with me, and I turn back to my broom. A Swedish Fish lands in the pile of the glass and dirt, and I kick it away, sending the candy skittering across the floor and under a game.

And then another one.

And another one.

And another—

"Chris, dammit," I snap, swiping at all the candy with my broom. "I don't want to fucking talk about it."

"Fine." He shrugs, shaking his head. He hops over the edge of the snack bar, dropping the mug on the counter with a loud *plink.* "I'll be around when you are." He grabs his jacket off the register countertop and nudges the front door open, but turns around. "Don't go on social media."

"Yeah, I won't," I grumble. "Last time I fell in…" I exhale. I'm not gonna finish that sentence.

"Hang in there," he huffs. "Call me when you need me."

And with that he's out the door, and I'm alone in the silent air of the arcade, interrupted only by the occasional song or chime from a machine. I finish sweeping up the glass, dirt, and Swedish Fish, and carry a dustpan over to the snack bar to dump them into a little can tucked behind it.

What am I gonna do?

There are options. I think. I could launch a GoFundMe or something, to try to save the business. I know a few bookstores in the area have done that, and a few of the boutiques. We're a beloved place in the neighborhood; people would chip in, wouldn't they?

But even if we are a beloved place…no one really comes here. So how beloved could this place possibly be? Would a fund-raiser only delay the inevitable? Whitney's dad wants to buy the whole building. I don't think a GoFundMe is going to raise enough for that. That's millions, not a couple thousand dollars.

And selling off pinball machines won't work. All the rarest games are either in not-so-great-for-collectors shape, or in the case of *Lost in Space*, they're just straight-up broken. I walk over to that game, which me and Whitney managed to get away from the door and to a safe corner of the arcade, to double-check the damage. If today is going to be an empty day, as the festival is slowly losing steam, I might as well get a little work in.

But there's something…different, that I didn't notice the other day, in the dark when the machine fell. The bottom isn't a metal sheet. It's a wood board, and there's writing on it. It's not some scrawl detailing repairs, which I know my dad would sometimes do, noting what he fixed or replaced.

Lost in Space.

Made in 1998.

Based on the original TV series, not to be confused with the excellent Netflix reboot or that horrible '90s movie with the guy from *Friends* in it.

Manufactured by SEGA, with about 600 made worldwide, which isn't necessarily a small number. Not when you're talking about a game like *The Big Lebowski*, that only had a dozen or so. Games getting runs a little under a thousand is normal when you think about just how many arcades were even still in existence in the '90s and early 2000's. It has a robot that moves around, an absolutely massive ramp, a way to interact with said robot by spelling out "warning" with the lights, and...

And it did not come with a built-in board on the bottom for measuring your children.

It takes me a minute to figure out.

I'm not sure when he did it. Maybe a screw broke that held the steel undercarriage in or it rusted out... I don't know. I don't think I can ever know, unless Mom knows something about it. But I can't shake that if she did, she would have said something. She would have wanted the bottom of this machine to hang up in our home, next to all her dead and dying plants.

There are scores. Endless scores, written in different colors, different kinds of ink; some look like marker and others like thick charcoal pencil. For different machines, too, there are a few for this one, but a *lot* for the *Street Fighter II* pinball game, one of my favorites, and a whole bundle for the *Starship Troopers* game that we had to retire a few years ago after an irreplaceable circuit board broke. I still have the back glass hanging in my room at home.

I can almost hear the voice of the game and the movie in my head, asking, "Would you like to know more?"

I would.

The thing about high scores on games, is that they get beaten.

But Dad wanted to remember mine.

These accomplishments, as small and silly as they are. I remember them meaning a lot to me when I was little, trying to rack up numbers the way he did, standing on a step stool to see over the edge of the games, onto the playfield. At the bottom of the board there are some wildly small scores, in the low millions, which is bad in pinball despite how large that number might sound, in ink that's a little faded. The *Super Mario Bros* game has a few, and I can't even remember the last time I played that without…

Without my dad there.

There are a couple little notches on the side of the wood board, too, with years and heights, and it took me a minute to figure out this board was someplace in here, maybe in the workshop or a piece of the wall that he had replaced, and he used it to measure how tall I'd been getting. There's a mark for when I was two, another for when I was three…it keeps going until I'm… I think ten? It's hard to read, and I don't really remember him measuring me.

I brush my fingers against the grain, at the little chips in the wood there, at the marker left behind.

Good God. I've been so wrong.

I've been doing this all wrong, all these years here. I've been making my mom stay attached to the place that had become a wildly painful memory. And me, giving up so much, so much of my life, for something Dad wouldn't have wanted for me.

My dad died running this place.

I brush my fingertips against the marks he made.

Where he checked off my height, our high scores, all those years of pinball.

And now I need to find a way to live without it.

I look around the arcade for a minute, wiping at my face, the sound of the wind outside still rattling against the door and the windows, the dying gasp of the winter storm.

I think maybe… I think I got it all wrong. When I think about him and this place. He loved pinball. He loved the arcade and the community and people around him, and all of that seemed to truly love him back, but…everything he made, everything he did, it was always for me and Mom.

I drop the broom.

There are more important messes to clean up.

And I need to head home.

My eyes flit over to a photo of me and Dad, the frame propped up against our cable box in the living room, with a number of other family photos. It's from the arrival of that *Lost in Space* machine, and the two of us are posing in front of it, his grin set to break his face. I must be… I don't know, twelve years old, in the photo. I wonder when he'd replaced the bottom of the machine with that wood board. Where that plank even came from. I don't think I'll ever know.

I pick up the frame and run my thumb over the glass and then the edges. It's made out of wood repurposed from broken vintage pinball machines, and I wonder for a moment if there's anything worth saving from the broken games in the office for something like this. They're newer, all metal and electronics, though, while the frame for this is wooden and lovely, the grains all different shades of light browns and deep reds. Polished, but with scratches under the varnish, gloss not covering up the history.

The house was full of wild excitement when he finally managed to get his hands on the machine, buying it at some convention across the country. It was all he could talk about for weeks until it arrived.

Mom humored him, in the way she always did with his games, whether it was something new he was picking up or a breakthrough with the game he was building. Always smiling warmly while he gushed about a machine's function or quirk, the weight of different kinds of pinballs, the strength of a good spring…always with an "okay, I love you" that was never condescending, but supportive.

He made us watch some of the old television show, then the awful movie from the '90s, and then we inhaled the Netflix series over a single weekend.

In those moments it was as though he was younger than me. Just bounding around the house like *he* was the pinball, the living room the playfield. A coffee table spinner. Family photos the drop targets. Side tables as bumpers.

"Adam?" my mom says, calling me over from the kitchen table, where there's a small spread of breakfast biscuits and meats, bacon and pork roll. "Where have you been? I've been calling and texting."

"Breakfast for dinner?" I ask, nodding at the table.

"Yeah, I'm…not feeling so great," she says, leaning back in her chair. She waves me toward her, and as I get closer, she scowls. "You're taking off that sweatshirt."

"Oh," I huff, peeling it off. I move to toss it aside when she reaches out.

"No, no," she says. "Just—" she grimaces "—put it in the sink or something, I'll carry it with some tongs to the laundry downstairs."

I roll my eyes and throw the sweatshirt into the sink, and make my way to grab a chair at the table. She slides a hot cup of coffee across to me, a dead succulent in the middle of our kitchen table. I can't help but laugh at it as I grip my hands around the steaming cup, immediately warming them after being outside without much of anything. I take a sip, and even though it burns my tongue, it feels so wildly good.

"So last night. And this morning," my mom starts, pulling her chair closer to the table. It squeaks against the hardwood, and it legit feels like I'm in one of those *Law & Order* shows she loves so much, about to get interrogated.

"Nothing…happened," I groan out, squirming in my chair a little. "We just—"

"Oh, God, Adam, no." Her face sours and she waves her hands at me. "I don't care about your little sleepover. You're old enough to be—" now she squirms in her chair a little "—ugh, responsible."

"I hate this."

"Okay, okay," she laughs. "This morning, though. The announcement with Whitney's dad." She sighs, her fork up in the air, a piece of pork roll speared on the end like a little red flag of overly salted meat. There's a pile of mail on the table next to her that looks like it needs sorting, but breakfast meats always come first. And besides, there's always a pile of mail.

"It wasn't supposed to happen like that, and I hope you know this. Mr. Mitchell and I had a meeting yesterday to talk about him acquiring the arcade, and then this morning he said he was driving down to pick up Whitney and you. I hopped along for the ride." She shakes her head. "I still can't believe he had a snowmobile at the ready. In Philadelphia."

"But…it's true, isn't it?" I ask.

"Yeah." My mom nods, sighing. "I just… We can't do it anymore, Adam."

She nudges some eggs around, sifts through the mail for a beat, and then glances up at me.

"Look, I'm…" She sighs. "I'm still on team us. You and me." She reaches out and pats my hand, giving me a small smile, and then leans back in her chair. She steeples her fingers together and holds her hands up to her face, looking at me from behind them, and I swear I can see the academic adviser playbook rolling out here. "You've done this amazing job."

"There's a but coming?" I ask.

"There's a but." She nods and leans forward again. "Adam, we can't keep doing this forever, not without your father. I know the arcade means a lot to you, but you have to think about what you want. Your dreams."

"I have." I nod and reach into my jeans pocket. I toss one of those LED throwies onto the table, and she looks down at it and smiles. "Let's do the Drexel tour."

She smiles, her mouth quivering a little.

"He'd be so proud of you, you know." My mom reaches out and grabs my hand, squeezing it. "Your dad, he wanted to go to college for that. Engineering. But you know, all those years running that place, followed by buying it, and he just never had the time. It's probably why that pinball machine of his never really worked."

I think about the pinball shooting into the wooden tool shelf, and can't help but laugh.

"But, Adam, if you want us to keep holding on to that place—" she lets go of my hand and folds them in front of her "—I can tell Mr. Mitchell we're not interested. You know, there's always the chance pinball gets hot again. Gets trendy. It happens every few years."

I can't stop the sharp inhale.

My heart hammers in my chest.

"Just… I want you to think about it a little, okay?"

I nod, swallowing.

This is it.

She pushes her chair away from the table—

"Mom, wait," I say, holding a hand out. She glances at me and sits back down.

"You're right." I exhale. "It's time to let go. I'm…" I wince. "I feel like I'm supposed to say that I'm ready. I'm not. I know I'm not. I don't know anyone who is ever really ready to say goodbye. I think that's a lie you find in books and movies, and Bon Jovi is the only one ever really up for saying the truth there."

She gives me a look.

"'Never Say Goodbye'?" I venture, and she shrugs.

"Your dad's music." She grins and leans back in her chair. "God, I wish I had one of Chris's Swedish Fish right now." She laughs and then lets out a long sigh. "All those years ago. Old City was different. The people were different. Philadelphia was different, really. The world changed and left us behind."

She sighs again.

"And I mean, I know maybe you don't want to hear this part, but the money for that building…" She looks around the kitchen for a minute before staring back into her mug. "Oh, Adam, it'll more than cover your college. You won't have to get student loans the way I did. We can get you a car, if you ever want to learn to drive one."

I laugh a little.

"A down payment on your future house?" She sniffles, wiping at her eyes. "Enough money to start a new business. There's just a lot of life saying goodbye to that place is going to give you. Us. And I just know your father would want it for you. And I could even *just* teach again." She exhales at that. "That. That feels good to say."

"So...when's it all going to happen?" I ask. "How much time do we have?"

"Oh, a while," my mom says, waving her hand a little. "Selling that building will take a minute. We have to have it inspected. Figure out a fair price, but...well, it'll be a lot. It's a building in Old City. I could probably retire," she huffs. "And we'll want to have some really solid last hurrahs there." She grins. "Really say goodbye to the place."

"What about...all the machines?" I ask, looking up at her. I turn back and peek at our living room. "I mean, Mom, I'm not an idiot. Like, there's no way we can fit them all in the house. And I don't think Mr. Mitchell is going to want them."

"Yeah, that's another thing. We're gonna have to figure out which ones to keep, and which ones to maybe sell?" She winces. "I know we can rehome them to arcades we've been friendly with over the years. Maybe some of the youth centers in the area."

That part makes me smile.

"We could make a lot of kids happy."

"We sure could."

She reaches out and grabs my hand again, and I can't help the tears.

It's over. Or at least, it's going to be.

Whitney flashes through my mind. Dad's old machine,

with the memories etched on the bottom, and the disastrous, never-ending project in the workshop, full of his attempts. Full of his dreams.

I know what I want to hold on to.

CHAPTER 20
Whitney

I'm standing outside my dad's café and glaring at a sign on the glass front door.

Coming Soon to Old City!

I look up and through the glass, into the place. Dana's in there, in the back at her barista station, fussing over something. I spot Dad, making his rounds as he does, talking to people stationed at computers. That kid Michael from the other day is at the register. It's been a little over a week since the whole disaster in Old City, and everyone, absolutely everyone, is acting like nothing happened.

Well, I guess that's not entirely true. Mom's texted me every single day asking if I've heard from Adam, which would be hard, considering he's blocked me on every social network and won't return any of my calls.

But Dad? Nick? My girls, who aren't really my girls anymore, and are really just "those" girls at this point? Business as usual. And with the holiday break over, and the last se-

mester of high school kicking off soon, it's time to get back
to the café.

I grab the handle to the front door and stop.

That stupid Coming Soon to Old City! sign tears at me. So
I tear at it, and leave the scraps of paper floating in the wind.

The *whoosh* of heat warms me over as I step into the café,
the familiar smell of my plants in the tables and along the wall,
paired with whatever coffee Dana is busy making and just…
people. Deodorant, cologne, whatever. All blended together
with a spritz of antibacterial spray. Michael glares at me as I
walk in, but I make my way right over to Dana, who beams
as I stroll over.

"Well, well." She crosses her arms. "The prodigal daughter returns and all that."

I snort out a laugh and lean against her coffee bar. I haven't
spent time traversing the world and wasting away my wealth,
only to be welcomed back home. No. I feel like maybe this
situation is just the opposite. I've spent plenty of my days
working wildly hard, while feeling unwelcome and unseen.

"I missed you," I say, tapping my fingers on the bar.

"You, too," Dana says but her face is turned up in worry.
"But look, um. Maybe today isn't the best day for you to get
back to it."

"What?" I glance over at her. "Why?"

I look over the café, and nothing looks particularly different.
Some familiar faces at computers, Dad hovering and not no-
ticing me. Same bad music pumping through the café's stereo.

"I just…" She sighs, rubbing her hands over her face. "You
know who starts today, right?"

"Starts?"

Before I can finish asking her anything about that, the door to my dad's office opens, and out strolls Helen and Andrea. They stop dead in their tracks when their eyes set on me, and I get up.

"Whitney…" Dana starts.

"I got this," I press, and walk toward them. Helen takes a noticeable step back, but Andrea just crosses her arms. "What's going on here?"

"Your dad offered us the internships," Andrea says. "He said we show a lot of promise."

"What?" I snap, and glance over at Helen, who takes another step away.

"Whitney!" my dad's voice booms, and all three of us look up as he strolls across the room. "I'm glad you came in. There's so much to talk about, and—"

"You don't want to ask how Mom is doing? How I'm doing?"

He winces.

"I figured…fine?" he ventures. "I mean, I don't like that you're staying over there but I understand you're angry at me, and I'm going to make this right."

"How?" I ask, nodding at Helen and Andrea. "By hiring them?"

"They're your friends!" he exclaims.

"They're not my friends,." I grumble. "I tried to tell you about it. Other people tried to tell me. And I think in a lot of ways, they tried to tell me, too."

I notice Sophie is missing from the trio, which says a lot. I'm not sure about who. Does she respect me enough to not be here, to not try to insert herself into my family life after she's meddled in my love life? It weirdly makes me want to talk to her. Though the absence of an apology isn't an apology, and I quickly shake it off.

"Whit, I think...there's a better place to talk about all this," my dad says, sounding awkward. I look beyond him, to the café, and a lot of people are staring.

"Fine," I snap and follow him toward his office. I catch a quick glimpse of Dana, giving me a thumbs-up and a nod, as I stroll inside. I wish I would have listened to her sooner, I really do. Inside I'm surprised to see that my dad's shifted things around a lot in the office space. There used to be a bunch of overbearing, completely unorganized shelves on the other side, and just his desk and a few cabinets on the other. But now there are some small, cubicle-esque nooks set up. They look like the sort of office pods you see in movies and television shows about Silicon Valley startups.

"What is this?" I ask, walking over.

"Well," he starts, stepping next to me. "That desk there, in the bigger pod—" yup, pods "—is for you. And the smaller ones, they're for Andrea and Helen, the interns. I figure we'll have a few interns come in and out of here every semester, or school year, depending on how the initial program goes."

"They're gonna...sit with me?" I ask.

"I mean, I thought they were your friends, Whit." He sighs, walking back over to his desk. I look at mine; it's a nice IKEA-looking thing, modern and sleek, with a brand-new shiny iMac sitting on top.

"What's with the computer? And the desk? Why would I have any of that?"

"Well, I was hoping maybe you'd be interested in taking

over some more leadership roles with the café," my dad says, shrugging a bit, a little smile on his face. "It's going to be a whole endeavor, transforming that arcade, and I feel like we can make this space here our little home base, you know?" He looks around, hands on his hips, like he's surveying land or something. "The intern desks are temporary, I think. I imagine we'll have other people in here. Maybe we can knock out a wall and put in some more—"

"So I'm in charge?" I ask, interrupting.

"Well, maybe just of the interns, for now." He smiles.

"Great."

I storm out of the office, and catch Andrea and Helen ordering from Dana. Dana looks at me, her eyes wide, and there's a warmth of anger surging in my chest. Andrea and Helen both turn around, and look taken aback to see me there.

"Whit, what—" Helen starts.

"You're fucking fired," I snap. "Get the hell out."

"What?" Andrea laughs. "You can't fire us."

"Sure I can." I cross my arms. "Get. The. Fuck. Out."

"Come on," Andrea says, trying another approach with her tone. "I'm sorry. We're both sorry, Whitney. For things with Patrick and Sophie, we should have told you and—"

"Out."

"Ugh, fine," Helen snaps, slapping the barista bar. "Let's get out of here."

The two storm out, and I glance back at Dana, who looks like she's about to crack up. My dad is standing in the doorway of his office, arms crossed.

"Where the hell were you?" I snap, taking a step toward

him. "During the snowstorm. I couldn't get a hold of you the entire time."

"What? Oh. I got locked in the café!" He laughs. "I went back to lock up, and the stupid smart lock snapped shut as my phone died. You know there wasn't a single charger in the space? And then the power went out! I just had to sit there in the dark surrounded by technology that could do nothing for me."

"Well, serves you right, I suppose." I cross my arms. "The way you sandbagged Adam like that? Releasing the news?"

"Oh, I don't know if I'd say I sandbagged him," he grumbles. "It was practically an accident, that announcement. A reporter overheard me talking about my plans, and I had to get ahead of it before it was online. I'm sorry it upset you. I thought it would be a fun reveal."

"Right. Dad, we have to talk."

"Oh, God, can it wait?" He exhales. "You're firing your friends, and I'm gonna have to deal with that fallout. Your mom is giving me hell over—"

"No, you know, I think I need to do this now before I lose my nerve." I exhale. "I'm…not going to do the social media and online stuff for the cafés anymore."

"Oh," my dad says, grabbing a coffee off the barista bar. He takes a sip and exhales loudly. "God. Needed that." He laughs a little.

"That was for a customer," Dana grumbles and starts working on another drink.

"What happened?" my dad asks, his tone calm.

"I just… I realized it doesn't make me happy. None of it does. The work at the café, the online stuff. It just keeps bringing me back around to people who don't actually care about me. They care about what I can potentially do for them, like Helen and Andrea and Sophie…" I clear my throat. "And that's not friendship. That's not…" I grit my teeth and shake my head. "That's not what family should be."

"Wait, wait." My dad takes a step toward me, putting his coffee mug on the countertop with a *plink*. "You think…you think I only care about you because of what you can do for the business? For the café?"

"I mean…you do," I say as he stares at me, his face distressed. I look away, down toward the café floor. "The only time I can ever get through to you is when it has to do with the business. With work. And sometimes that doesn't even work. You didn't even want to come to the Winter Festival until you had a reason to crash it and make it about you."

I look back up at him, and he's looking dumbstruck to the point his mouth is open. His eyes are darting about, like the answer is somewhere. And I watch Dana out of the corner of my eye, slip out from behind the bar and walk into the general space.

Smart.

"That's…that's not true. That's not fair. I don't come to the festival every year because of your mother."

"And *that's* not fair!" I exclaim. "She works hard on that festival every single year."

"And that's exactly why it's not fair for me to be there," he presses, his face stern. "Whitney, I don't want to ruin it for her. Not for you, and not for her. Seeing me there…that won't make her happy."

"Then explain the other day." I cross my arms. "You ruined it for *everyone*."

"Listen, I've apologized for that. I'm sorry. It was a misstep and I was excited and just…if I could take it back, I would. But Whit. You really think I only pay attention to you when you're working?" he asks, grabbing his coffee again, holding it as though it's going to be the thing that steadies him. "Really?"

"That's how it feels," I say.

"Whit." He walks toward me. "I'm just… I'm just so busy. The business, the travel, trying to expand. The whole arcade thing, helping Adam's family…okay, yes, it's a business decision but I also thought maybe it would help your friend? You know, I was asking about the two of you the other day, because I wanted to do something good there. You two were just so close and…" He shakes his head.

"You are more to me than your work," he says, reaching out, grabbing my hands, which are shaking at this whole confrontation. "I love you. And I'm sorry. I'm sorry if you had to grow up these last few years, feeling like you had to earn it. A parent's love shouldn't feel like a reward for a job well-done, and that's just…a massive failure on my part."

He reaches out and hugs me, and it's awkward, but it's a hug.

I can't help but think about Mom in all of this. How it didn't feel like I had to earn her affection or attention, how she made me feel like I just deserved it. And how Adam, those days leading up to the festival, made me feel much the same. That I didn't have to fight to be seen.

And I'm not sure if I can really forgive my dad for all this.

But if this is a start to some kind of way back, maybe I can explore it.

I pat his back and he lets go, his face turned up in what I think might be a struggle to avoid crying.

"Thanks, Dad." I walk by the barista station and back into the office, grabbing my jacket and backpack. I turn around and head out, hurrying toward the front door, when I stop.

"But you're gonna work with me to make it up to Adam, and I still quit."

CHAPTER 21
Adam

Dear Adam,

Thank you for your email. I don't get many. I don't think…honestly, I don't think any younger people read my book? It's not really for them, it's for the very specific niche of people who work in pinball and appreciate philosophy. Sales have…not been great.

But your words here, they meant a lot. And I want to let you know I appreciate them. I don't think anyone has ever called me a hero before, save for the time someone asked me for a hero at a publishing event. That's what you call sandwiches in Philly, right? Or is it hoagie?

I digress.

I am unsure of what to tell you, when it comes to letting go. Your friends sound wise, and you're lucky to have so many at such a young age. Also, if I sound like I'm talking down to you, I'm sorry. That comes with old age, I find. I don't mean it. It's an old man's attempt at sounding wise.

I loved pinball. I still do. I have a few machines in my basement that my kids love and my wife could live without. Some
rare ones even. I bet you'd get a real kick out of seeing The
Last Starfighter game. It's one of only eight. That said, if I had
to walk away from all the games, from the books that I write (I
wrote a few more books other than the pinball one you know.
Do you like mysteries?), it would be easy. And should be for
you, too, in theory.

Those machines. That arcade. Those are things and that's a
place. That isn't what makes a home, even though it can sometimes feel that way. The people there, the memories you carry.
That is what makes a home, Adam. Your family. Your friends.
This...girl that seems to have wronged you, who you've mentioned like three dozen times in this letter.

Forgiveness, it's important. Being able to realize a mistake
and move on, is what keeps us going in life. And really, when
you think about it, in pinball. Every time you lose, every time
you fail, you don't just build up the courage to play again.
There's a step that happens in between the loss and the next attempt that's so subtle that we don't even realize it's happening.

We forgive ourselves. And it lets us carry on. Play games
with quarters, not hearts.

And I think, not only do you need to forgive when it comes
to this person who is so close to you, but you need to forgive
yourself. Because it's okay to let go.

Your idea. Electrical engineering. That's still a means of
letting go. Even if it started with the arcade. It isn't the actual arcade. Just as that girl isn't. Just as your family isn't.
Just as YOU aren't.

I am unsure if I've answered your question here. I hope I have. Most emails I get are about how to fix something, but I never really thought my book was about fixing machines.

It was about helping people fix themselves.

Email and say hi anytime. I wish you lots of luck, and I've included a gift card to your local bookshop. I'm not saying you should use it to buy one of my other books, but...do with it what you will.

Watch out for bumpers.

—James Watts

I print out James Watts's email, and hang it up in my room.

I print out a second copy, with a smaller font, and fold it into a little square that I cram inside my wallet.

I should order a frame.

I should forward it to Chris.

I should...

I should tell Whitney.

Old City Pinball:...

I try and fail to type out a message several times.

Hey, you're not going to believe who sent me a letter.

Hey, how are you doing, we should talk?

Hey, this is ridiculous, I'm sorry, I know it wasn't your fault, I was a storm of emotions and feelings and didn't know what to do.

Hey, I'm not sorry I hit your dad with a snowball, and I would do it again.

I'm not entirely sure where to get started, but I know I'm not going to find the answers in a game or a letter.

I need to reach out. I didn't lose the arcade; I let it go. And I'm okay with it. But losing Whitney? No. I'm not okay with that.

I tap Follow.

CHAPTER 22
Whitney

It's a little after 3:00 p.m., and I'm nudging open a door to a classroom I've never stepped in before. But the flyers smattered around the hallway, in between posts regarding open calls for this year's spring musical and an antiracist book club, promised something I couldn't resist.

"Hello?" I call out into the classroom, spotting a small bundle of students sitting in the very back. It's a science class, some kind of biology or chemistry room? There are lab tables clearly set up for experiments, with big holes in the middle and beakers stations along the edges.

A few heads turn, and someone stands up and waves me over.

"Horticulture club?" they ask.

"That's what I'm here for." I smile.

"Get on over here!" They sit down and I make my way over to the circle, the classroom smelling of bleach and chemicals, like maybe the class that got out at 3:00 p.m. just finished a dissection lab. Everyone sitting in the circle looks like they're from different grades, a few younger faces mixed in with some teens who are clearly seniors.

I take a seat, and awkwardly wave and nod to everyone. "Hey."

The girl sitting next to me looks at me as though she knows me, and suddenly my heart sinks. Her bright green eyes are wildly eager and she smiles, like somehow we're old friends, and dammit. I knew this was a bad idea. I've been stressed about this new school thing since we moved, but as the days got closer and it got realer, my thoughts were consumed with what would happen if people recognized me from my dad's cafés. It's supposed to give me a fresh start, not be another opportunity for people to want to use me again. I thought maybe I should keep a low profile at the new school, just keep my head down until graduation and not bother trying to meet anyone.

"Is that a Krumm's tote bag?" she asks.

"What?" I ask, and look down at the bag clutched in my hands. It's from Mom's shop, a big golden K against a black bag. "Oh! Yeah, yeah, it is."

"Oh, my God, I love that place!" she exclaims. "Dario, don't you go there a lot, too?"

"Hell, yeah," a guy across from me says, nodding. "Best succulents in downtown. What's that button on your jacket?"

"Huh? Oh!" I tug out the collar of my coat. A little succulent with "here's to growth" around it, a gift from Dana now that I've given up using the café's social media accounts. No more Growth social media managing software. Just actual growth. A good reminder.

"They sell them at the shop." I grin.

"Man, we are gonna have to make a field trip," Dario says, shaking his head. "I love that. It's a good message."

"Yeah." I nod, thumbing at the pin. "Yeah, it is."

This year. This half year. It's going to be different.

It's going to be better.

My phone buzzes.

Old City Pinball has followed you.

A smile threatens to break my face. He's back. And there's just one more thing I have to do.

CHAPTER 23
Adam

"And this is our makerspace," the tour guide, a young woman named Becca with blue in her hair and thick black leather boots, says. "Those of you who want to explore a little bit, feel free. We'll be meeting up in the cafeteria across from the building for lunch."

The group of students in the tiny crowd disperses, a few making their way into the makerspace building, the rest walking off here and there.

"She reminds me of someone from NextFab," Chris says as Becca walks off toward the cafeteria. "This place is so cool."

"It really is." I exhale, looking around.

We walk in through the sliding doors, and the Drexel campus's makerspace expands out in front of us, full of desks and tables and noise and smells. I close my eyes for a minute, taking in that scent of ozone, the sound of a laser cutting something.

It feels like home in a lot of ways. Almost like the arcade. All lights and sounds and atmosphere.

"I wonder if they have a rummage box here, too," I say out loud, and Chris just looks up and shrugs at me. We make our way through, students and what looks like faculty, or maybe grad students, I don't know, making their way up and down the area.

"Hey, you must be Adam." An older guy comes up to me, hand out. I take it and shake it, but look at Chris and then to him.

"I... Yeah, but who are you?" I laugh.

"Sorry, I'm one of Jorge's friends, from NextFab, Lamar. I knew your dad, great guy. I'm sure you hear this all the time, but I'm sorry."

"Oh." I exhale. "Yeah, yeah, thank you."

"Come on, come with me." He motions for me to follow him. "I'm the manager of the space here, but I'm also finishing up my PhD in Electrical Engineering here. This kinda pays for the other thing." He smiles.

"Cool." I nod, looking back at Chris, who just smiles.

"You'll find just about everything you need here for any project you're working on, and if you have questions, or requests, I just want you to ask," he says, stopping. He looks at me expectantly and I'm confused.

"What do you mean *ask*?" I ask. "I'm not gonna be here until—"

And then I spot it.

"Wait...what is..." I mutter and look at Chris, who looks like he is about to lose it, a smile fit to burst from his face. My eyes flit up to Lamar, and he just grins and shrugs.

"Go ahead," he says. "Check it out."

There's a desk.

A bunch of LED throwies are against the wall it's backed up into, spelling out "Welcome." I walk over to it slowly. There's a pinball machine–shaped tarp near it, and all kinds of machine parts scattered on the surface, but also other kinds of electronics I don't recognize. Tools. Wires. Gadgets. Lights. I run my hands over it, and turn to the machine.

And Whitney steps out from around a nearby corner, smiling.

Lamar grins, crossing his arms.

"What…what is this?" I ask, glancing over at Chris, who shrugs. "Did you know about this?"

"I may have been working you, as an inside man." He grins.

"I don't understand," I say, turning back to Whitney. I take a step toward her, and her smile warms up even more. My heart is hammering in my chest.

"Go ahead." She nods at the covered machine behind me. "Take a look."

She's dressed differently, which feels like a silly thing to notice, but there's no white jacket. She's wearing this peacoat, and a T-shirt with a succulent on it.

"That's, um…a new look you've got there." I nod.

"I'm seeing how it fits." She smiles.

"I like it." I exhale. "It's more…you."

"Oh, my God!" Chris exclaims. "Please take the tarp off of that."

Whitney laughs, and I do, too, turning to the machine. I flip the plastic off and…

It's Dad's machine.

The unfinished Beast.

"What..." I look back at Whitney and over at Chris, who is now excitably bouncing up and down. "What is this? How did you—"

"Look, I know you're not gonna start here until the fall. After we graduate. But...well, Chris and your mom and I agreed. Couldn't hurt to get a head start. And my dad owed me one so...this space is yours, rented for the semester."

I look at the machine; all the parts are missing from the surface, but they are elegantly placed in order on the desk, labeled and everything.

"You did this?" I whisper out.

Whitney holds out a resistor, the little electronic pressed between her fingers.

"Only a little bit." She smiles. "Chris helped. But it was you. You got yourself here."

I reach out to grab the resistor.

And there's a spark.

★ ★ ★ ★ ★

ACKNOWLEDGMENTS

I was surprised at where this book took me, written during a strange time. During a pandemic. What started off as a quirky romance turned into a story about what it's like when old friends drift apart and families try their best and still fail one another, intentionally or not, and how you navigate that.

I'd like to take a minute to thank the people who have never failed me.

For beloved writer friends Lauren Gibaldi, Kelly Loy Gilbert, Roselle Lim, Bryan Bliss, Misa Sugiura, Tom Torre, Jadzia Axelrod, Olivia A. Cole, Ashley Woodfolk, Jeff Zentner, Lamar Giles, Marieke Nijkamp, Whitney Gardner, Sam Maggs, Lauren Morrill, Ashley Poston, Rebecca Podos, Farah "Horrible Goose" Naz Rishi, Fran Wilde, Kelly Jensen, Katherine Locke, Dahlia Adler, Sarvenaz Taghavian, Akemi Dawn Bowman, Cindy Pon, Mike Chen, Blair "Two Sheds" Thornburgh, Joshua Isard, Stephanie Feldman, Alex London, Caleb Roehrig, Emily X. R. Pan,

Nicola Yoon, Rosiee Thor, Jeannine A. Cook, Rachel Strolle, Anna Birch…whether it was long talks about writing, late-night exhausted calls about parenting, long emails about teaching, or angry text messages about video games, thank you.

To dear friends Darlene Meier, Andres Jimenez, Miguel Bolivar, Dario Plazas, Alberto Lorenzo, Carlos Ortega, Nwayieze Ndukwe, Amy Colon, Liliana Vidal, Glen Tickle, Jorge Estrada, Stephanie Rath-Tickle, Jill Ivey, Allison Krumm, Steve Rauscher, Preeti Chhibber, Swapna Krishna, Christine Loy, Dana Murphy, Saba Sulaiman, Christopher and Shannon Wink…thank you for always showing up for me.

To Chris Urie, whose friendship is so pure and wholesome, that my editor almost didn't believe you were real when I wrote you into this book.

My pals at Indy Hall, for giving me a place to write and encourage others, especially Adam Teterus, Alex Hillman, Anaia Daigle, John Fahl, Anna Goldfarb, Amanda Thomas, and Neil Bardham.

To my agency colleagues at P.S. Literary, and the authors I'm blessed enough to work with, for dealing with an agent who also writes his own books. Dawn Frederick for finding this book a home, Liz Rahn and Kim Yau for championing me out in Hollywood.

The team at Inkyard and Harlequin, especially my legendary editor, Rebecca Kuss, Bess Braswell, Laura Gianino, Brittany Mitchell, Linette Kim, Natashya Wilson, Connolly Bottum, Kathleen Mancini, Steffi Walthall, Leigh Teetzel, and Gigi Lau. Lauren Smulski for opening that door.

My lovely family. Mom, Dad (especially for all those games of *Pinbot* on the old Nintendo), Lauren, and Jordan. My darling wife, Nena, and sweet son Langston, who keep me on my toes and inspired. Melissa Salazar, for the love she showed Langston and our family in the difficult year that was 2020. Afsaneh Oskouei for taking care of our little one through the spring. Kristelle Mallah, for teaching me to focus on what's really important. Renee, Dan, Erik, Elizabeth, Vinnie, Sean…the most beautiful surprise. Grandma Watts and Boling, brothers James and Ali, cousins Randelle, Charles, Jessica Nicole, and Ron, for the endless support, and Elbert James Watts for the constant enthusiasm.

And last, to Auggie. The best boy. I miss you every day. Say hi to Coco for us.